# OUR DAUGHTERS

Yàzhōu nǚ'ér – The Asian Daughter

# OUR DAUGHTERS

## Lori Ann Mathews

 Our Daughters

Yàzhōu nǚ'ér – The Asian Daughter



Published by LAM Productions

Paperback ISBN-13: 979-8-218-06255-2
Ebook ISBN-13: 979-8-218-06809-7

First Edition • August 2022

*Dedication*


To my sons, Amaru and Samir, I love you beyond measure.

To my family and friends, always.

To Dorian Hurd, you are so missed.

# OUR DAUGHTERS

Yàzhōu nǚ'ér –
The Asian Daughter

Erin walked near the water's edge trying to read the newspaper, which was difficult for two reasons: one, because it was raining from the approaching storm and the water was bleeding the print, and two, she wasn't wearing her reading glasses. The wind charged at her, attempting to rip the paper from her grip as she struggled to read the headlines: Presumptive Democratic presidential nominee Camille Harrington was chosen as the nominee for President of the United States, only the second woman in American history.

She accepted with honor and is moving forward despite the untimely death of her beloved son, Abrams, known as the 'American Prince' along with Loren Roberts, his princess.

So engrossed in reading what she could of the story, a wave she didn't see coming hit her, knocked her down, and enfolded her before she understood what was happening.

Blinded, Erin gasped in dark water and tried to fight her way out even as the undertow pulled her down. Underneath the force of the swirling waves, a large hand clutched Erin by the back of the shirt and dragged her stumbling and retching back to shore, where she dropped heavily to her knees, spitting up more water as her heart galloped in her chest. Her head bent almost to the sand as she shivered from the cold and the storm around her.

"Are you trying to kill yourself?" a voice screamed. Erin turned and stared at Sam, who was soaked to the skin from his rescue; a panicked look of hysteria on his face.

Erin didn't say anything. She couldn't speak because she was suddenly crying in wracking, loud sobs as thunder bowled toward them across the ocean. Sam got to his feet, helped Erin to hers, and pulled; almost dragged her off the beach, across the tarmac, and onto the street as the rain arrived in a sheet drenching them both. The thunder and lightning came on seconds later. It exploded around them until they moved in a kaleidoscope of sound and fury.

They ran the block back to their house. They lived in Hull, Massachusetts, where every neighborhood was a block away from the ocean. The sound of the pounding waves was constant background noise as the wind and rain thrashed against them, making speaking impossible. The streets were nearly deserted. Those few people who did pass by them didn't look their way; they were hurrying about their business, getting out of the weather.

Sam turned them onto their road, a long dark lane with mostly gray-slated houses on both sides, their windows lit from within by the flickering blue light of large flat-screen television sets. Their house was far down, number eight on the right-hand side of the street. One window was lit, throwing muted light onto their small front porch. Sam quickly mounted the one-step and pulled open the screen door, only to have it ripped out of his grasp by the wind; it smacked back against the wall hard enough to break from its moorings.

Sam grabbed it with one hand while pushing Erin through the unlocked inner door with the other, followed quickly behind before slamming the door closed on the frenzied outside world. They stood catching their breath, cold water running off them in freshets drenching the rug at their feet.

He led Erin by the hand into the living room, pushing aside the brown boxes strewn all over the place. This was their favorite place in the house with its large windows and even more oversized fireplace. The room was filled with two of their favorite things:

pictures and books, so many of the latter it would take half a day to count them all.

Sam stood Erin in front of the fireplace, already set with a roaring fire.

"I'll get us some dry clothes," Sam said, and with his face suffused with worry, he left the room.

When he returned carrying towels and dry clothes for Erin, after quickly changing his own, he found her still standing in the same spot, shivering; Sam suspected it was not just from her bout with the storm-tossed ocean but her grief due to Loren's death and sadness over Jesse. Even though the girls had been Erin's nieces, the daughters of her sister Lillian, they had loved them both, having no children of their own, and Jesse had been their favorite. Erin had loved Jesse like a daughter and taken the loss as if she'd been their baby.

Sam helped his wife undress, towel off, and get into dry clothes. He then sat her on the couch, "I'm going to make us a couple of hot toddies. You rest, and I'll be right back; just in the other room if you need me." He hurried out, more worried than ever.

After making the drinks, Sam retraced his steps back to the living room and halted, tray in hand, dumbstruck by the sight before him. Erin was no longer sitting by the fire but was standing in front of it, tossing books into the roaring flames.

"Why are you burning books?" he asked, shocked. He watched as Erin grabbed another one from the brown box at her feet, flipped the book open, ripped out its papery guts, and tossed the pages into the fire.

"These aren't books. They're Jesse's diaries. She sent them all to me before she disappeared."

Sam hastily set down the tray, picked one of the notebooks out of the box, and flipped it open. He read the page out loud, 'First day of high school. I'm terrified, but Loren will be there, so maybe I won't get killed.'

"Why would you burn these?" he held the book out, not understanding why Erin was doing this. "This is her life."

"It's over, her life as we know it."

Sam carefully set the book on the table, "Come, sit down and have your drink before it gets cold."

He led Erin to the couch and then got the drinks, handing one over before picking up the open bottle of Jim Beam off the tray, "We ran out of lemon to add to the Earl Grey and honey, so I'm adding an extra shot of whiskey," he said pouring a finger-shot to each cup. "My version of the hot-hot toddy."

Erin laughed. Sam could always make her laugh though it still felt like a new thing she'd just learned. She watched as her partner – younger by twenty-plus years - added two fingers of whiskey to each cup before handing one over to her and watching as she took a sip.

"It tastes wonderful," Erin said gratefully.

Sam swept a finger through his thick, dark beard before grinning through it at her, "It should. It's whiskey-fired up."

He glanced toward the window where the rain pounded as if trying to get inside while the wind swept around the house in a screaming fit.

"The storm was building, you were out there, and I needed to find you." He looked at his beloved partner, "You weren't yourself, Erin."

Erin touched his warm neck, "Thank you, honey. I wasn't thinking straight. The paper mentioned Loren, nothing on Jesse." She paused briefly, "We have a right to know what happened to them both."

"You don't believe the police's version?"

"No, they're not willing to tell us the truth – they can't - because of Camille Harrington, who's soon to be our first female president. Meaning no scandal must interrupt that progress even disavowing what happened to her son."

"A cover-up then."

"Wait a second, since no one's talking, I have an idea."

Sam stared at Erin as she got to her feet, pulled over a box, and scrambled through it, tossing out notebooks, small photo albums, and pieces of loose sheets of paper.

"Lillian sent Jesse's things, what she couldn't bear to look at anymore," Erin said, switching to another box. This one seemed filled with hair ribbons, barrettes, silver-toothed combs, and antique brushes. She held up a tiny, toddler-sized sweater with pink baby roses around the neckline and down the sleeves. Stitched on the right-hand side was a delicate series of characters that Erin gently ran her finger over.

"This is her name – was her name – Zian, beautiful ha?"

Erin folded the small sweater and laid it carefully on top of a shelf before removing another book from the box. This one had pink and white roses on the cover; she held it out to him.

"Jesse will tell us."

Sam stared at the book, wondering how Jesse could tell them anything; she was gone, disappeared. With a swirl of two emotions: stupidity at reading a girl's journal, even one he'd loved and learning her secrets; good and bad, her dreams, her nightmare, her life. And eagerness to find answers, the truth, he reached out and took the book. As he began to read, the storm outside deepened ferociously with longer and louder bursts of lightning and thunder. He barely heard it, because in his mind's eye, he was seeing and remembering only Jesse as she walked along the calm water's edge underneath the smooth, gentle blue sky while the waves lapped a caress at her feet. Her long dark hair blowing around her face, her smile bright and warm, and her with them again.

# CHAPTER 1

When did it begin? The two things that changed my life forever? The first had to do with a shocking discovery involving my beloved sister. The other was when love literally and figuratively saved my life.

The first thing happened at Loren's; we'd been agreeing to disagree over the arrangements for the thirty-fifth-anniversary party we were throwing for our parents. I'd been wandering around her spacious living room, which looked like something out of Beautiful Home Design Digest. Our grandfather, Loren's biological grandfather, Victor Sinclair, had been a so-called Lion of Wall Street. When he'd died, he left a sizable inheritance to his two daughters, one of whom was our mother, Lillian.

He'd left his first grandchild, Loren, his blood, this Manhattan townhouse worth a fortune, when she was sixteen. On the other hand, I was thirteen, and he'd left me a nice sum of money, which I'd used to buy my small house, worth eight times less than Loren's. Her home boasted four spacious bedrooms on the second floor, two and a half baths, two hearthstone fireplaces, a chandelier in the foyer, and a terrace. She'd furnished the room with tasteful and expensive furniture, which she balanced with strategically placed photographs of her, me, and our family.

Moving slowly from picture to picture as I always did, even though I'd seen them so many times, I suddenly lingered, frowning, over those taken when I'd first come to America. I counted six photographs of me as a toddler, noticing not for the first time; that I wasn't smiling in any of them. In most of the pictures, I looked scared to death. In one, I was bundled in a cheap-looking sweater, crying my heart out as my new parents held me in their arms. Welcome to your new life as an adopted daughter, I thought. In many of them they'd held me up as if I were a prize they'd won: a girl child. I realized I hadn't started to smile in any of the pictures until I was around three years old.

In time, I'd learned to smile but grin every time a camera was pointed my way. In most of the pictures we'd taken as a family, we were all grinning as if we'd been lobotomized. I shook my head, ridding myself of such a nasty thought.

There was a large, framed photograph of us on a family ski trip to Telluride. One of Loren, our mother, and I on a school trip to the Nantucket Whaling Museum. A picture of our father, Martin, standing with the members of the Harvard rowing team in front of one of his award-winning scullers. Pictures of us on snorkeling vacations and Disney World trips. The two of us at a local playground screaming with laughter as we swung side-by-side.

Taking from the mantelpiece my favorite picture of Loren and I, I thought how it was the only one I truly loved. The two of us sat in a kiddy pool in the high summer. Loren was seven years old, and I was four. She had one arm around my shoulders and was planting a big kiss on my cheek while I grinned at the camera.

"Jesse?" she called from upstairs.

"Yes?" I called back, replacing the picture and following her voice into the foyer, where she stood looking down at me over the upstairs railing. "Why do you insist on keeping all these baby pictures of me?" I asked. "In half of them, I look ready to pee my pants with fright."

Dressed in a light blue summer wrap-around dress that complimented her flawless figure, Loren stared down at me. Her blond hair was piled high on top of her head, making her look cool and sophisticated as she held a designer gown the color of a ripe peach over the railing.

"I'll never forget," she sounded grave, and my heart sank a bit for no particular reason I could define as I looked up at her.

"Forget what?"

"That you're unique, little sister. It's as if we found you in a pumpkin patch."

"But you didn't," I said drily. "It was an orphanage of starving and neglected children where adoption, if you were lucky, was the only escape."

"Well, that's a mood killer," Loren stared down at me a moment then said, "The picture of us in the kiddy pool is my favorite too." She pressed the dress to her body; it turned skin already glowing into a luminous portrait. "I think I'm going to wear this to tonight's event."

"You'll look fabulous in it," I called up, saying something I'd said a thousand times, always truthfully, almost automatically.

"Since we still have to hash out the seating arrangement, let's have some wine. You choose. I'll put this away and be down in a minute."

Frowning after her, I wondered how long this was going to take. I was tired and wanted to go home. Walking into her kitchen and over to the wine rack, I choose a rose' from the Wolffer Estate before taking two glasses down from the cabinet over the sink.

Pulling open the drawer where Loren kept her corkscrew, I stumbled back in shock, almost dropping the bottle. There was a gun among the corkscrews, ice tongs, and cocktail sticks.

I sat the bottle carefully down on the counter and stared at it as if I'd never seen one up close before. The fact of the matter was that I had, once. A friend of mine, who'd dated a Bronx detective, had come to a party with one strapped to his side and taken it out to let us see and touch it. Yet, I'd never expected to see a gun in my sister's utensil drawer.

"Oh, that's where I put it," Loren said nonchalantly from behind me, making me jump.

"What in the world, Loren?" turning to her, shock threading threw my words. "Why do you have a gun? And out in the open in your kitchen?"

"Where else should I keep it? In the bathroom?" she asked evenly, amusement filling her lively gray eyes. "It's a Lady Glock. They had one in pink, but I preferred the steel gray. It cost me more than six hundred dollars. I had no idea guns were so expensive. You listen to the news; you think people can get them on every street corner for a buck."

She took the corkscrew out of the drawer, shutting the gun away. She opened the wine and poured each of us a glass.

"Answer me: why the gun?"

"Don't worry, I'll move it," she waved my concern away with the stem of her wineglass before taking a sip. "This was a good choice."

"You still haven't answered me, for chrissakes," anger flared in me at her blasé attitude. "Is it loaded?"

"It would be useless if it wasn't. I got it because the neighborhood has seen some trouble lately. A couple was robbed at gunpoint right up the block. You remember Mr. Redmond two doors down? He had his house broken into, and he was so badly frightened, he had a heart attack."

"Oh, no. Is he dead?"

"No, but he was in the intensive care unit for two weeks. I won't be surprised if he sells his place and moves away. So, a friend suggested I consider some kind of home protection other than the alarm system. I thought of a gun and bought one."

"But a gun is dangerous, Loren. What if somebody gets in and steals it? Or you get hurt trying to handle it?"

She waved me and my concerns away, her blond hair loose and glossy in her top knot. "I watched YouTube videos on how to use it, even took shooting lessons and was good too. Don't worry, sis, I won't shoot myself or anyone else." She flashed a perfect grin, "Unless I have to."

I stayed for dinner, though I didn't eat much. Loren had made a chicken stir-fry, but I hadn't been too hungry to begin with, and I kept thinking about that gun sitting in the drawer only a few feet away.

Still thinking about my sister and the fact she, of all people, owned a gun, I'd walked over to one of my favorite parks, the James J Walker near St. Luke's place, not far from her house. I'd had a thing for parks since I was a little kid when I visited my first one, the Boston Public Garden. I'd never visited a park in China, so when I did here in the states, it was as if I'd been dropped into the most beautiful place on earth, and I've loved parks ever since. Growing up on Nantucket with the water all around, the wind, the sand, and seagrasses, I'm used to nature right on my doorstep. I love the wide-open spaces, the trees, the flowers, and even the kiddy playgrounds but most important to me is the open free beauty that's there for everyone, no matter who you are. There are thirty-two in Manhattan proper, including the park-of-all parks, Central, the most visited park in the US. I know it like the back of my hand; it's wonderful but doesn't make my top five list. I enjoy the smaller, off-the-radar spaces where people go for peace and solace, to think and just be themselves. I hadn't planned to stop at the J. Walker but wanted a quiet place to think.

I walked under the summer trees, which formed a lush canopy of Scarlett Oaks, American Yellowwood, and European Ash, making me feel like I was in an enchanted forest. In the fall, the trees blaze with color and light, while in the winter, they're so sharp and stark and skeletal it makes you realize life is no less than a dancer on edge.

I thought I'd walk for a little while and then go home. It was close to nine o'clock and the sun was beginning to set. I noticed people going about on the streets outside the park's fence while the park's interior was relatively empty except for a few walkers here and there: a harried mother pulling at the arm of an angry, tearful toddler who didn't want to leave the playground; a man walking a large, white French poodle that looked show dog ready. Two teenage boys, one black, the other white, smoking weed and talking to each other in low tones between intermittent bouts of giggling.

When I'd first entered the park, I'd passed by them, and one of them had called, "Hey, Asian chick."

I hadn't responded or even turned around. I'd heard similar comments before and knew it was best to ignore the comment and who tossed it at me. I'd seen those two hanging around the park before and considered them mostly harmless.

A breeze freshened the air, fluttering the leaves that hadn't yet fallen. The setting sun caused the 1920's era lamps, with their twenty-first-century lighting filaments, to come on and throw a glow where the gloom was gathering. I found a bench away from the cluster of those near the park's entrance and sat down, suddenly feeling lonely and melancholy. August would soon arrive, and before long, this summer would be nothing but a memory.

Thoughts of my hometown, Nantucket Island, filled my mind. The Island, with its three lighthouses, was only six miles wide in each direction, and I knew every inch of it, where every dune had grown up, where the moors began and ended, and every path that led down to the beach.

I'd walked or biked those six miles all summer, especially when I couldn't take the harassment and bullying anymore because I was different and didn't look like everyone else. Instead of being just a good citizen, an athlete, a loving daughter, and a loyal friend; I was the 'exotic one,' the girl whose real

family in China didn't want her; the one who was repeatedly asked if I was Chinese, Vietnamese, Japanese, Laotian, Korean.

The jokes at my expense with the ugly slanty-eyed gesture for more laughs. The one asked: 'How much did they pay for you?' Or the one called 'the dark sister.' The one who was told too many times to count their lucky stars and, 'You were lucky your real mother wasn't forced to abort you.'

Closing my eyes to close out the thoughts in my head, if not my heart; I didn't hear them come up behind me until the world flipped me upside down. I screamed. My eyes flew open as I hit the ground hard; searing pain flared in my knees and shoulders as they contacted with the cement.

Crying out from the pain, I rolled over and looked up into the grinning faces of the two teenage boys I'd passed by near the park's entrance. They had come up behind me without my noticing and tipped over the bench, tumbling me to the ground. They pounced on me, pawed at my clothes, pulled my hair, their hands all over me as their skunky, weedy stink enveloped me.

Pure terror caused me to kick and lash out at them in a frenzy of arms and legs in an effort to get away. I screamed at the grinning, distorted faces above me, backgrounded by the canopied cover of the swaying trees and the menacing darkness behind them.

One of them gripped my wrists and squeezed until the bones ground together, causing me to moan in pain, "Shut up, shut the fuck up," he yelled down into my face.

The other laughed wildly as he chanted in a high-nasally voice, "Me love you long time; love you long time, you bitch."

I tried to scream again, but it came out as a tiny sound underneath their grunts, harsh breathing, and curses. A brutal punch to the side of my head forced my voice up and out, not on a scream this time but a screech of pain that filled my mouth and seemed to fill the park. A greasy, cold hand slapped over my mouth, stopping my breath.

With all my strength, I doubled my efforts and fought back, fueled by the certainty that I would be hurt worse, when a voice suddenly shouted from the settling darkness, "Hey, what the hell are you doing? Leave her alone right now."

A shadow loomed over us out of the shadows. Large hands grabbed the boys and swung them off me. I heard but didn't see them take off running while shouting obscenities at the man who gave chase. Rolling over, I pressed my face into the grass beyond the cement path, its coolness soothing my hurt side. My body felt hammered and brutalized; I wasn't sure if I could move again. But hearing footsteps, I rolled back over as quickly as possible, ready to yell and fight again as the man bent to me, his hands outstretched.

# CHAPTER 2

"It's okay; it's only me. I'm not going to hurt you," he said. "I chased them out. Let me make sure you're okay; then I'll call the police."

He put his hands lightly at my elbows and gently pulled me up to sit. He waited a few seconds, then said, "I'll help you." He stood first, then carefully pulled me unsteadily to my feet.

"Let's go over to that other bench and sit for a minute so you can catch your breath."

I nodded but didn't move until he did. Walking stiffly, I let him lead me over to another bench where I gingerly sat, feeling sick to my stomach, headachy, and shivering from reaction. A thought hit me then and shifted my already galloping heart into overdrive.

"My God. My purse. Did they get it?"

"Wait," the man got up and walked over to where I'd fallen. He bent, picked up my bag, and brought it over. "You must have rolled over onto it. I don't think they were trying to take it anyway. They were just crazy high."

"High," I said and burst into tears.

"Hey, hey, it's okay," the man said. He looked alarmed and started to get up. "I'll get a cop."

"No, no," I grabbed his arm as a bolt of terror shot through me. "Don't leave. Please, I -"

"I won't," he said soothingly and sat back down. "But the side of your face…" he gently turned my head and tried to get a better look under the meager light from the lamp."

"I'm alright, just a bit shaky."

"You need to put some ice to that bruise; it's starting to swell."

"I tried to fight back," I said, my voice quivered as I flashed back.

"Of course you did," he said.

"But they started grabbing me. I have to go to the police," I stood, wobbly but straight as I could manage. "I need to report what happened. I've seen them in the park before; they might try it again on someone else."

"Yes," the man stood. "There's a precinct house five minutes away. We can walk there."

I nodded, and we left, moving hurriedly down the block and around the corner without speaking.

# CHAPTER 3

We entered the Sixth Precinct on West Tenth Street through two sets of double-glass doors, passing two officers on their way out. The place was dim and virtually empty except for an officer sitting at a long desk behind a black railing at the top of the room. He hadn't looked up when we entered. As we approached the desk, he still didn't acknowledge us as he scribbled on a sheet of paper.

"I want to report an assault," I said.

"Who was assaulted?" the officer – Ryan, I saw from his badge – asked, still not looking at us.

"Could you at least acknowledge me if it's not too much trouble?"

I was starting to feel violated again at this policeman's treatment, and I knew it wouldn't take much more for me to scream, this time in pure rage instead of fear.

Officer Ryan still didn't look, instead he put up the 'wait-a-minute' fore-finger with his other hand; it was too much for me. I lifted my bag and slammed it down on the page he was writing on. His pen went stuttering off the desk.

"Goddammit," Ryan reared back in surprise. He finally looked at our faces. I didn't give him a chance to say anything else.

"Two young men attacked me in Walker Park a few minutes ago."

"I'm a witness," my rescuer said. "I chased them off but afterwards."

"They knocked me to the ground and hit me."

"Wait a minute," Ryan put up a halting hand. "I gotta –"

"No, more waiting," I demanded, surprising myself but not deterred. "Take my report now before someone else gets hurt."

"Alright, already," Ryan said and drew a blank piece of paper in front of him.

"Start from the beginning."

He took down all the details I could remember and stopped once when my words stumbled over themselves as I relived the brutality of the moment. It took an hour to get it all down, with Ryan promising he'll send out officers to check the park; even as I advised, it was probably too late because the two were long gone by now.

"You want to add anything else?" he asked after I'd given him all I could remember and all that was left to do was for me to add my signature.

"I'm making this report because it's the right thing for me to do; I don't want them hurting anyone else like they did me." I stated, then signed the report, and we left the station.

Outside, the man said, "You ever been to Mr. Kirby's? It's right down the block. Let's go there and get some ice for the side of your face. And maybe a drink to make us both feel better."

"No, it's fine," I started, his mentioning my face caused it to start to throb again with the beating of my heart. "I'd better get home."

He took my right arm in a light grip, "It's right on the corner," he said quietly. "A warm, well-lighted place."

My rescuer was right, I was not usually a drinker, but what I'd been through tonight, something warm and reassuring, even if it were a cup of coffee, would go a long way to making me feel normal again; at least less afraid. I also owed this guy for his help, and a drink wasn't too much to ask, was it?

# CHAPTER 4

Mr. Kirby's was a small cafe with six tables, almost always occupied with laughing, talking people. Along with great coffee and good sandwiches, Mr. Kirby's sold penny candy from around the world for ten cents apiece. This included American favorites: chewy wax with flavored juice inside, squirrel nuts, and candy necklaces; making it a popular spot in the neighborhood.

We managed to get the only unoccupied table near the back.

"Sure, you're alright? You might need a doctor," the man said, studying my face closely in the bright café light as I shook my head.

Studying him right back, I pulled in a breath. Firstly, because I believed I'd seen him somewhere before or maybe not because I couldn't place him. Secondly, because he was extremely good-looking, I hadn't noticed that at all, but under the circumstances, how could I?

He had to be in his mid-thirties with thick dark hair, a warm complexion, smooth even features, and rich dark brown eyes; Jake Gyllenhaal's eyes which were filled with kindness and direct appeal.

"You shouldn't be out here by yourself. People are being assaulted at all hours of the day."

"Women are being attacked you mean. And many of them look like me."

He nodded soberly, "Yes, that's true. I've told some of my friends who live around here to take whatever precautions they need to feel safe. I'll go get some ice."

He moved off toward the front counter and staring after him; I literally felt myself tumble. Maybe it was only a delayed reaction from the attack, yet my head swam, my stomach did a loop-de-loo, and my knees wobbled as a flash of heat permeated my body, rushing up from my chest to warm my throat and face. What was this now? It wasn't only delayed reaction was it?

My rescuer returned with a plastic bowl of ice and sat it on the table. Taking off his jacket, he rolled up the sleeves of his pristine white dress shirt, revealing muscled forearms and smooth skin.

Pulling his chair up close to mine, he sat facing me. We stared at each other for one, two, three heartbeats, taking each other in, before he asked, "You sure you're okay?"

I nodded.

Taking an ice cube from the bowl with one hand, "Do you work around here?" he asked as he used the other to lightly push my hair away from the side of my face with two fingers.

"No, for the Rutherford Foundation –", he pressed the ice to my face and I winced at the sting and bite of hard coldness.

"Sorry, I was trying to be careful," he held the ice to my face a few seconds longer and then put the dripping cube back into the bowl. "You should start feeling better in a minute."

"Better," I repeated, my teeth suddenly chattering as my body jerked in a violent reaction.

"You're safe. You're alright now," he ran his hands quickly up and down my arms in an attempt to warm me. He then took my hands between his, "They're freezing," he chaffed them with his strong fingers. "It's reaction; let it happen."

It happened as I felt his hold. I stared at him intently and not because he'd come to my aid but because it had only taken the touch of his hands, the touch of his eyes on mine, to fall insanely, head-over-heels in love with this man, this stranger.

Yes, of course it sounds crazy. I was falling in love at first sight. A fairy tale, a myth, a Disney movie. Yet, it was happening to me right there while he put soothing ice on my face. It was love. The kind of love you read about in greeting cards and laugh at in the movies.

"You don't talk much, do you? Can't blame you for what you've just been through," he looked at me questioningly. "My name's Abrams, by the way." He smiled at me, showing even white teeth behind sculpted lips, the bottom slightly fuller. His face was a play of masculine beauty and appeal.

It was love; I'd swear to it despite the fact we'd only just met, and I'd never been in true, deep love before. Almost thirty years old and having dated often enough, the sad fact was that I had not been truly in love with any of them, hadn't understood what it meant until this moment, with this man. Glancing up at the small clock beside the cash register, I saw it was a quarter after eleven and made a mental note of the time to put in my journal. The time I fell in love for real and true.

So, you think it's not unusual for a person, a woman especially, to feel emotional about her rescuer. The damsel-in-distress complex saved by her hero is natural. Okay, so he didn't save me from a burning building or a collapsing bridge but from a couple of kids high on drugs causing trouble.

Yet, it could have ended badly for me if he hadn't come along. It could have escalated to a full-fledge, unrelenting assault, if not worse. Thank goodness it hadn't, and that was due to this man, Abrams. All of it had nothing to do with why I'd fallen in love with him though; this was meant to happen on this day; at this moment, I was sure of it.

"Jesse. My name," I said and reached for him.

He was too startled to pull back as I took his face between my hands and ran a finger across his lips, feeling their soft texture before putting my lips to his and pressing; his were warm and tasted sweet. I felt him tighten up in shocked surprise before he pulled back to stare at me.

"Thank you for coming to help me," I managed breathlessly.

He'd tasted exactly as I suspected: wonderful.

"You're more than welcome," he said with a bemused expression.

I felt a flash of embarrassment suffuse my face and throat to bright pink. Yet, it was mixed with the thrill at my boldness, at my touching him for the first time.

"You sure you're alright?" he asked again, and it sounded as if he thought the blow to my face had scrambled my mental faculties.

I laughed, "I'm sure." Touching the side of my face with my fingertips. "It feels much better after the ice."

"Are you hungry, thirsty, or anything? I can get us a drink. Mr. Kirby keeps a bottle in the back for special occasions."

"No, it's really late." I opened my purse, took out my phone, and seeing I had no urgent messages, I put it back. "I have to catch the ferry home."

I got to my feet, stood a few seconds to see if I would fall over and when I didn't, I turned away.

"At least let me get you a cab," he said following me out onto the street.

"Can I give you my number in case something happens on your way home?" He reached into a pocket and took out his phone. "Or give me your number. I'll be out of town for a couple of days, but when I get back -"

"There's no need," I said, cutting him off. "I'll be fine." I was now feeling stupid. I'd practically thrown myself at this stranger. I needed some mental and physical distance from what had happened and from Abrams. I needed to try and get some perspective before it was too late.

Quickly tapping his phone's screen, Abrams held it up toward my face, "This is my number. Call it anytime if you need me."

Glancing at the number, then at the earnest look of concern on his face whose features I'd had already memorized, I quickly memorized his number. Turning away, I saw a cab coming, stepped out, and hailed it.

As it cruised up to me like a submarine sliding underwater and stopped, I opened the back door. Before getting inside, I turned to him, "Thank you again, Abrams, for what you did for me."

As the cab pulled off, I looked out the back window. Abrams stood there looking after me with a confused look on his face. I understood it perfectly. It was exactly how I felt.

I took out my phone and tapped what I remembered as his number into my contact list before addressing the driver.

"Whitehall. The long way around."

The driver glanced at me in the mirror, "It's your wallet."

I wanted to take my time getting to the ferry, to think, or at least try to; my head was still spinning, and it was not from the attack.

## CHAPTER 5

I ferried my way home, past the grand Statue of Liberty to Staten Island, probably the least diverse of the five boroughs. Yet, it was an island. I'd grown up on one and could live no other way; I seemed able only to live where the ocean was near my doorstep, and I could breathe it in every day. And then there were the parks. Staten Island is home to thousands of acres of parkland, forests, and wetlands. Some of the country's most pristine and untouched land was right in my backyard.

Picking up my car from the terminal's parking lot, I drove home to Mulberry Street, which is on the island's North Side. My house is a neatly structured condominium with large sunflowers leading up the walkway. It sat in the middle of a quiet block of small condominium complexes and sturdy homes with attached garages.

Putting my car away, I hurried inside the house, dropping my purse on the couch on my way to the bathroom, where I ran cold water over a hand towel, squeezed it out, and put it gently to the side of my face for as long as I could stand it, wincing at the cold pain. In the bedroom, I grabbed my journal off the bedside table, opened it to a crisp, clean page, and wrote down everything I could remember of the day with my Montblanc pen.

It took me forty-five minutes to get down every detail, beginning with entering the park, the incident, the rescue, Mr. Kirby's at the table, him pushing back my hair, and ending with my getting into the cab. I underlined the fateful meeting with Abrams twice for good measure.

When I'd finished, I flopped back on the bed, suddenly feeling exhausted and stupidly happy at the same time. Love was real. Love at first sight did happen because it happened to me only a couple of hours ago. My phone pinged from the living room; I hadn't taken it out of my bag. I went and got it; Loren was calling.

"I was going to call you," I answered.

"When? You should have texted me an hour ago telling me you got home alright. I do worry about you, Jesse."

"I'm sorry. I missed the ferry and had to wait for the next."

Why didn't I tell my sister what had happened to me instead of telling her a lie? Shouldn't I be excited about meeting 'the man of my dreams? Why was I holding back? Was it because Loren would think it was totally nuts? She didn't believe in love at first sight or any of the sort. For Loren, love was planned. Maybe even manufactured. Someone of high standards, in high standing, introduced you to a man of your status. Or you met him at a high-end function where everyone was substantial. There was no 'it just happened' or 'met by chance' because that was too chancy in itself, and you could end up with a person you were too good for - her philosophy, not mine.

"I thought you were still upset about the gun, so you hadn't called me."

"The gun is a bad idea," I said. Then, "Weren't you going to the Guggenheim tonight for that thing?"

Loren sighed across the line, "A climate change thing to benefit Miller's Freeze, but I suddenly felt ready to drop from exhaustion after you left. Richard has been on a rampage for days. Did I tell you he's already booked two years in advance with shoots with only a few weeks' rest in between? So, nursing his anxieties plus his ego from when I walk in until I can get away; it's overwhelming, sometimes to the point I want to scream and...." she just trailed off until there was silence on the line.

I didn't say anything. I'd never heard my sister speak this way about her job or her boss. Loren had one of the most enviable positions in the photography world as the private manager for Richard James Carter, a.k.a. RJC, one of the most famous and sought-after photographers in the world.

One of the reasons he was so in demand was because of Loren. She oversaw not only his professional life but his life in general. Keeping it well-ordered and balanced, which wasn't easy, was sometimes near impossible, keeping him afloat and in lucrative demand; I guess she paid the price for that success in her way.

"On top of that, my date for tonight wasn't able to make it back from an out-of-town trip; some emergency."

Oh, so that was it. "That's why you're not going: no date." I was amused now. My sister didn't like going anywhere without arm candy. "Where's Troy? The Gorgeous Troy."

"I'm not speaking to him right now."

"What did he do? It had to be him at fault. He thinks you're perfect. Call him up and forgive him, and he'll go with you. All you have to do is snap your fingers, and he'll be on your doorstep in seconds. Begging."

"Come on, Jesse. Troy and I aren't like that."

"Really?" I couldn't help the touch of sarcasm. "You've known the guy for six years. And he's been in love with you all that time. He's just waiting for you to give him the signal. Why not put him out of his misery?"

"Troy and I are not like that, Jesse," she stated again with a touch of finality. "I'm not like that."

She paused, and I could see her standing in her kitchen, phone on her ear, and her head to the side as she thought about it while staring at her reflection in the kitchen window.

"He's not the kind of guy you settle down with, who you settle for. Yes, he makes a nice living with his real estate companies, more than nice, but it's so…so ordinary. And I want more than ordinary. I deserve more."

"So, Troy's not at the top of your list?"

"Far, far down, but there is someone…and so far, he has every quality on my wish list and more."

"Wow," I said, impressed. "No one has ever had more than six qualities from your wish list, and to have all fourteen is amazing."

"Jesse, you have to set high standards," Loren said with a touch of queenliness, "we're talking life partner here; your ultimate teammate, soul-mate, the person you want to spend your life with and be with more than anyone else. You can't wimp out on any of those qualities and accept just anybody."

"Alright, I get it," I said; on the one hand, understanding where she was coming from, I did feel the same way, at least on my good days. While on the other, I understood only a person like Loren, who was born in a family with means going back to forever, could realistically hold these ideals with such surety.

"Ever thought about just going alone? To support the cause on its own merits?"

"No," she laughed. "You have your nerve getting on me. What are you doing tonight, and with who?"

"No one and nothing."

"Then, boo-hoo for you. Another night without a beau. Stephen's been out of your life for more than a year and a half. As a matter of fact, isn't he getting married at the end of September? He's over you, Jesse, and has so obviously moved on even after your living together for two years. It's time for you to do the same." I didn't respond, only listed patiently as Loren went off on one of her sisterly lectures. "He, in my opinion, wasn't worth five minutes of your time, let alone two long years. And for him to go off and marry someone else after you'd just broken up."

"He has the right," I interrupted her. "No more talk about Stephen. I wish him nothing but happiness."

"You can because you didn't love him, Jesse."

"Don't you have to get ready for the function you'll bravely attend alone?"

"I'll send a nice, fat check instead."

"How noble of you," I grinned into the phone, stretching my face.

The injured side pulled up, causing it to sting while my mind played the attack again along with my rescue by Abrams. Abrams, what a nice, strong name for him.

"Okay, I'm getting ready to take a long bath. I'll talk to you later."

"Alright," Loren said and yawned loudly through the phone. "Night. Talk to you tomorrow."

"Bye, love you."

"Me too," Loren hung up.

<h1 align="center">CHAPTER 6</h1>

Iran a hot bath, and while waiting for the tub to fill, I looked at my face in the mirror. It looked swollen and bruised, and the spot felt tender to my touch.

Sitting on the bath's edge, I brought up my contacts list and looked at what I hoped was his phone number. I'd call him tomorrow and thank him again. No, not call; he might not pick up but text him instead.

Testing the water with my hand and finding it hot but not too hot, I took off my clothes and sank into its soothing heat up to my chin. Had it really been only hours ago I'd fallen in love? Me, who believed I'd never fall in love with anyone. Loren had been right. I hadn't loved Stephen. I'd just been used to the relationship, having someone to sleep with, go to the movies with, and have meals with to avoid being alone. This had been what I'd called love when it was a cold, deliberate, and decisive play at having someone in my life as opposed to having no one.

Wow, I thought, with some self-contempt, that was not being a good person. I suddenly felt sorry for Stephen. I'd done him wrong, as the saying goes. He'd left me, but I hadn't given him many reasons to stay, including the fact that I hadn't loved him enough. We'd met at jury duty of all places and had hit it off immediately. He'd been funny and thoughtful with his bright red hair and green eyes. A regular Irishman who was able to trace his family back centuries to Tipperary.

Like all the other men I'd dated, he'd been white. My only exception to the rule, which I realized was a rule but would only admit to myself now, was John Standford. And he'd been a boy. We'd met when we were twelve. At the Asian-American Cultural Club, a meeting place for adoptees from mostly East and South-East Asia, we called 'The Kulture Klub' ala Boy George.

The meetings were held twice a week, supervised by two women who had been adopted from Cambodia and Vietnam as children. John had been the only boy in a room full of girls.

I remember how shy John had been. For the first three weeks, he'd said only one word: John, his name. Most of the girls had giggled wildly at him every time he'd come into the room, and he'd looked humiliated as if he'd been caught in his underwear each time.

I'd felt sorry for him. The only boy caught up in a group of laughing, talking, disjointed teenage girls on the brink of growing up, most of who were going through a weird, 'I love the eighties' phase, including me. Meaning we dressed, talked, and laughed; Madonna, Keanu Reeves, Guess Jeans, The Police, Little Darlings, and The Breakfast Club, headed by our appointed goddess, Molly Ringwald. John had been caught up in the mish-mash of those adolescent confluences which caused most of us girls to either play for his attention with heated precision or ignore him altogether with cold determination.

It was not only because of his looks: his thin face and features, his thick black hair and eyebrows, and his shy and quiet demeanor which made him the center of endless fascination for us girls. John was different from many of the boys we knew, who were boisterous, outgoing, and mostly Caucasian. For many of us, John was the only young Asian male we'd ever been around.

He told us the minimum about himself, which included the fact he had a brother and sister and lived in Milton, Massachusetts;

that was mostly it and little else. To me, that was not good enough; I was curious about him. More to the point, I was a nosey teen determined to learn all I could about the only young Asian man in my world. The first time we were alone, I took courage in hand and asked him if he would help me put up the week's bulletin board.

Each week one of the students was given the task of updating this board which listed current flyers for chess or violin lessons, information for ESL or to learn Chinese, Japanese, and Korean, and lists of student accomplishments. To me, the board was a big reminder to enforce the understanding that we were Asian 'other', and we had to stick together because of it.

John had looked at me, then nodded. I'd picked out a flyer, tried to tack it up near the top of the board for some strange reason, and he'd taken it and the pinout of my hand.

"Allow me," he'd said, and I'd laughed. He'd sounded like an English butler. My laughter had caused him to laugh too, and from that moment on, we were friends.

Later on, John told me about his history and the small pieces of background information his adoptive parents gleaned from the orphanage's staff. John was from North Korea. His birth parents had somehow miraculously escaped and ended up in China, in the Szechuan province like many had, but they'd been caught when he was eight months old.

People from North Korea are repatriated, but before this could happen to John's parents, they'd disappeared, leaving him alone, and if it hadn't been a cleaning woman who'd heard him crying, John might have starved to death. I'd asked him once what he thought had happened to his parents. He'd told me he believed they had died, killed themselves instead of being forcibly taken back to North Korea.

The first time John invited me to his house for dinner, I'd been so excited that I couldn't sleep the night before. My parents had been all for it. They'd wanted to make sure I was, as my mother put it, 'immersed' in my culture, its people, places, and things, and John, took care of the 'people' part of it. I'd told my mother more than once; that John was born in Korea while I was from China. She'd stared at me with a look suggesting that fact was an unimportant, a minor detail.

I was introduced to everyone at his home, a huge Georgian mansion on a quiet, prosperous street in Milton. His family had included a set of visiting grandparents, his older sister Jane's boyfriend, Elliott, and the two dogs, Buddy and Myron. His adopted parents had both been environmental lawyers and extremely chatty. John had hardly said a word.

His mother, a thin, tall woman with grey hair streaked with dark strands, told me about John's beginnings, at least his beginning with them.

"We got John away before all the newly established criteria and standards were put in place by the ratification of the Hague Convention for the Protection of Children," she said, sounding very lawyerly.

"Thank goodness for that," her husband had chimed in. "Or it would have been even harder, maybe even impossible, to adopt a child under those circumstances."

He was as tall as his wife, with the same grey hair with darker streaks. They looked more like brother and sister than husband and wife.

John's mother had smiled at me, then at him with a motherly warmth, "We're an open family. John was made aware of his adoption, from A to Z. We held nothing back from him."

Later as we sat idling swinging next to each other on an elaborate set in his backyard, I'd asked John only one question about his past, "You ever want to find your birth parents? If they're still alive, I mean."

John had shaken his head as he looked down at the indentation in the dirt made by countless feet as they swung and stopped and swung and stopped again. The look on his long, thin face, handsome in its way, was thoughtful.

"It might hurt them, the ones who raised me if I go looking," he'd finally said. "They've been good to me. They wanted me when no one else did. They're my real parents, and I owe them."

I nodded, understanding exactly how he felt. John was like me, believing the people who'd taken us in when no one who looked like us had loved us very much. Though there were times, perhaps too many when I was younger when I'd wished those who'd given me up had agonized over it. It had been there- forever- tragedy, and they were forever looking for me. It was a fantasy I'd held on to as long as I could. Our parents, who looked nothing like us, proposed to love us, and we loved them because we had no choice. They had brought two unwanted children thousands of miles into their lives and given us a home and privileges we could have never imagined. Our parents were enough.

Reaching over, I'd taken his hand. We'd swung there quietly, our fingers entwined. My first love. Innocent and sweet. It hadn't lasted long, of course; puppy love doesn't, and in my case, for the simplest reason: John and his family had moved across the country so his mother could take a professorship at Whitman College in Walla Walla, Washington.

# CHAPTER 7

My first young and budding romance didn't get a chance to fully bud and ended my dating of anyone of Asian descent or anyone who looked like me. I thought through this meandering sadness as the cooling water drained out. Getting out of the tub, I dried off and put on warm pajamas. I got into bed with my journal on my lap, and with my pen stabbing at the heart of the white page, I mused over the past, scribbling down my thoughts.

In high school, my sphere of males widened. Yet, because my school was private, meaning very expensive, most of those males were white. Nantucket's population was nearly ninety percent white even in tourist season, which isn't surprising.

I was in the minority from elementary through high school, though at least there, I wasn't alone. Along with two students of Indian-American descent, there were three African-Americans and four other Asian-Americans besides myself. I couldn't tell you any of their names because I didn't hang out with any of them. Yet, I do remember their faces in their various shades of brown.

The young men who did ask me out and I accepted were always Caucasian the only difference was in the color of their hair and eyes. I understood why some of them asked me out in the first place and why a couple slept with me; it was because they saw me as 'other,', different. The rest saw me as a conquest, a challenge, or worse – as Loren's little sister, who wouldn't turn them down.

I'd said yes to them excruciatingly aware of how they saw me; but at least I was being seen and if it was on the arm of the blond-haired captain of the team – any team – I was with the guy who always belonged, who was always accepted no matter where he went or what he did and it meant I was accepted too, for that moment I was somebody even if it was with someone who thought I was a joke.

In college, I narrowed my romantic ideal down to pale-skinned, dark-haired, and dark-eyed men and hadn't seen any reason to change my preferences when I left college. The only exception had been Stephen with his red hair.

I put the book aside, turned off the bedside lamp, and stared out the window, not seeing the night sky but Abram's face. Closing my eyes, I held his image before me; I knew him, I thought, not in the romantic sense but from somewhere else. However, it might be my imagination working overtime. I'd just been through a shock, after all, and on that thought, I fell asleep.

Around five a.m., I woke up feeling groggy and needing to use the bathroom. After taking care of my needs, I checked my face in the mirror, saw the swelling had disappeared, and realized it didn't hurt as much as before.

On Saturday, I stayed resting and reading. On Sunday, my phone buzzed, and I tried to ignore it. My body still ached, and my face felt tight and under pressure even with my eyes closed. But my phone wouldn't stop beeping. Sitting up abruptly in bed with my heart beating fast, I grabbed it off my pillow. Thinking the worst, an emergency, dying, dead. I looked at the number and knew for a fact based on the caller, she wouldn't stop until I answered.

"Hello."

The best line from the 1979 Warriors movie came out the tiny speaker: 'Warriors come out and play-yay. Warriors come out and play-yay.'

Then Loosha's voice, "Jesse, come out and play-yah."

"It's way too early," I yawned hugely, "for your machinations, Loosha."

"Whoa, you wake up with big words and attitude. It's noon, and I've been up since eight. I've been to hot yoga, eaten my steel-cut oatmeal with fruit, and had two lattes. I'm ready to roll. I got two words for you, my friend: Fuzhou Festival."

"What?" I thought I misunderstood her. "Fuzhou Festival? I'm not going into the city today, let alone over on East Broadway."

Having said my peace, I settled back into the bed and felt myself beginning to drift back to sleep again.

"You won't have to. The festival's taking place in your neck of the woods." This piece of news woke me up a bit as she went on eagerly.

"Right over on Settler's Island. Gui told me about it last week and messaged me a link. I checked it out, and it looks fun. Come on, Jess. It's going to be a beautiful day, and we should take advantage while supporting the Fuzhou community, right? And I'm willing to brave the V-to-the-N to come get you. What more could you ask for?"

"Loosha, don't you ever take it easy?"

"Why?" she sounded mystified. "Girlfriend, pretty yourself up. I'll be there at two. Bye."

She was gone without giving me another chance to argue her out of it.

I smiled sleepily at the thought of my friend. Lucia 'call-me-Loosha' Gustafson. We've been friends since meeting at the Kulture Club. Loosha was born in China, too, the Hunan province, while I'd been found in the Guizhou province.

She'd been adopted when she was four, having been orphaned at seven months old, left on the doorstep of the Li Shui Orphanage. From what she'd been told, her arrival had been heralded by fire-crackers and that she'd almost frozen to death waiting to be found. She'd been left by someone who'd called herself Loosha's 'Lao' or grandmother by the note attached to her blanket. Though her birth parents were unknown, the same as mine, my birth mother had at least left a message in my basket, asking someone to take care of me and that I'd been born under the sign of the rooster. The old lady who'd left Loosha had disappeared without a trace.

Loosha and I had jelled from the first moment we met. Where I was reserved and cautious, she was funny and out-going with her chin-length hair and country-peasant round face, that of a farmer's wife, she told anyone who met her. We naturally complemented each other, allowing us to remain friends all these years.

The only thing we couldn't agree on was our feelings regarding our status as adoptees. We were at opposite ends of the spectrum on the subject. Loosha, who spoke both Mandarin and Cantonese fluently and, of course, Icelandic, was on a mission to find her birth parents or any family member in China. She believed she hadn't been abandoned but forcibly taken from her parents, snatched from their loving arms because she was an out-of-plan child. And to this day, they missed her and only want to be reunited with their stolen daughter.

While I couldn't care less about finding my birth parents. Why should I? They were the ones who'd abandoned me, willingly given me up because I was 'a maggot in the rice'. They'd done me a favor, hadn't they? I had a wonderful life and was truly lucky. I had no bitterness toward them because I cared not at all; that was the past. I couldn't connect with China when I couldn't remember it and chose not to try.

Loosha's adoptive parents were from New England by way of Reykjavik, Iceland. As a matter of fact, her father's family was part of those who'd founded the capital. The Gustafsons were the epitome of pure Scandinavian genes with white-blond- hair, sharp Nordic features, pale eyes, and hair. Loosha was their only adopted child, but not the only child; she had an older brother and sister, Sondre and Silje.

She'd grown up in Eastham, Massachusetts, along Cape Cod. A beach town, beautiful in the summer but brutal in the winter with its deep, deep cold days and the occasional nor'easter hollowing across the Atlantic. The Gustafsons had no problem with the winters; it reminded them of their roots with their Nordic Viking edge and rhythms.

I lay in bed a little longer, thinking about Friday and Abrams and getting in touch with him. Glancing at the time on my phone, Loosha would be on her way in a few hours, and if I wasn't standing outside, ready to go, she'd honk the neighborhood down while texting me repeatedly that she was outside waiting.

I got up and took a long shower before making up my face more heavily than usual to hide the bruising.

Dressed in a white summer dress with tiny blue lotus flowers printed on it, flat blue walking shoes, and my hair tied back with white butterfly barrettes, I was outside when Loosha pulled up in her red Audi 360 right on time.

As I settled into the passenger seat, she gave me a smiling glance, "You are a flower among flowers," she said, throwing the car in gear and roaring down the street. Loosha drove like a typical New Yorker with the lead foot of a NASCAR driver.

"You're looking spiffy yourself," I said while giving my seatbelt a good tug, ensuring it was in place. She was wearing red Capri pants and a white, sleeveless midi-blouse, and her black hair in its bob cut shimmered with liveliness. "The festival is where again?"

"On Settler's Island," she whipped the wheel a hard right, going around a blue Jaguar idling at the green light, the driver with his head down was staring at his phone. She honked, and the guy looked up, startled.

We took the Staten Island Expressway to the West Shore Expressway and got onto the Leisure Thoroughfare, a long stretch of connecting road.

"We gotta take the causeway," I said.

"Only way to get there," she countered.

We grinned at each other, our trip, the day, and our time together as the best of friends put us in the best of moods. We drove for another forty minutes until we got to the two-way bridge that connected Staten Island to Settlers Island, a sparsely inhabited green, verdant, and beautiful place.

The traffic was light, and we let down the windows as we approached the causeway. Loosha requested from Sirius XM, Loverboy's 'Working for the Weekend.' She rolled down all the windows, and as the warm air pushed through from all sides, making our hair fly up, we laughed and sang at the top of our voices all the way to the end of the causeway.

Once we got onto the island, the traffic flowed heavily. I looked out at the green fields and trees that looked more like farmland than what it was: thousands of acres of federal, state and local parkland which made up the island.

"Reminds me of Kentucky."

"Like you've ever been," Loosha scoffed.

"You know what I mean; it's full and lush as I imagine Kentucky to be with the ocean was millions of miles away."

We drove on until we saw signs at the side of the road that read: Fuzhou Festival, with an arrow pointing ahead. We went that way and came to a hill, and as we drove up, a red dragon with a huge set of rolling eyes suddenly appeared floating on the other side, high above us. It was gigantic, Macy's day parade size, with golden flames coming out of its mouth. We crested the hill and saw the dragon was not one but two, and they entwined around each other, creating an archway that was the entrance to the festival.

"Dude," we said simultaneously.

**CHAPTER 8**

Traffic had thickened six- fold, and there seemed to be thousands of people moving toward the festival's entrance, having left their cars parked in the nearby fields. The police were there directing traffic and waving people to alternative parking locations. We followed the directions of a cop and found a space on the side of a low hill.

We got out and followed the crowd underneath the archway into a world of fluttering flags and balloons featuring the five Chinese elements: earth, water, wood, fire, and metal and the twelve animal zodiac signs: the Tiger, the Dog, the Rooster, the Monkey, the Dragon, The Pig and all the rest. All around us were the competing voices of the festival-goers speaking in English, Mandarin, Cantonese, and other dialects unfamiliar to me.

The smell of competing foods filled the air. Music blared from loudspeakers as game barkers hollered for takers. Large tents held displays of traditional dancing and games, including ping-pong, a mahjong tournament, and an elaborate puppet show that delighted a sea of children.

From one end of the festival grounds to the other, there was something to be seen, listened to, and in our case, hungrily devoured from the food stalls and food trucks that lined one side of the makeshift midway. There were all kinds of delights, from well-loved egg drop soup to fried Oreo's-on-a-stick. Loosha and I enjoyed it all.

We started with Chinese pork and noodles and moved on to elephant ears topped with vanilla ice cream. Once, we queued up to a stand serving bowls of rice, and on a huge flaming grill, what looked like a thousand kabobs with vegetables, chicken, fish, and other pieces of meat I didn't recognize.

Loosha spoke Cantonese to the man grilling with both hands while shouting at his helpers.

She whispered to me, "Get the fish on the left."

When it was our turn, I pointed to the skewered fish, "Two, please."

The man tonged the sizzling fish onto paper plates while one of his helpers handed us boxes of steaming vegetables and rice with chopsticks sticking up in its center.

Once we'd paid and walked away, I asked, "Why didn't we get the ones on the right?"

"Those brown, shiny things next to the fish that looked like large nuts? Well – they weren't. They were roasted cicada larva. But hey, if you wanna go back and give 'em a try?" she grinned at me. "They'll be nice and crunchy by now."

The thought of sinking my teeth into female cicada larvae, a Chinese delicacy, its juice flowing into my mouth and down my throat, made me shiver, "I'll pass and stick with the fish."

She laughed as we munched and strolled, feeling the sun on our faces.

We drank water from an open tap, walked, and danced until I couldn't anymore.

"Let's find a couple of seats and rest for a few minutes," I said, taking hold of Loosha's arm and pulling her away from a game that featured tossing a small red ball into even smaller red cups lined in a row.

Under a large oak tree, we found an empty bench down from the main festival fairway and dropped onto it with heavy sighs of relief. We rested and watched people go by.

I took off my shoes and freely wiggled my toes, "My feet are starting to hurt," they felt hot and tired and appreciated the breeze across their bareness.

"The one good thing with all the walking we've done, we burned some calories," Loosha said.

"No, we didn't, with all the junk we've eaten. Don't you think it's time for us to make our way home?" I pulled the phone out of my bag and looked at the time. "We've been here for more than three hours. It's going to take a while to get back to my house, and you still have to get home if you don't want to stay over."

Slouched back, her face up to the waning day with her eyes closed, Loosha didn't answer. Her phone beeped; she took it out of her pocket, glanced at it, and put it back.

"There's going to be fireworks later," she glanced at me with eyebrows raised.

"Another time," I said.

She slapped her hands on her thighs, stood, and stretched, "Then let's go."

We walked down the midway, which was still tight with people making progress slow. Once in a while, we were at a standstill, waiting for whatever obstacle ahead of us to sort itself out.

At one point, Loosha grabbed my hand, "Let's take a shortcut through the stalls."

She pulled me along before I could protest, down a side aisle between two stalls selling cooking ware and knick-knacks.

"I have someone I want you to meet."

"Who?" I asked, going from surprise to confusion. I was also tired of bumping into people and was starting to feel sick from all the food we'd eaten and was in no mood for Loosha's shenanigans.

"What are you talking about?"

"It'll only take a minute, Jess. Right over there."

She pulled me out back of the festival, where some of the food trucks were now parked and being cleaned out.

"You can't still be hungry, Loosha."

"One-stop."

She led me to a white trailer with: Food Bank painted on its side in plain, blue letters.

My friend knocked on the door and called, "We're here."

From inside, a male voice answered, "On my way."

We stepped back as the door was swung open by a tall man, a few years older than we were. Under one arm he held a large clear plastic box full of white plastic utensils. When he saw us, he smiled, sending a good-looking face instantly into handsome.

I stared at him and flashed to a character from an eighties movie I'd seen a dozen times, 'The Year Of The Dragon', starring Mickey Rourke. He'd played a corrupt New York City cop working in Chinatown. A movie that had offended my sensibilities then, which I now found beautifully photographed, and one of director Michael Cimino's best, in my opinion.

The character this man reminded me of had been called Joey Tai, played by actor John Lone, except the man in front of us was more muscular in the arms and legs with the physique of a ballet dancer. He had dark, almost black eyes and underneath his right was a scar in the shape of a half-moon, and it smiled when he smiled.

"Nice you could make it," he said in a calm, even voice before stepping out of the trailer and down its stairs.

He kissed Loosha on the cheek, then turned to me, "You're Jesse," he said. "Finally." He grinned at me with straight, even teeth. His entire demeanor radiated an anticipatory welcome.

"I'm sorry, I don't -" I began with an intense, questioning glance toward my friend, who was smiling at us.

"Let me put this down, and I'll be right back."

He walked to a picnic table where large foil-wrapped pans of food sat in tubs of ice. He sat the box on a bench then came back over to us. He pointed toward the pans.

"Whatever was not sold by the vendors but usable for meals is headed for the food bank. Others will be along any minute to help load the truck."

"I'm glad it's not being wasted," I said, though more confused than ever.

I had no idea why I was here and what I was doing talking to this stranger. Did this somehow have to do with water? Had Loosha told him I worked for a foundation whose mission was clean water for all? Though he hadn't mentioned anything about water conservation. What was going on here? I started to ask when the man gave me a slight bow before sticking his hand toward me.

"My name's Siyu Lew. Loosha's told me about you so I wanted to meet you."

I didn't take his hand. "She didn't tell me about you."

Siyu folded his arms across his chest, his smile still in place, "It's no problem; I'll be glad to tell you whatever you want to know."

"Why would you do that?"

"I think it would be great getting to know each other and you seem nice just like Loosha said. And you're beautiful too; just like she said."

I whipped my gaze around to my friend, who shrugged and looked at the two of us as if she were a proud parent off a set of twins.

"Hey, Lew," a voice called from off to our left.

A group of people moved toward us, men and women, wearing white t-shirts with VOLUNTEER printed in blue letters.

"Excuse me a minute," Siyu addressed me. "Don't leave, please. I'll be right back."

He walked away, calling, "Gary, we need to pack this food right now and get it going. They can use some for meals tonight if we hurry it up."

We watched for a few minutes as Siyu organized the volunteers and got them to pack the truck with orderly haste.

I turned on Loosha, "I haven't forgotten about you. I'm tired, and I'm gone. I'll wait for you in the car.

"Wait a minute," she said, alarmed. "Lew will be right back."

"So what? You stay and talk to him if you want; he's your friend."

"You can't leave. You're right: we're just friends," she said. "I told him all about you. How great you are, how fun, smart. Lew's a wonderful guy. He owns the Lynnis Tire store chain, didn't I tell you? The company that makes those tires with the inside sensors that adapt to road and weather conditions so the car can be safer. Plus, his work with the food bank. All that's wonderful, right?"

"You wait for him if he's so wonderful."

"He's here to meet you not me."

"What're you trying to do?"

"See if you two would like each other, that's all," she said innocently. "You two have a lot in common. The moment I met him; I was positive you two would be perfect for each other."

"So, you didn't want me to come to the festival just to enjoy myself? But to set me up with some guy. To manipulate me into this meeting."

"He's not just some guy, but a very one doing well, giving back, and wanting a great girl in his life. You're my best friend, and I was hoping you two would hit it off."

I turned and looked at Siyu and watched him load the truck with the other volunteers as they joked around with each other. He was handsome and, at first impression, seemed a person worth getting to know.

Yet, standing there and analyzing how I felt: I realized I felt nothing. No need, no desire to find out more about Siyu Lew because Abrams was in the way, in the form of possibilities.

Those possibilities included what? I wasn't sure and was even a bit afraid of what I didn't know, if I ever saw him again. Nevertheless, I wasn't going to let the chance pass me by. I'd once read a book titled, Blink by Malcolm Gladwell, and as concept he'd formulated I'd never forgotten, called 'thin-slicing'.

It's essentially making up your mind about someone in a matter of seconds, even though you know very little, if anything, about them even as we feel we know all about their lives and intentions. We do it all the time when we meet from a stranger, a new co-worker or someone at a dinner party. And my making a snap judgment about Abrams was as solid, complete and stead-fast as if I'd been with him for thirty years instead of a couple of hours. I'd felt him instantly, his essence, his true -self, and already believed I could love him for a lifetime.

So, although Loosha bringing me here was built on a foundation of good intentions, it was a non-starter for me. I'd made my decision: Abrams was the one, and I was throwing it all in for that one man.

After getting the truck loaded up to its rafters and thanking the volunteers, Siyu hurried back to us, and this time, I held out my hand first. He took it, and I shook his warmly.

"It's wonderful what you're doing," I said.

"It's the food bank whose saving people. You work at the Rutherford, Loosha told me. You're saving lives all over the world."

"It's the foundation and there's always room to do more. It was very nice meeting you, Siyu."

I turned back the way we'd come, not caring if Loosha followed or not; I'd wait for her at the car.

"Wait," Siyu briefly touched my arm. "May I call you sometime? I would love to take you out to dinner or a play or a movie. Whatever you want."

I shook my head, feeling badly embarrassed but determined at the same time.

"I – no – Loosha shouldn't have tried … but thank you for asking, Siyu. And again, it was very nice meeting you."

His hand dropped away, and I walked off back the way we'd

come. I found the car and waited for Loosha, who had the keys. She arrived a few minutes later, a sullen look on her face as we got in the car without a word to each other. On the way home, I forgot about Siyu Lew; he didn't make it into my journal that night; as a matter of fact, I never thought about him again.

## CHAPTER 9

On Monday morning, around five a.m. I woke up feeling groggy and touched my face, the swelling had disappeared, and it barely hurt. Back in bed, I slept dreamlessly until seven-thirty. I breakfasted on Special K with strawberries and had a cup of tea before dressing and leaving for the ferry into Manhattan.

It was going to be a beautiful day. I stood on deck, feeling the clean breeze and watching the city open and blossom as we approached. The sunshine sparkled off its glass and steel, giving it an unreal beauty. As I stared, I saw Abrams's face; his large dark eyes, the flash of his smile as the sun flashed off the water and the buildings ahead.

My office is at thirty-two Old Slip in the Financial District, or FIDI, as New Yorkers call it. The building is thirty-six floors of prime real estate occupied mostly by profiteers except for a few non-profits like the one I worked for, The Excel and Estelle Rutherford Foundation; its mission: clean water for all. I was the logistics expert for the foundation, in charge of making sure wherever we went in the world, we were relatively safe, and I do mean 'relatively' because there are never any guarantees any place in the world.

In my office, closet-sized but with a window and a view of the East River, I quickly stowed my purse before placing my phone on my desk. While shedding my jacket, I turned on my computer with its two monitors and signed on to read my email. Finding nothing too urgent, I picked up my cell, took a deep breath, and tapped on my contacts list. My finger was hovering over the number I hoped was Abrams when my desk phone rang, making me jump. As it rang again, there was a knock at my door.

"Come in," I called, sitting down my phone. I picked up the receiver of my landline, recognizing the number. "Hi, Mom, could you hold a sec? Someone's at the door. Come in," I called again.

The door opened, and Clarence Murphy stepped inside, a sheaf of papers in one of his hands. He was a tall, angular man with a smooth bald head and craggy features surrounded by a ginger beard.

When I'd first come to Rutherford, I'd heard him call me 'geisha girl.' I'd gritted my teeth in anger, not only because the comment was highly inappropriate but because he hadn't bothered to find out if I were Chinese-American, Japanese-American, Korean-American, or any of the other 'Americans.'

"Here's the report from the African Commission," he said. "I tried to send it to you in a pdf, but my computer's down; Jerry's working on it now."

He placed the papers on my desk.

"Thanks, Clarence."

"What'cha doin' for lunch?" he asked, backing toward the doorway and stopping there.

"Since it's only eight forty-six, I haven't given it much thought."

"Right," he said and blushed underneath his beard. "Are you aware there's a tiny bruise on the side of your face?" he pointed. "It looks painful."

"No, it's okay. Sorry, "I held up the receiver. "I'm on a call. Can we talk later?"

"Sure, sure," he backed across the threshold, grabbing the doorknob. "You want this open or closed?"

"You can close it."

With a brief wave, he closed the door after himself.

"Sorry about that, Mom. Why didn't you call me on my cell? How are you?"

I pictured my mother sitting at her antique desk, which sat in an alcove off the side of the kitchen, the two small, authentic Chagall prints at her elbow. In front of her was her most recent journal.

"I'm fine," she said. "Dad's fine. It's you I'm concerned about, Jesse."

"Me? Why?"

"You were going to call me back two days ago, and I haven't heard from you."

"Mom, I was going to call you this afternoon. Work has been so crazy, and I was-"

"Your sister is in the paper," she interrupted. "Well, the online paper if you prefer. Mine is the old-fashioned hard copy, of course."

"Is she?" I said, not having to ask which paper. My mother only read two: The New York Times because her daughters lived in New York, and The Nantucket News, her local paper.

Logging onto the Times' website, I went immediately to the style section.

"She didn't tell me she'd be in a feature story today," I said as I scrolled through the pictures of various dinner galas, city-wide events, museum, and art institute openings, stopping when I came across the photos for the Miller's Gala.

I scrolled, stopping at the fourth picture. It was of Loren standing with her boss, Richard James Carter, and the mayor's wife, Rosalyn Stansfield. Their arms were around each other's waists as they smiled politely at the camera. The caption below the picture read: Mayoress Rosalyn Stansfield; Richard James Carter; Loren Roberts, head of the management team for RJC as the world-renowned photographer is widely known. He was instrumental in helping raise more than one million dollars in one evening for the Miller's Freeze project against climate change.

I saw that Loren was wearing the peach dress she'd shown me.

"She's wearing the one Vera Wang designed for her," my mother said.

Loren looked good, and she knew it. I could tell by the tilt of her head and the tiny smile that played across her lips that all eyes had been on her. She was the quintessential example of the European standard of beauty ingrained in all our psyches: blond hair, light eyes, and willowy figure.

"Richard is lucky to have her," my mother went on. "I read that your sister put tremendous work into this fundraiser, and it raised more than it has in the last three years."

"Sis is great at charity causes and benefits - no one's better at staging a show - even without a date."

"She was an integral part of the project. Doesn't she look poised and elegant even next to the mayor's wife? Who is a clothes horse if I ever saw one."

"She looks great," I agreed as I always did.

"You're beautiful too, Jesse," my mother said quickly. "In your own way," she added as she always did.

I felt the stupid urge to ask, 'What is my own way?' but didn't. "There are more important things than looks, Mom. But I get you."

"Get what?"

"Nothing."

"So, what have you been up to?"

I took a deep breath and opened my mouth to answer even though I wasn't sure what would come out, yet I was helpless not to say it, "I met someone."

"I was thinking we'd," she suddenly stopped. "I'm sorry, honey, what did you say? Who? Where was this?"

"Friday, I was in the park."

"Park? Were you by yourself? Oh, Jesse, how many times have I told you about going by yourself. It's dangerous."

"I was fine," I lied.

"Loren said people in her neighborhood are being robbed, assaulted, and if anything happens to you -"

"I'm sorry I brought it up."

"Jesse, these days it's dangerous out there. You must be extra vigilant about your safety. Be aware of your surroundings -"

"Listen, I have to go; I'll call you later."

"You haven't told me about this 'someone'?"

"Later, Mom. Love to Dad," I said and hung up.

Picking up my cell, I tapped Abrams's number and was asked to leave a message.

"Good morning, Abrams; this is Jesse from the other night. I want to invite you to dinner tonight to thank you formerly." I felt on a meter and hurried on, "It'll be my pleasure to meet you again in a less stressful situation. And oh, if this isn't Abrams's number, sorry."

I tapped off, put down my phone, and answered emails until ten o'clock when I picked up my desk phone and called Bradley Wachowski, the foundation's point person in India.

"We can send two people into Rajkot," Bradley said, walking into my office for an impromptu meeting and taking a seat in one of the two guest chairs. "They've recently dug two new wells. It's just that the water's flow is limited to only a few hours a day. I'm unsure how much good we can do in that situation."

Bradley had worked for the foundation for more than twenty years and knew almost everything possible about the Indian continent. He was a terrific researcher and field coordinator.

"What about another meeting with Rajkot's government officials?" I asked.

"The people distrust the local government more than they distrust us. And anyway, they may want a substantial bribe in return."

"What if we give them some kind of incentive? If they can increase water production by six percent each year and are successful, we'll put on some sort of award ceremony."

Bradley pointed his ink pen at me, "That's a good idea," he said as I surreptitiously checked the clock on my computer. We can have something made up, almost like an Oscar or better yet, a Golden Globe, and we'll put on a big ceremony when we give it out."

"We need to send Carol Dreyfuss with the new campaign. She speaks Hindu and Bengali."

My phone rang; I turned eagerly toward it before remembering I'd left a voicemail for Abrams on my cell phone, not my office phone, and picked up.

"It's Sharon at Interpol," I said to Bradley. "We'll finish later."

He got up and left the room with a brief good-bye.

"Sharon, how are you?"

I listened as she informed me of the current state of the countries where the foundation's staff worked and lived. Sharon knew if a coup was ready to take place in Addis Ababa, Ethiopia; if the army was readying to overthrow the government of Chad; if the rebel groups were seeking control of the Republic of Congo, or if there would be a spike in terrorist threats in Beirut, Lebanon come the fall.

My job was to make sure our workers didn't fall into the middle of any of those deadly conflicts; while at the same time doing my best to ensure they established themselves as best as part of the communities they lived in and were not just visitors doing a job who'd disappear once it was done.

Hanging up, I picked up my cell: no messages, at least not from Abrams; my stomach dipped in disappointment.

I moved from behind my desk; I must have gotten the number wrong, hadn't memorized it - only thought I'd gotten it right. Now, I'd never see him again. Shit. Shit. Shit.

I grabbed my jacket and with phone in hand, left my office needing some fresh air.

# CHAPTER 10

Outside, I walked down Old Slip, which was crowded with early lunch-eaters, and over to Old Slip Park, a small discreet place that boasted baskets of flowering plants and incongruously, on occasion in the summer, stands of waving palm trees.

There were a couple of benches and a fountain which took up quite a bit of space. Sitting on the fountain's rim, I glanced at my reflection in the water.

Had Abrams seen a Chinese-American girl or just a girl he'd rescued? How would he have known I was Chinese-American in the first place? Could he tell the difference between someone who was of Vietnamese, Chinese, or of Korean ancestry? I hadn't said, and for Abram's part, he had not asked, which boded well for him.

I turned my face to the sun welcoming its heat, which was countered by a breeze that was strong enough to pick up the strands of my hair, streaming it out away from me until I caught and held it back.

I felt better being outside, it helped me figure out what I would do for the rest of the day: focus on my work; it would take my mind off Abrams not getting in touch. And anyway, I was acting a love-starved, overwrought teenager instead of an immensely able young woman who needed to get it together. On the way back, my phone beeped an incoming text, it saw it was from Loosha.

'Girl, what's up?'

'Not a thing. On my way to the office. Will get back as soon as I get back.'

She sent an emoji of a polar bear in sunglasses: 'How about dinner at Val's? For some of his 'jing gaau.'

Jing gaau was: dumplings in Cantonese. I thought it over. Val Wong's was on Mott Street in Chinatown. He was a good friend of Loosha's and did make the best dumplings in the city, though most people hadn't caught on to his restaurants existence, at least not yet. Val and his family had only been in the United States for five years, having emigrated from Taiwan.

'Thanks, not feeling it tonight. Home and a bowl of Special K with strawberries.'

'Boring, boring, boring as hell. It's going to be a beautiful night. Let's meet up for a cocktail then. A place with a patio so we can drink to the moon and stars.'

'Alright, alright. I promise to come for only one drink. Maybe two,' I typed back.

'The Mad Passion at six-thirty. Don't be late.' She ended with a dancing girl emoji.

I walked back to my office feeling lighter and managed to work until nearly time to meet Loosha. I checked my email - not for the last time that evening - in case I needed to take care of anything before leaving for the day when my office phone rang again. I looked at the number and didn't recognize it. Oh no, my heart picked up speed. The call had to be about one of our workers. Someone was sick, hurt, taken hostage, or worse.

I grabbed up the receiver, "Hello?" I said with a touch of nervousness. "This is Jesse. May I help you?"

"Jesse?" the voice was familiar. "This is Abrams. I got your text but was hurrying for my flight and only just checked my phone." There was a pause, "The guy from Friday night. Can you hear me?"

"How did you get this number?" I finally asked. I'd recognized his voice after only a few seconds. It was him, the man I'd told I loved.

"It wasn't easy," he gave an embarrassed laugh. "I had to call in a few markers. Listen, I wanted to respond in person instead of a text which sometimes seem impersonal…" he trailed off then said quietly. "So here we are."

"Yes," I said, clearly seeing his face, his beautiful eyes. "Here we are."

"You mentioned getting together for dinner? I hope I didn't miss my chance?" I didn't say anything. "If you can't or don't want to, I understand."

"I can. Where should I meet you? "

"Good," he sounded relieved as if I'd said no would have broken his heart. "How about Mandalay?"

"On Thirty-ninth. What time?"

"Six-thirty."

"See you there."

Slowly replacing the receiver, I glanced at the clock on my computer, six minutes after six. I retrieved my purse and went to the bathroom. Stepping up to the mirror over the sink, I critically accessed myself. I wished I'd kept a change of clothes in the office. Or wore something better to work today instead of my oldest pair of khaki pants that bagged in the seat and this varsity t-shirt extolling Notre Dame College of Ohio, which was at least seven years old. I didn't have time to go out and buy something new to wear, so this was, unfortunately, it.

After refreshing my make-up, I gathered my hair high on top of my head. No, not a bun. Maybe in a long ponytail? But when I pulled my hair back, my eyes narrowed and I looked more Chinese than usual and for some reason I didn't want to leave that impression. But then why not, what did it matter? Abrams knew I didn't look like Gigi Hadid or Elle Fanning. Letting my hair go, it cascaded down my back in a long, silky ribbon.

With one last disappointed glance at myself, I left the bathroom and was halfway down the stairs when I remembered the meet-up with Loosha at six-thirty. Hell's bells, it had entirely left my mind when Abrams called. I turned into a corner and took out my phone.

"Hey, you on your way?" was the first thing Loosha said when she answered.

I could hear music, laughter, and the tinkling of glasses in the background.

"No, somethings come up and I can't–"

"But you promised you'd come out with me tonight; you suck, Jesse," she said with mock disappointment and a touch of genuine anger that didn't surprise me in the least.

As out-going and unbothered as my friend seemed with her let's-party-till-we-drop attitude I knew it was mostly a fake front. Loosha had a streak of steely anger running through her psyche.

This streak had been hard-wired there by the circumstances of her birth, feelings of abandonment, run-ins with prejudice, and the victim of chronic bullying growing up. All these factors colored every aspect of her life, and although she seemed happy-go-lucky, she kept her true emotions under a tight rein even though they sometimes got out and got the best of her.

"I know, but it can't be helped. There's a crisis brewing in Sierra Leone," I lied. "We've been preparing to send a team to dig wells and I can't send them if I don't know they'll be safe on the ground. As it is, I'll be on the phone most of the night monitoring the situation."

"Alright, I'm sorry, I sounded mean. I hope everything works out. I know your people do great work in terrible places. If you need anything, let me know. Call me even if it's just to keep you company."

"Thanks, Lo. You're the best."

"I know it," I could hear the humor back in her voice. "Bye."

# CHAPTER 11

I hailed the first cab I saw. I would be at least ten minutes late. I hoped Abrams would wait and not think I'd stood him up.

Mandalay was on Front Street, less than a twenty-minute ride from Old Slip. In the cab, I tried to calm myself. My entire body strummed with anticipation. I couldn't believe I was going to see Abrams again and hoped, deep down, I wouldn't be disappointed.

I'd built him up so much in my mind the idea of coming face-to-face with the real person versus what I've been imagining was jarring. But to him, what if I was an even bigger disappointment? But how could I be? It isn't as if he's expecting a version different from me – this was just me – the Chinese-American woman he'd met in the park under harrowing and fraught circumstances.

But what if I was reading all of this wrong and Abrams wanted to go out with me because he had a sick fetish thing for Asian women, where we weren't people, but some unreal fantasy culled from too much Anime or too many Manga magazines. To top it all off, I'd lied to my best friend over a man.

Okay, I 'd have this one dinner with him. There wouldn't be anything in that; only a last-minute date probably never to be repeated. Loosha and I had canceled on each other for last-minute dates before; as a matter of fact, if one of us received a better offer, we'd take it and tell the other about it later. It was almost a rule with us. Got a hot date? Go for it. For one, we didn't get many of them, and I was asked out less than Loosha was so she'd understand and would wish me good luck. So then, why hadn't I just told her I was meeting Abrams for a drink? Why had I lied to her in the first place?

As the cab pulled up to the entrance of Mandalay, I put aside negative thoughts and got out. I glanced at the small plaque with the place's name etched discreetly into the dark wood. If you didn't know Mandalay was there, it was easy to overlook, and it was how the owners preferred it.

It was an English-styled pub that served a shortlist of English staples: beans-on-toast, fish and chips, and kidney pies, along with dark brews of Guinness, ales, and lagers. Yet, it was truly known for its cloistered atmosphere and lush privacy even when it was filled with people. Mandalay was a place where discreetness was served and appreciated.

Stepping inside, I stood for a few seconds allowing my eyes to adjust to its cool dimness. Looking around, I didn't see Abrams, so I moved further into the interior, which smelled of pork steaks, dark malts, and apples. The place was centered around a long, darkly burnished bar that seemed to go on forever. Bottles of all shapes and sizes sat behind the vast bar while leather-topped stools wreathed the rounded wood. Two men sat at the polished bar nursing high ball glasses of whiskey.

The only sounds were the low murmur of voices, muted laughter, and the clinking of glassware by those who sat at the few tables near the back and in the plush, red leather booths which ran along the walls.

There was still no sign of Abrams. Taking out my phone, I was only eight minutes late. Was he running late, too? Or had he shown up and assumed I had not? Or had he not shown at all?

I tapped his number and listened to it ring in my hand and in the room. A man appeared coming toward me. He held a phone in one hand and two empty long-stemmed wine glasses in the other.

As the man put the phone to his ear, he walked fully into the bar's subdued light, and looked right up at me. Abrams, at last. He stopped. He was wearing a cerulean blue shirt which deepened the richness of his black hair and dark eyes. There was love at first sight, no doubt about it.

Abrams spoke first, "I'm glad you came," his voice was low and smooth with a touch of an accent I hadn't noticed when we first met. "I went back for the wine glasses." He tipped his head toward the room, "Come on, Jesse let's sit down."

He led me to a booth with a reserved sign on the tabletop. I slid inside the booth, the cool leather surrounding me. Abrams slid in across from me, his body lithe and strong looking. His fine features were emphasized by a light tan, his smile wide and healthy. He was beautiful and sexy.

"You look wonderful," he said.

"You too. How'd you get my office number?"

"A couple of people on Rutherford's board were willing to trust me with it and the fact you're from Nantucket and live on Staten Island. I couldn't text you; I was running in between planes back to New York."

"I'm happy you made it back safely," I said, suddenly nervous now that we were together. "Of course, you did or you wouldn't be here…." I trailed off.

"True, and that's enough about me."

Abrams rested his forearms on the table, cupped his chin in one hand, and leaned slightly toward me, giving me his undivided attention.

"Tell me all about yourself, Jesse. Everything."

"Everything? That'll take about ten minutes."

"No ill effects from Friday?"

I shook my head, "A bad dream. A bad moment or two. But I'm alright now."

"Good, glad to hear it."

"I'm adopted," I said suddenly, baldly.

I'd tossed it out there, wanting to get it out of the way.

"Okay," he said slowly.

"From China. I was found in a basket from what I've been told; by the people at the orphanage. A man found me, and if he hadn't been sympathetic to my plight and taken me to their door, I would have died." Abrams didn't say anything, so I went on, "We're ubiquitous, don't you think? You see us all around, mostly girls, trailing after our adoptive families like what we are: yàzhōu xiǎo nǚ'ér."

"What does that mean?"

"Little Asian daughters; who in reality could be Korean, Vietnamese, Cambodian; though many of us came from China where adoption seemed as easy as buying puppies once upon a time."

After a few seconds, Abrams said quietly, "It's only a small part of you, Jesse. Of your story." His eyes held mine levelly, "I'm not interested in parts of you, but all of you. You're beautiful, you know."

"So are you."

"Uh, oh," Abrams sat back laughing. "You're confused and light-headed from hunger; I'd better get you something to eat. I brought a few delicacies back from France."

He slid out of the booth and disappeared down the hall toward the kitchen in the back of the building. He returned a few minutes later, holding a bottle of wine and a corkscrew. "Tara is preparing the rest; she'll be right out."

He opened the wine and poured a few drops into my glass to taste and then some into his. The wine's aroma was rich and pure. I took a sip as Abrams watched.

"Like it?" he asked before taking a sip.

"It's wonderful," turning the bottle toward me. I translated the label in my limited college French, "Paris Sunshine from the Tournay Seine Vineyards. A full glass please; I'm old enough."

He poured me a generous helping before pouring more for himself.

"You brought food back along with the wine?"

He nodded, "I spent a day in Paris and two in Lyon at the vineyard where my friend grew up. He wants to expand his family's label by exporting it to this country."

"I visited France as a teenager. I love to travel. We take a lot of family trips - or used to - so I always keep my passport with me. You, of course, speak fluent French?"

He shrugged, "I minored in languages in college. What about you? Any other languages?"

"Mandarin."

"Fluent?"

My turn to shrug, "Lessons when I was growing up but stopped after four years, so learned enough to get by."

A sound came toward us, and we looked toward the hall, "That's our dinner." Abrams got to his feet as Tara pushed a cart loaded with delicacies up to the table. "Thank you, Tara."

"You're very welcome, Abrams," the woman said, and I recognized her as one of Mandalay's owners, "Enjoy.".

"This is all for us?" I was taken aback at the vast array of food, from succulent-looking mussels to fresh whole apricots.

"For you. And you'd better hurry and eat up. It's traveled a long way to get here."

After he'd crowded as many plates as he could onto the table-top, Abrams slid across from me and pointed out a container of thinly sliced meat, so thin it was almost transparent and so brown and moist it glistened.

"We have wild goose from an organic farm in Province. All the animals live as they want until they're humanely dispatched and used for food. The potatoes are grown organically."

"They're light blue and perfectly round," I said, having never seen potatoes like them. "They look more like rounded stones."

"Or blue seed pearls."

Abrams picked up one of the tiny potatoes, "You can peel them like onions; their flesh is soft and buttery." He put the slippery pearl potato on my plate, and I picked it up with my fingers and ate it.

"Good, yes?"

"Good, yes."

I was captivated by the food and by him as the barest hint of his cologne mixed with the unique smell of him reached me. The sounds of the bar, the other patrons, everything else became insubstantial beside him.

"I'm glad you like them," he said. "Speaking of like, do you have any guilty pleasures you want to share with me? I'll keep them to myself, I promise."

"Not necessary. My pleasures are guilt-free. Horror stories are one of my most treasured ones, the scarier, the better."

"Which are your favorite writers?"

"Graham Masterton, Stephen King, John Saul." I smiled gleefully at him, "Old-school-hardcore- masters who know how to give you nightmares."

"What about the movies made from the books?"

I shook my head, "They don't even come close to the visceral, shivering fear a great story can give you. How about you?"

"Classic Hollywood movies. You know the stuff they show on TCM. My nieces call them 'old-timey pictures,'" he smiled. "I consider them classic up until 1986."

He pushed a plate of petit points of crusty bread toward me before pushing beside it a plate of thinly sliced plums, their skin the color of rubies.

"The bread is from a master baker in Lyon.

"There's a large park there too, isn't it?"

"Parc de la tete d'or. One of the largest on the continent. It's as beautiful and as busy as Central in the summer. And finally," he pointed to a plate of flaky pastry with cream and a rich, gentle glaze on top. "Puit de' Armour or Well of Love. Try one; they're delicious."

"This is too much."

Picking up one of the slivers of plum, I placed it on my tongue; it tasted as sweet and rich as the wine. I then took a bite of the Well of Love, which melted in my mouth, sweet and magnificent.

"Heaven," I closed my eyes in gastronomic bliss. Then, "Did you get to see more of France?"

"A few more stops before finally visiting my sister and nieces in Avignon." Abrams picked up a pastry and took a bite. "Uhm, persimmon."

A tiny flake of the pastry was left at the side of his mouth; my fingers itched to remove it, to touch his skin, his lips.

"What about you?" he asked. "Any brothers or sisters?"

# CHAPTER 12

"No," I lied quickly, feeling in my marrow I didn't want Loren to be part of this beginning whatever this was. I picked up my wine and downed what was left.

"Honestly, siblings can be a curse as well as a blessing," he laughed.

Abrams took up the wine bottle and refilled our glasses. "I'm glad we were able to get together." He sat down the bottle and looked at me; his dark eyes were steady on mine, "I've been thinking about you ever since we met."

"Ever since you came to my defense you mean. I've been thinking about you too."

"Good. Would you like more to eat? There's plenty more in the kitchen."

I pushed my plate aside, "No, thank you. It was wonderful. If I'd any idea I would be wined and dined with French cuisine, I would have dressed better."

"You look terrific, and it was my pleasure," he said and reached out and brushed a thumb lightly across the side of my mouth. "A pastry flake. How long have you been with the Rutherford?"

"For almost six years," I answered, taking a moment to recover from his touch. "I worked for a temporary agency before joining the foundation."

"They do excellent work all around the world. Their commitment to women and families, to education."

"Don't forget the development of water projects," I added. "With digging wells, sanitation projects wherever needed, which sometimes seems everywhere. Plus, other forms of humanitarian aid. Sorry, I get carried away talking about the foundation's work; I can't help it; I'm proud of what we do."

"You should be, the Rutherford Foundation has never floundered on its commitment to clean drinking water for all, that's a wonderful thing." Abrams sat back and crossed his arms which pulled his shirt across his broad chest, emphasizing how smoothly muscled he was, "You're the logistics coordinator; what does that entail?"

I paused for a second, surprised he knew so much about me.

"I ensure our field operators get where they need to go in our base countries and are safe as long as they're in country. Though safe may be a relative term depending on the place; what's happening in the world and who's in charge at that precise moment in time."

"It's inconceivable to me that millions of people live without clean water."

"Many die trying to get it," I said, heating up to the topic so close to my heart. "The overwhelming number are women and children who walk hundreds of miles there and back for water to cook, drink, and wash with; many are assaulted even killed trying to get it for their families. It's crazy to me people don't get the fact clean water won't last forever. We can't make it, grow it or produce it. Every living thing on this planet literally cannot live without -"

I suddenly shut up, realizing I was again on my soapbox, "There I go again."

"No, I like it," Abrams laughed; it was husky, warm, and genuine and reminded me of my father's. "There's nothing wrong with feeling passionate about something you care deeply about. Or someone."

"It gets away from me," I reached out and briefly put a hand on his arm, feeling the reality of him, his strength and tautness of his skin underneath the cloth of his shirt. "So, now you; what do you do?"

"Right now, I'm one of the millions of guys working a start-up. Mine is a media consulting firm. It's only eight months old, wobbly and uncertain," he made a face. "There are times when I wonder if it'll still be going by the end of the year. There's three including myself: Kimberly Chapman and my friend Peter Summerson plus two part-timers. Peter and I grew up together. We both went to Columbia Law, and we're working around the clock to make a go of the firm."

"Will you?"

"Somedays, I think, no doubt about it, it's going to be great. Other days, that I should shut it down because nothing's going right, file for unemployment, and spend the rest of my life walking the streets. Speaking of walking, it's not as hot out right now; want to go?"

"Yes, I would love a walk." I looked at the still half-filled plates on the table, "What about the rest of the food?"

"Tara will take this away, and what's left outback, she'll give it to anyone hungry. Anything you want to take with you? I'll have it wrapped up and waiting for you when we return."

I shook my head, "I'm stuffed, thank you, Abrams. This was a wonderful surprise."

"You're more than welcome," he slid from the booth and extended a hand to me, helping me out. As he pulled me up, he pulled me close. His eyes moved over my face, the look on his thoughtful "It was a pleasure for me too."

CHAPTER 13

After having a word with Tara, we left the pub for the mild sunshine and the streets where New York lived during summer days. Everyone was out; people were walking and talking, laughing with each other or on their phones as they took advantage of the coming evening that promised to be cool and sweet.

Abrams held my hand as we walked. I looked down at his big, thick fingers wrapped around mine. We were connected, and the truth made me feel secure and cared for. It seemed as if everyone we passed were a couple. In love. In the city.

A few people glanced at us as we walked down Front Street; some even stared as we went by, and it made me take notice. Was it because this good-looking white guy was with the Asian girl? No, that couldn't be it. We were nothing new. Not in today's world and not in Manhattan.

Then I realized it wasn't 'us' they were staring at but Abrams. He was handsome, but thousands of handsome men were in the city. Yet, Abrams was more than that, and there was a sophistication about him, a sexy appeal that put him in a league of his own. Abrams stood out.

A question popped into my head, making me stop in my tracks and causing Abrams to halt beside me. Pulling him around to face me as people maneuvered quickly around us, "I don't even know your last name."

"It's Allen," he pulled me along again.

"Abrams Allen, it goes together."

"A blessing then," he pulled me closer to his side as a group of runners moved to pass us in a six-man line. "Yours is Michaels. I read it when reading about Rutherford."

We turned down Fletcher Street, Abrams making sure he walked on the outside with the traffic as we strolled along.

Finally, after twenty minutes into our walk, I asked. "Where are we going?"

"Haven't you heard about the small oasis somewhere around here? Come on, let's take this street."

We headed down a side street with only a few pedestrians going back and forth.

"Somewhere? You're not sure?"

"I have a general idea though it's been a while since I've been around this way." Abrams looked around, a slightly perplexed look on his face, "Hope they haven't turned it into a parking lot or condominium complex. We both get how outrageously valuable an inch of space is in this city. It's a small park, Jesse. It's lovely, believe me."

"I believe you."

"Right around here," we turned a sharp corner onto a street lined with small side-by-side shops featuring homemade soaps and candles, a shop for Indian powders and elixirs, a knitting store, and a used bookstore.

We passed these as Abrams turned us down an alley.

"Yep, this is the way. Come on."

The alley was narrow asphalt, where sat large and fully-loaded dumpsters against the building's walls. The smell from them was a hot, rich stink.

"Down there?" I pointed apprehensively.

"Not far down, Jesse."

The asphalt we were on suddenly turned to cobblestone. Ten

feet down on the left-hand side was a wrought iron gate entwined with a flowery pattern. The flowers were painted in bright colors of red, yellow, white, pink, and purple; the colors were so vibrant the flowers looked real, as if they'd grown there.

Abrams put his fingers on the gate's entrance and lightly pushed it open, "It's never locked."

He stepped aside for me to pass through into what was more garden than a park. A profusion of flowers was laid out in pathways in front of us, from cornflowers to chrysanthemums to roses and a few I'd never seen before.

Around the edge of the flower garden were tall maple trees; their leaves shimmered green in the light breeze as they stood like sentinels among the flowers. I looked around in wonder, delighted at what was before me.

We strolled down the nearest path, which was made up of sea stones that sparkled and threw back tiny rainbows. The scent from all the flowers was fresh and abundant in the light breeze. Bees went about their business as butterflies danced about, giddy at what was on offer. We were in a world of flowers, and the sight drove out of my mind the smell of rotting garbage.

We wandered over to a green-painted bench and sat down close, thigh-to-thigh. A small silver plaque was attached to the side of the bench, which read: Serenity Place, the name fit the park. It was as if Abrams and I had stepped through the magic wardrobe into the secret garden, which was essentially what we'd done, though down a dumpster-filled alleyway.

"I had no idea this place was here," I said with a touch of bemusement. The breeze brought the fragrance of hibiscus and roses wafting over us. "We're the only ones here."

"It's one of the few places you can really be alone." Abrams glanced at me. "In parks, I mean, wide-open spaces. You can walk there alone. Be there by yourself to think, to breathe. People go out of their way to let you be. A rare thing in today's world."

I knew exactly what he meant; it was one of the major reasons I loved parks too.

"Thank you for this, and it was another wonderful surprise. I'll always remember this place always." Mostly because I'm with you, I thought.

"It's been here for ten years," Abrams said as the wind ruffled his thick dark hair while it lovingly plastered his shirt against his body.

He took my hand and played our fingers together. His thumb rubbed against the inside of my wrist, making my pulse jump.

"It's a gift from a man named Cesar Bichon, an immigrant from the Dominican Republic who came illegally to this country thirty-five years ago, but who worked hard, paid his taxes, and did what he could. Twelve years ago, he became an American citizen, and when he did, he took some of the money he'd worked hard to save and helped create this park, a tiny oasis at the end of an alley. It was Bichon's way of thanking this country, this city, where he's raising his family and carving out his own small piece of paradise."

I nodded as a hummingbird winged past us and headed for a group of marigolds. It was as if Abrams and I were the only two people in the world living in our own Garden of Eden. Though, not Adam and Eve, I thought; look what happened to them.

"What else do you do other than walking in parks?" he asked before taking a strand of my hair, smoothing it between his fingers before gently tucking it behind my right ear.

"It's as silky as it looks. I've wanted to find out if that was true from the first moment we met."

"How many other women have you met lately?"

"Quite a few," he said with an amused twist of his lips. "In a day? Countless: getting in and out of cabs; at business meetings; getting a haircut - my barber's a woman - the optometrist where I get my eyes checked -"

"I mean Asian- American women."

"Lately ha?"

If he was one of those me who had a 'thing' for Asian women; who only wanted to date – us - for the novelty or worse; as part of an unhealthy, sick fetish that was dangerous for the object of their desire, then I was out of here.

Maybe he wanted to date someone different from the everyday blondes, brunettes, and redheads, if only to show his friends how cool, how hip he was from everyone else.

"Why is a man like you -"

"- what's wrong with me?" he countered quickly, his disconcerting gaze settling on my face.

"That's it right there, Abrams. Not one serious thing from what I can tell. Of course, I don't know you well, that's why the question popped into my head: why isn't someone like you in a serious relationship? Married to some former debutante or up-and-coming clothes designer, or Victoria Secrets model?"

"Whoa, give me a chance."

"Or are you?" I overrode him, unwilling to be stopped as the strangeness of this situation came home to me. Was this real or not? Was he playing with me?

"And if you're just playing around because I practically begged you to meet up like some lovesick fool, and you were flattered by my declaration of love and wanted to find out if it was a joke or if I were crazy…"

As I went on, I watched him gather his thoughts, preparing what he'd say to me. Would it be a rebuttal? A confession? Or would he end this thing right now before anything truly serious started?

Yet, when he finally spoke, his words threw me for a loop.

"Do you like going to the movies?"

Maybe he was the crazy one.

"Depends on the movie," I answered cautiously.

"As I said, I'm into classic Hollywood. At the Uptown Rialto, they're playing Breakfast at Tiffany's. Have you ever seen it?" I shook my head, and he went on. "Would you like to go with me Saturday night? Dinner and a movie? Unless you have other plans and I'd understand if you did, with me dumping another invitation on you out of the blue. And with your not being sure of my intentions."

I bit my tongue to keep the words from jumping out of my mouth: 'Of course, I'll see you on Saturday night and Sunday morning and Monday through Friday if you want me to.'

I didn't say anything, instead I pulled back my emotions. Yes, it sounds ridiculous when I've already professed my love, and here I was hesitating over a second date because being with Abrams was like being with no one else in my past while at the same time it was like being on a roller coaster during a hurricane, and I was suddenly afraid for my future.

"I have a family obligation to attend to," I said. "So, I'll have to get back to you."

"Fair enough, Jesse; I get the family thing all the time."

Abrams got to his feet and pulled his taunt body into a long healthy stretch before walking over to a purple chrysanthemum bush and gently pulling off a tiny sprig of the flower he handed me.

"To remember me by."

Man, he was something. I took his offering and inhaled its sweet and heady fragrance, "Abrams, believe me, I won't have any trouble remembering you."

"Come on, let's walk for a while, then we'll get a cab to Whitehall."

"You don't have to see me to the ferry."

"Yes, I do," he slipped my arm underneath his and rested his hand on top of mine as we walked as if we were a nineteenth-century Victorian couple through the newly created Central Park. "I want to make sure you get home safely."

At the gate, Abrams pulled it open and followed me out before securely closing it behind us. As we walked down the alley, I glanced back at our secret garden, placing it in my mental memory book in case this was the first and last time I would see it with Abrams.

On the busy main street, which seemed frantic with people and filled to overflowing with noisy traffic, Abrams hailed us a cab which took us to Whitehall, where a ferry was already boarding.

As we stood, letting other people go ahead of me, Abrams said, "If things change and you can make it on Saturday, message me or even call if you want. If we don't get together, I'll give you a call next week, though meetings and commitments might get in the way. I don't fully have my schedule down yet."

"I understand," I said.

The people flowing around us seemed almost invisible, the sound of the announcements from the ferry hardly noticeable; my attention was entirely on him.

"So, we'll see how things go," he said and took my face between the palms of his hands before touching my lips to his, slowly, carefully, tasting me for the first time.

He wrapped strands of my hair through his fingers as I reached up and cupped the back of his head with one hand while laying the other on his chest against his strongly beating heart.

We stayed that way, locked together as people went around us, as the boat's engine sped up, readying for departure. Finally, we pulled apart but only as far as a breath.

"Time for you to go," Abrams stepped back from me.

"Thank you for today."

"And more to come, I hope."

Waving briefly at him as the attendant closed the gate, I stood at the railing as the ferry moved off. Abrams watched for a few minutes longer as the ship glided away before turning and walking back into the terminal. I stayed at the railing as Manhattan grew smaller and smaller.

# CHAPTER 14

It was growing dark when I finally arrived home. Flicking on the lamp, I picked my journal off the coffee table and wrote down everything that had happened with Abrams. I began walking into Mandalay, then decided to start with Abrams's phone call instead and ended with my watching him until he disappeared into the terminal.

It took me nearly an hour to write down the sights, sounds, and tastes of the afternoon, and when I'd finally finished, I sat back against the sofa cushions, closing my eyes, satisfied I'd gotten it all down. And only then did I realize my purse was beeping. Retrieving my bag, I fished out my phone, wondering how long it had been ringing while I'd been lost in my afternoon's dalliance - I couldn't help but smile at the word. I'd missed two phone calls: one from Loren, the other from Loosha.

Loren's line rang three times before she answered, "Where were you?" she asked immediately.

"Out enjoying the weather."

"By yourself?" she sounded skeptical.

"Did you call for a question and answer session, or do you want something?"

Walking from the living room into the kitchen, I got a glass of water.

"Not an answer," she said. "Hiding something, little sister?"

"What do you want, Loren? I was just getting ready for work tomorrow."

"Yeah, yeah. I have a couple of notes on the party. I got the tickets for Randolph's exhibit."

"That's wonderful, Loren; Mom is going to freak out when she realizes she can go to the Island's biggest event of the year. I wonder if he's going to show 'Us By The Sea'? She'll never forgive him if it's not there for her to drool over."

"I have no idea," Loren said vaguely then. "The caterers will be at the house at four-thirty on the dot."

"Do you need me to meet them?"

"Jesse, it's Po Rafifi Dawn; they're born knowing exactly what to do. And anyway, I already gave them step-by-step instructions." I was sure she had. Loren was relentless in everything, and taking care of details was no exception. She said, "The flowers will arrive at three and Reverend Davis at three-thirty; he's going to give the first speech of the evening."

"It was more than thirty-five years ago when he married them. He must be ancient, Loren."

"He was only twenty-six then. So, he's what? Sixty-one now; not that old." She paused for a few seconds, "We're getting up there ourselves. I'm rounding on thirty-five myself?"

"You're only thirty-three."

"Yeah, and what do I have to show for it?" She sounded despairing, an emotion I'd never heard from my sister. "In two years and seven months, I'll be thirty-five, and then what?"

"Oh, so ancient. The pictures of you at last night's gala were fantastic," I said in an effort to cheer her up. "You looked stunning, Loren."

"Yes, I did," she chirped, sounding like her old self again. "I had a good time. Oh, one more thing: you're giving the second speech."

My stomach tightened in sudden dismay at her statement. She hadn't asked; it sounded more like an order.

"I'm not going to give a speech."

"Why not?"

"Because I don't want to."

"Come on, Jess," she coaxed. "I'm giving one. As their daughters, who appreciate all they've done for us, we're obligated to let them know, right in front of family and friends."

Immediate guilt struck me just as Loren knew it would. How could I put up much of a fight when it came to honoring our parents?

"What am I supposed to say?" I asked reluctantly.

"Something about being adopted."

"Why?" I questioned her high-handedness, something I should be very used to by now. "Everyone knows the entire story, and for those few who don't, my standing next to you all might give them a clue. So, why is it necessary for me to talk about it?"

"Because it was life-altering for our folks."

"Yes, it was," I agreed, having heard that for years, but for once, I asked a question that had never before crossed my mind. "How was it for you, Loren?"

"Jarring," she said so quickly, her word gave me pause, "in many ways." She changed the subject, "Are you inviting anyone? You haven't added anyone to the guest list though I'm assuming Loosha's coming."

"Yes, my one guest. How's Richard these days?" I inquired, moving as far away from the subject of my giving a speech as I could, hoping she wouldn't bring it up again.

RJC, who'd photographed from Rhianna to Queen Elizabeth, was in high demand for his talented work, which included: his paintings, musical collaborations, and creative, one-of-a-kind, limited-edition coffee table books that sold for a thousand dollars or more. For him to accomplish it all, he had a team of over thirty people who Loren managed; she was a mix of Mary Poppins and Captain Ahab, depending on what the situation called for.

She kept RJC's life on track by acting as his right-hand person, his henchwoman, and his conscious, which included overseeing the cease-fire between him and his two former wives, coordinating his highly anticipated exhibitions, and buying birthday presents for his three children. Carter, a thin, rapacious browned-skin man who wore small diamond stubs on both sides of his nose and tight dreadlocks which bounced with his frenetic energy; trusted or needed no one as much as he did Loren, and he was the first to tell you so.

"You know Richard; he's always the same. He's shooting Katy Perry for his next book, so we're working to make her time with us as wonderful as possible." Loren gave a mocking laugh, "Magical."

Jesse didn't laugh. She'd learned from her sister that dealing with some celebrities was the same as dealing with high explosives.

"You're going to be busy then?"

"Off the charts, but not too busy to ensure our folks will have a perfect anniversary party - beyond perfect."

"I want them to have a terrific time too, Loren," hoping it didn't sound like a whine but figuring it did. "I've done everything I can to help pull this off."

"You have to do more, Jesse," she stated, sounding like high-tone royalty speaking to a commoner. "Like give that speech where you talk about your adoption and how joyful it was and all that."

"I was two so didn't yet know joyful."

"Take my word for it: you were."

"I didn't look joyful in any of those pictures all over your living room, just terrified."

"You were, trust me."

"Okay, whatever. I'm tired and going to take a nice long bath before bed."

"I'll talk to you tomorrow then…. unless I think of something else tonight."

"You haven't forgotten a thing; bye, Loren."

I tapped off, walked into the bathroom, and started the water running in the bathtub before heading into the kitchen. Pouring myself a glass of red wine, I stopped in front of the hall mirror on my way back and stared at the face so different from Loren's and our parents'. My skin burnished from the sun, my upturned dark eyes, narrow nose, and thin lips, all framed by my straight black hair. China doll. Not American-girl-doll or even Barbie doll but China doll. But not so fragile and breakable, I hoped.

I fingered my hair, remembering how as kids, Loosha and I used to pull my mother's sunny yellow pillowcases over our hair, secure them with bobby pins and pretend we had long, golden locks like Darryl Hannah in Splash. Back in the bathroom, I turned off the water, undressed, and eased down into the tub.

A speech about my being adopted, I mused. What was I supposed to say? How grateful I was the Michaels had made me part of their family and not some other kid? If it wasn't for them, I wouldn't be here today living well and relatively secure. I wouldn't have had my expensive education, a great job, or this house? Yet, who's to say if the Michaels hadn't adopted me, some other family wouldn't have taken me in. Did my parents save me? Or would I have survived in some way and saved myself? Would I've made it out of the orphanage and still been able to have a good life?

Jesus, too many unanswered questions though in my heart-of-hearts, I knew one answer: no; I probably wouldn't have a chance, nothing like the life I was given. But was I supposed to spend it shouting my gratitude from the rooftop? Praising them on the constant for taking me in? For choosing me? Maybe I was supposed to do all those things and more though I figured they already knew how obligated I felt toward them; I'd shown them in a thousand ways, a thousand times from the moment I realized how lucky I was.

But then again, maybe I hadn't shown enough gratitude. I was, of course, much more indebted to them than Loren, their birth child, could ever be. And my publicly acknowledging all they'd done for me would at least pay down some of that debt.

Those thoughts whirled around my head until they got me out of the tub. Quickly drying off, I headed into the kitchen for another glass of wine. Moving into the bedroom, I put on a silk wrap decorated with blue peonies; the color was the same blue as the shirt Abrams had worn. Glancing at the shelf where I kept my laptop, I considered googling him. Was he an entrepreneur as he claimed? Or was he jobless? What if he was married? Or a criminal? A con man? A felon? A serial rapist?

Reaching toward the laptop, I stopped and drew back my hand. There wasn't an urgent need to check was there? I'd wait, and if we went out again, then I'd run him down, ask if he had a Twitter account or was on Instagram, which for some reason, I suspected he wasn't. Abrams didn't seem the type who spent his time trolling Twitter feeds. Or was I just afraid to ask him? Afraid of what I might find out.

After finishing off the wine, I turned off the lights and got into bed, where I slept dreamlessly until something woke me. I lay there slightly groggy staring into the semi-darkness broken only by the diffused light from the streetlamp. I could faintly hear the distant waves pounding on the shore and another sound that got me out of bed and over to the window.

Looking out, I saw that it was softly raining. The water slid down the glass, dripped off the leaves of the trees, and puddled in the street in a lonely, desolate rhythm that afflicted me with what I could only call melancholia.

My phone pinged; that was what I'd heard. I picked it off my pillow: a message from Abrams that caused my heart to jump a beat and then settle. It read: 'Thinking of you. I can't sleep. It's raining and supposed to go right through to morning, be careful on the ferry going to work. Think of me too.'

Smiling sleepily down at the small screen, I returned to bed, the phone again on the pillow beside me. He didn't have to ask me to think about him; I couldn't think of anyone or anything else but him.

## CHAPTER 15

The following day, it was raining harder. I was careful getting onto the ferry and stayed inside the lounge, as did most other passengers. The wind had picked up, and the waves rolled with an unsettling feistiness as they pounded the boat, spewing froth and causing some passengers to quickly exit to the restrooms. I couldn't see much out the windows, making the twenty-six-minute ride into Manhattan seem to take much longer than usual.

I'd planned to spend most of my morning getting ready for my monthly meeting with the foundation's executive director, Eric Weber, but once at my office, I was greeted with a crisis. One of our team members, Eric Elevado, working in the Australian Outback, was trying to reach me. He'd sent me a text only a few minutes earlier.

Tapping him on, "Hello, Eric."

"Jesse, Tracy's missing," he said without preamble, and I could hear him trying to keep panic at bay. "She… she went to -"

"Slow down and tell me what happened."

He told me Tracy had been touring a section of the Murray-Darling River Basin, which was going through a California-styled drought. She'd been visiting a couple of farmers who used their water in a successful water-trading program. He believed she'd gone to see the system in action and had somehow gotten lost.

"Exactly when did you last see her, Eric?" I asked, twisting myself out of my raincoat, trying not to miss a word of what he was saying. "The day, time, and where."

"Here at the hostel. More than twenty hours ago. Hell, almost an entire day ago. And I never thought to check on her," he said bitterly.

"It wasn't your job, Eric."

"You see, my stomach has been bothering me," he cut in ignoring my words. "Some seafood I ate, I think. So, I spent most of my time in the room, well, in the bathroom, and that's how Tracy ended up going by herself. We'd intended to go to a town meeting where the farmers were discussing water rights, but I didn't feel well enough to go."

"Tracy went by herself then? No one else from the group you're with went along?"

"No one. She messaged me after the meeting, saying she was heading to the farms. Jesse, I've been blowing up her phone every twenty minutes and nothing." I realized the panic he'd been trying to tamp down was coming through loud and clear. "She's in trouble, hurt. Maybe even dead."

"Eric, nothing has happened to her other than her phone might have stopped working or her jeep might have broken down. It's not like there's a Midas or a towing service station every five miles."

Turning on my computer, I quickly signed in and rechecked my email, even though I hadn't seen any from Tracy earlier when I'd checked from my phone.

"It could even be as simple as she forgot to charge her phone, or maybe she's someplace where she can't get a signal; it seems impossible in today's world, but where you guys are working, there are limited cell towers."

"No," Eric insisted. "I think something bad has happened to her."

"Please stop jumping to conclusions, Eric," I refused to accept that Tracy was - no - I wouldn't even allow my mind to go there. A tragedy had already happened on my watch; I'd been too close to it and it had nearly driven me insane with guilt and grief. I couldn't live through that again.

"Listen, I'm going to give her another two hours -"

"What?" he shouted in my ear from almost ten thousand miles away. "What if she's lying in some ditch somewhere?"

"She's not," I shot to my feet, unable to sit still. "I don't believe it, and neither do you. Tracy is extremely resourceful; she's observant, careful, and can take care of herself. She's been doing this work a long time and in worse places. Listen, Eric, I have some calls to make, and as soon as I know something, I'll be in touch. Contact me immediately if you hear from her before I do."

I needed him to get off the line; there were several avenues to check, people to call, and steps to follow I'd created in case there was an emergency involving a team member working out in the field.

Eric was silent; his worry and confusion came clearly across the line before he reluctantly said, "Alright, I'll wait to hear from you."

"Good, and if she shows up within the hour -"

"I'll call you back."

"Try to take it easy, Eric."

Disconnecting, I looked down at my phone, feeling a cold coil of fear winding through my belly. Was Tracy okay? Of course, it was possible something could have happened to her, something terrible, because bad was always around wasn't it?

Yet, I'd told Eric the truth; Tracy was a seasoned operator. When I'd started, she'd already been on Rutherford's staff for more than fifteen years. She was one of the foundation's most effective workers, an expert in facilitating water sanitation and hygiene programs in the countries we serve, spending her last two years in Australia.

Tracy knew the territory, was well aware of its dangers, protected herself at all costs, and wouldn't be caught out in the field; Eric knew this as well as I did. It had been a long time since one of our workers was hurt, let alone killed, and I refused to believe this was a similar situation to that other terrible time.

There was a brief knock at the door before it was pushed open, and Mark Patel stuck his head into the room. "Is it true about Tracy?" he asked. "Everybody's worried."

"I get that; I'm checking now."

I quickly typed an email, distributed it foundation-wide, updating everyone on what they'd already heard, and hit the send button, "It's out."

"Good, people are starting to panic."

"Don't anyone panic," I said sharply, looking at him. "It's too early. We don't know anything yet."

"Let her be okay," Mark said and left the room.

"She will be," I said to the empty air.

Pulling up my contact list for the region, I noted the time on my computer. It would be eleven-thirty p.m. in Australia, too late to call anyone official on my list but not too late to ring the local police station which I rang quickly.

I spoke with Inspector Rutledge, who took my information and created a report, or so he told me, which was not good enough. He told me it was too late to form a search party, but he'd organize one in the early morning if she hadn't turned up. Dissatisfied, I hung up and then made a couple more phone calls but to no avail.

There was another knock at my door, "Come in," I called, distracted as I dialed the phone.

The door opened, and Shannon Dekker, one of our interns, walked in with a large cup of coffee, "Thought you might need this," she sat the cup down in front of me.

I nodded my thanks as the line on the other end rang fruitlessly before going to voicemail.

"Dammit," I said and hung up the receiver, "Voicemail."

Shannon shook her head regretfully.

My cell phone rang; I picked it up, expecting it to be another contact I'd left a message for; instead, the screen read: Tracy Kotevski; I almost dropped the phone in my haste to answer.

"Tracy," I nearly screamed at the overriding relief that flooded my veins. "Oh, my God – is that you? Are you alright?"

Shannon, with a wide grin on her face, quickly left the office. The news that Tracy was on the phone would spread throughout the foundation in seconds.

"It's me," she said, sounding breathless.

"Are you alright?" I repeated with anxious concern, clearly picturing Tracy, a small woman with auburn hair and a winning grin. "What's going on?"

"Yes, Jesse," she laughed with relief and what I thought was a touch of hysteria. I laughed back, realizing I sounded the same. "Exhausted, but okay."

"Can you tell me what happened? Are you sure you're not hurt in any way?"

"I'm fine. My right front tire blew, I went off the road, hit a tree, and my head hit the steering wheel, and I guess I knocked myself out. Thank goodness I was wearing my seatbelt, or it could've been a lot worse. Anyway, when I woke up, I was dazed but managed to get out of the car and start up the road, not knowing where I was going, not even caring."

"I walked for a long time until two little kids found me. Why they were out in the night, I don't know - but they found me, took me to their place, and their mother doctored my head. It took us a long time to find the jeep again, where I retrieved my phone, it was dead, and I had to find a place to charge it and call for help. When I finally returned to base, I calmed Eric down and called you."

"You're in your room?"

"Right."

"I want you to stay there. I'm calling Dr. Howard to give you a thorough check-up."

"I'm fine, really, Jesse. A bit banged up, but that's all."

"You were knocked unconscious, Tracy; that's extremely serious. You have to be checked out as stated in your contract, by the way. So, take it easy until the doc arrives. If you start to feel unwell, call an ambulance and get to the hospital."

"Yes. And I'll wait for the doctor."

"And if anything - I mean anything - happens, call me immediately."

"I will."

"And Tracy, you don't know how wonderful it is to hear from you."

"Same here, Jesse."

Hanging up, I called Eric, who answered immediately.

"You don't know what a relief it is to have her back."

"We're all relieved. Now, Dr. Howard will be there as soon as possible to ensure she's fine. I want her to rest for forty-eight hours before you two restart your program."

"I agree," Eric said hurriedly, happily. "I'll make sure she rests, and we'll start fresh in two days."

"Good, I'll talk to you soon."

Disconnecting, I left my office for the outer room where most of the staff was standing in small groups, whispering amongst themselves.

I stopped in the center of the floor, instantly grabbing everyone's attention as worried faces stared back at me. We were a small, diverse, and tightly-knit foundation, and one reason was that we believed wholeheartedly in the mission. Each of us was committed to saving as many lives as possible, and it made us a family.

"If you haven't already heard: Tracy has touched base."

There was an eruption of applause and a few cheers, faces that had been filled with worry lightened and cleared in relief.

"She's been in a minor accident, but she's fine though a doctor will examine her to ensure she's one hundred percent. All-in-all, she sounds good, so no more worrying, please. If anything new comes up, I'll bring it to your attention right away. I'm not going to keep anything from you because that's not how we work."

Mark clapped, and everyone in the room joined in. I clapped too, then went back to my office, closing the door. Picking up my landline, I made a long-distance call to Dr. Howard; it took a few seconds for the far-away connections to be made.

When the line was finally picked up, "Hi Catherine, this is Jesse." I listened a few seconds then, "Good. Listen, I need the doctor to make a house call."

"Do you know what time it is here, Jesse?" Catherine asked at the other end. She worked for the doctor's answering service.

The question immediately annoyed me because I needed her to get the doctor going.

"It's late because it's early morning here, and none of it stops me from needing Dr. Howard to see a patient, Tracy Kotevski. She was in an accident and needs a thorough check-up as soon as he can get to her hostel."

"Sorry to hear about your troubles. I'll let him know right away. He's out in Sydney and will fly over as soon as possible."

"Thank you, and have him call me after he's seen her. Make sure he sends me a report, Catherine, along with the bill; I'll be waiting."

"Will do."

"Goodnight, Catherine."

"Good morning, Jesse from Down Under."

Replacing the receiver, I laid my head down on my desk and said a prayer aloud, "Thank you, God."

My relief at Tracy being alive almost made me feel light-headed. It wasn't only that she hadn't been killed or seriously hurt that caused me such head-spinning relief, but that I'd come through fairly unscathed. There was no one else dead on my watch. Of course, I couldn't control world events, acts of nature, or human nature; all I could do was keep abreast of affairs the best way I could and try and circumvent, head off any problems that could arise, and pull our people out in a moment's notice if I could.

Should I have pulled Tracy out and told her to come home? But why? It was a blown tire. Unforeseeable and minor in the scheme of things. I couldn't be blamed for that, could I? I was thinking about it too hard. I'd been with the foundation almost right out of college. They'd taken me in, and I'd found my purpose in this small but vital organization that had endured uprisings, bombings, epidemics, earthquakes, and wars in order to continue assisting the most vulnerable. One incident, that was turning out okay - thank goodness - wouldn't set me back.

There was another brief knock before the door was pushed open, and one of our office assistants, Carol, stuck her head inside, "Mr. Weber is on his way, and he's heard about Tracy and Mumbai."

Staring at her, "Mumbai? What about Mumbai?" Turning to my keyboard, I tapped keys clicked up the CNN site for breaking news.

A news crawl ran at the bottom of the screen, which read: Possible terrorist bombing at the Royal Chambers Hotel in Mumbai, India, frequented by American tourist.

"There isn't much coming out yet," Carol said. "Giovanni and his team are in Mumbai, right?"

Clicking onto the New York Times site, it said the same thing as CNN with no new updates. I clicked over to the BBC site, and still nothing new.

"No, it's Samir and Francis. They're there for a symposium at the Mumbai Hilton tomorrow."

"It's in the same area as the Royal, isn't it?" Carol asked, and when I didn't answer, she said, "Mr. Weber has some paperwork to sign, but he said he'll meet you in room 3212 in ten minutes."

I nodded, and she pulled back, closing the door. With a muffled groan, I slumped back in my chair. I'd forgotten Mr. Weber was coming in today to review foundation paperwork with our office manager and meet with a few key staff members, including me. It was just what I didn't need after the incident with Tracy: to be interrogated by Weber. If necessary, I needed to touch base with our folks in Mumbai and have them follow the foundation's safety protocol.

I didn't have time to defend myself if Weber had decided what happened to Tracey was somehow my fault. Or was I being paranoid and under stress? No one had accused me of anything, at least not yet.

# CHAPTER 16

Smoothing down my hair, I straightened my blouse, gathered my notes, and with a deep breath, which didn't settle the nervousness fluttering my stomach one bit, I left my office for room 3212. Not a good sign, I reasoned; 3212 was where employees were taken for private talks, bad news, and occasional tears.

When I reached the room, I saw the door was partly open. Weber had arrived first; I knocked.

"Come in, Jesse," a deep-based voice answered.

Stepping inside the room, I closed the door behind me. Howard Weber, the foundation's executive director, stood on one side of the conference table. He was reading something on a piece of foundation stationery and didn't look up as I took a seat.

Weber was dressed in a charcoal gray suit, a stark white shirt, and a purple tie that complemented his nut-brown skin and straight-forward features. He finally looked up at me from behind designer glasses which didn't detract from his knife-sharp gaze. He was a cultured man who'd sold his company to Apple, retired early, and was known to be a mega-fundraiser, able to coerce thousands of dollars from the most tight-fisted of donors.

Once at a fundraiser, he'd told me why he'd stopped being like everyone else who cared less than nothing about their water and how they got it. He'd said it had all changed for him after a visit to a town called Ceine outside of Khartoum. He and his driver were on a road when he realized it was filled mostly with women and young girls. It was the hottest part of the day, over one-hundred and ten degrees, yet those women were walking, loaded down with bags, bowls, canisters, and jugs.

Suddenly there was a commotion up ahead, causing the slow-moving traffic to stop. Weber had rolled down his window to try and see what was going on and had heard a terrible waling and screaming coming from up ahead.

He'd jumped out of the car and run toward the commotion, and when he'd gotten there, what he'd seen had frozen him. Lying along the road as if they were broken dolls were three small children, babies, really Weber had said, and a woman, their mother. His face had been like slate when telling the horrific story.

The family had been run over by a speeding truck as they returned from collecting clean water. They had still been five miles away from home.

An entire family gone, killed, he'd said, while attempting to obtain a basic human necessity: clean water, a thing he summoned with a flick of his wrist; something he bought for three dollars from any corner bodega; the stuff on his dinner table he usually ignored.

Weber's voice had been filled with remembered loss and deep pain I've never forgotten. He'd decided then to make sure as many people as possible had easy access to life-giving water, and he'd been working at Rutherford championing the cause for more than four years.

"Hello, Jesse. Thanks for coming and please have a seat."

I sat, "No problem," I said as if I'd had a choice.

"I heard the good news."

"We were all relieved."

He took the seat across from me, "The Mumbai symposium has been canceled for now," he got straight to the point with a reserved, no-nonsense air that made him an effective director.

"I hadn't heard."

"It was only just posted," he pointed to the iPad.

"I'll tell the team to move hotel and set up outside the city, at the Continental," I said, jotting a note.

He sat back and stared at me levelly, "What happened to Tracy?"

"A minor car accident. Fortunately, she wasn't badly hurt. I contacted our physician in the area, and he'll soon be on his way to give her a thorough check-up."

He nodded, "You handled it well, Jesse. No surprise to me. It's why you're here. We were all thrilled to hear she's okay."

Weber settled his elbows on the table and intertwined his fingers underneath his chin. He's settling in for a while, I thought, and seeing this caused my body to tense in preparation for a blow.

"You've learned, haven't you? From the incident three years ago with Yolanda Jackson. Though that's too trivial of a word, 'incident,' for such a terrible tragedy." He looked at me speculatively, almost clinically, "Her murder."

## CHAPTER 17

I didn't say anything, just tried not to fall apart at his words or mention of her name, even as her face flashed in my mind's eye: her caramel skin, hazel eyes, and warm, generous way of being. I felt a stab of pain as fresh as the day it happened. Yolanda had been murdered in the worse way imaginable: beheaded by Boko Haram in the place I'd sent her.

Boko Haram had crossed the border from Chad and raided Toumour, the town where Yolanda was working as an educator. The terrorist believed she was there as a foreign aid worker and had killed her. We had been the best of friends since college.

Weber didn't know Yolanda's murder had driven me into a deep depression which resulted in a five-day stay in the Bellevue Psychiatric Hospital. My suicidal thoughts and the psychosomatic, physical pain I'd endured had kept me bed-bound, unable to leave my home to sleep, work, or visit my parents. Living became an agony. It was only because of the medications and my sessions with Dr. Cassavettes that helped me to find my way back. It took me almost a year to climb out of the abyss of my sorrow, haunted by nightmares of Yolanda's beheading. I had been beyond frail then, but now I was stronger; not only had I found my way back, I'd fault my way back.

As we looked at each other across the table, I told Weber only what I could: the truth. He was a shrewd man who had a way of

93

figuring out if you were trying to make a fool of him. He'd once told Clarence what he liked about me: I was truthful and smart.

I'd asked Clarence if Weber believed my intelligence came from my being Asian-American.

Clarence had narrowed his eyes at me and asked, 'Did I believe Weber was a good athlete because he was black?'

The question had ended that particular conversational track.

"Howard, I've learned I can't save anyone when the circumstances are out of my control. I can only do what I can: know as much as possible about what's taking place in the parts of the world our people are working in and have an escape plan ready. Yet, no matter what I do, there are no guarantees."

"It's the business we're in," Weber said matter-of-factly. "We're trying to save lives in parts of the world where life is worth less than a bag of rice or a can of heating oil. But we're doing a good job, especially you, Jesse. Have a good rest of your day."

He picked up the paper and began reading again. The meeting was over. Gathering my notes, I stood and turned toward the door.

"Once you get a new date for the symposium, please post it."

"I will," I said and left the room without another word.

In my office, I closed the door and leaned back against it taking shallow breaths before sliding down it to the floor, my forehead sinking onto my upright knees in an effort to steady myself.

Weber's bringing up Yolanda had caused it all to come back: Yolanda's happiness at going back to Niger, where her grandparents had been born; to work as a teacher. We'd celebrated her assignment all night.

I'd made as many connections in the country as I could and had been told time and time again by the state department and Niger government officials that Toumour was safe and was not in the path of the terrorist group, but they'd been wrong. Boko Haram had been starving, so they'd crossed the border into the town and kidnapped more than thirty teenaged girls and young women, including Yolanda. When they'd discovered she was working for an American organization, they had raped and beheaded her on video for the world to see. The horror of it had branded my soul. Her death was my forever nightmare. Closing my eyes, I let the memories come flooding back.

We'd been frantically trying to get in touch with Yolanda and her team for two days when the state department informed us of her kidnapping. On television, we'd seen the girls and women who'd been taken. Seeing Yolanda's face in the group, a face I recognized as well as my own, had caused a scream of shock to ripple from my throat.

I'd called everyone I knew and had reached out to past members of the foundation who had connections with the government, the state department, and even with Niger officials but to no avail. No one could help me, and no one could save them, save Yolanda. We spent days in the office, afraid to leave in case, by some miracle, Yolanda and the girls were freed or rescued. I didn't go home at all and slept on the couch in my office when I could sleep.

It was five days later when the video was presented to the world. I'd gone to my office to retrieve the charger for my phone, and when I'd come back into the main office, the first thing I'd heard was crying, then the blaring of the television set mounted on the wall which hadn't been silent since the nightmare began.

Someone had grabbed me from behind and pulled me out of the room; I remembered it was Mark. I'd fought him off and looked at the screen and what I'd seen was a man holding a machete over the head of my sweet, wonderful friend who'd talked me through panic attacks over challenging exams, who'd nursed me back to health when I had the flu and who'd made me laugh until my stomach hurt. Her head had been uncovered, her face bruised and wet with tears, her eyes closed, and tied around her neck was a sign that read: American whore.

He'd brought the machete down in one swift, decisive movement, and I knew no more; I'd fainted before seeing anything else. My unconsciousness lasted for twelve hours. When I finally woke, it was to rave and scream for Yolanda, and I wouldn't let anyone come near me, not even my parents; they'd had no choice but to seek help for me.

In the hospital, I went from raving to a form of catatonia, a deep, bottomless depression. After five days in the ward and with intensive therapy, plus a drug regimen, I'd only given up last year; did I learn to cope with my friend's death and my part in it. I got on with my life though I still think about her and sometimes dream about her.

Needing some natural air, I left the building. I walked down to one of the cafes on the corner and ordered a green tea while sitting on the patio. The rain had stopped, and the sun had come out with a purpose, prompting people to come out and fill the streets. It was a New York summer day, bright sun with a mild breeze that wafted freshets of clean air between the smells of warm-smelly cloistered air and car fumes.

Watching the world go by, I started feeling better, so after a while, I returned to my office. For the rest of the afternoon and into the evening, I soothed the frayed nerves of those still concerned about Tracy and the Mumbai situation.

Around six-twenty, there was a knock at my door, and Clarence stuck his head into the room, "We're leaving in twenty minutes, going over to Lenny's for drinks to celebrate. Want to come along?"

I glanced at my computer's clock and saw that time had gotten away from me, "It is getting late. I think I'll stay a while longer; a few more things left to do."

"Okay, then have a good weekend."

"You, too."

When my cell phone rang, I was working on the contingent plan for the Mumbai team. I picked it up, looked at the screen, and groaned. Loren. I almost let it go to voicemail, but that would only prompt her to keep calling or messaging until she got her way. It was easier to answer and get it over with.

"Hello Loren, what's up?" Holding the phone between my ear and shoulder, I kept typing as she spoke.

"I'm crazy busy, as you well know."

"Is Katy there? Is she as fantastic as she seems?"

"Yes, and she's taking all our madness in stride. I'm calling to make sure you're going to see the parents."

"We're giving them the party next weekend, so I was thinking I wouldn't go -"

Loren didn't let me finish, "It's only for a day and a half, Jess. We don't want to break our routine and make them suspicious."

"Why would they suspect anything? We've been extra careful planning this thing."

"You know our mother has a sixth sense for a party, especially one involving her. If we don't keep up appearances, she'll know something is going on in a heartbeat. I'm going to stay only one night myself while you stay the entire weekend."

"Loren, it's a bad time," I began, suddenly thinking of Abrams, whom I hadn't heard from all day. Maybe if I called him, we could get together.

"For me too," she stated sharply. "I have Katy Perry here for chrissakes, one of the most popular entertainers on the plane. Yet, I'm going to go for one night because this is all for our folks."

Hit by her directly targeted guilt, I stopped typing; suddenly feeling exhausted from the stress of the day. I didn't have it in me right now to argue with her, to go against her. "Alright, I'll go. I'll leave in the morning as usual"

"Of course, you will," she sounded in no doubt. "I won't make it until Sunday. There's an Ari Sunny Gala tomorrow night for the Manhattan Observatory, Katy and Michael are going, so I have to be there too. I won't bother you again about the weekend or the party, Sis, I promise - at least not tonight. See you at home. Did you know Katy loves poached eggs? Yuck," she laughed prettily. "Don't tell anyone. Bye."

Flipping my phone face down on the desk, I sank back into my chair. All I wanted to do was get home the fastest way possible. If I could have swam there, I would, and once there, I'll go to bed and pull the covers over my head.

My phone beeped again. My God, I groaned; I couldn't take any more. Another beep, then again, and because I had to, I picked it up. A text from Abrams: 'How are you?'

'It's been a brutal day but fine now;' I texted back.

'Can I call you?'

'Definitely'

A few seconds later, it rang, "Hello, Jesse."

His deep, confidant voice caught me; I automatically lowered mine to an intimate drawl, "It's wonderful to hear from you."

I pictured his face, those dark eyes staring into mine as if I were the only person in the world for him.

"I hadn't heard from you and suspected you'd had a busy day."

"It had its moments. How about you?"

"A day of headaches. If I were the kind of person who ran away from my problems, I'd be long gone."

Smiling helplessly into the phone, "I know exactly what you mean," my next words popped out before I could catch them. "So, why don't we run away together?" Abrams didn't say anything, I could hear his surprise, and before he could speak, I rushed on, "It was a joke. Is your offer still open for 'Breakfast at Tiffany's? I could use some escapism right about now."

"It would be my pleasure to take you to the movies." I heard the pleasure in his voice. "Or any other place you want to go. Hold a minute, and I'll check the movie times..." I held for one beat, then two. "There's screening at seven forty-two. It'll give us enough time to get to the Rialto if we can get cabs in the next five minutes."

"I'm shutting down now," I switched off my computer.

"I'll see you there," and he was gone.

Quickly straightening the few papers on my desk, I retrieved my purse and jacket and was out of my office in two minutes and hailing a taxi in three. One stopped in front of me, the door opened and a man around my age with red hair and a neat mustache and beard, reminding me of Stephen, got out.

He stepped aside as I hurriedly got in, "The person you're meeting sure is lucky," he said, giving me a five -star-white smile as he closed the door after me.

The driver, who'd paid no attention to the short exchange, pulled away from the curb.

"Sixteen Fulton Street," I told him.

"The movie house," he said and maneuvered expertly into the flowing traffic.

Sitting back, I pulled out my phone and checked myself in a mirror app, looking critically at my face. I looked frazzled but not too bad. Maybe I'd have time to dash into the bathroom at the theatre and spruce up a bit.

The traffic was heavy as New York after-work traffic was apt to be. When we pulled up in front of the theatre, Abrams was already there. He wasn't looking at his phone or the people passing on the sidewalk but standing there, hands in pockets, waiting for me.

When the cab pulled up abruptly at the curb, Abrams was at the cab's door. He pulled it open, extended his hand towards me, and helped me out before handing the driver some folded bills. As the taxi pulled off, he took me in his arms.

I wrapped my arms tightly around his neck and pressed against him in a tight but brief embrace. He pulled back to arm's length, his hands on my upper arms as his eyes ran over me from top to toe.

"It's wonderful to see you." He took my hand in his, "Come on; the movie will be starting soon."

We walked underneath the elaborate marquee that was ablaze with thousands of Hollywood light bulbs surrounding large, black capital letters that read: Breakfast At Tiffany's. Starring Audre Hepburn.

I held back a few seconds and took him in: he was dressed in all black; a long-sleeved shirt with the sleeves rolled up, black jeans, and loafers. The color made the darkness of his eyes and hair shine.

To my surprise, the theatre's lobby was full of people. Many of them were looking at the display of Hepburn memorabilia that was situated around the lobby. Most of it was from her former New York apartment: books, scripts, 'the gloves and cigarette holder' from the movie; even a shelf of her recipe cards for the meals she'd created for her family. Abrams and I walked slowly around the display, oohing and aahing with everyone else before we stood in line for our tickets.

In front of us was a handsome young couple; he was the color of dark chocolate and had a styled-high afro while she was silky skinned with auburn hair and bright green eyes in a heart shaped face.

He was searching the pockets of his jeans, a confused look on his face, "I musta lost the rest when I pulled out my I.D at the Raja."

He pulled the girl aside to allow those behind them to get tickets. He then went back to rifling his pockets, pulling them inside out while looking embarrassed at the girl who looked sadly back.

"I'm sorry, Layla."

"It's okay. We can go to -"

"Hey," I stepped up to them and held out three twenties. "The movie is good. You should see it."

He shook his head, "No, we -"

"No, yes," the girl said and grabbed the money with a sweet smile back at me. "Thanks very much."

"And popcorn too," I added, taking Abrams's hand as he came over to us after getting our tickets. "You can't enjoy a movie without popcorn."

"Thank you, Mam. That was really cool," the young man said. He took the girl's hand, and they hurried back to the ticket line.

Abrams and I looked at each other.

"He called me 'Mam.'"

"He did," Abrams said, and we burst out laughing. He then looked at me admiringly; the laughter gone, "That was a nice thing you did."

"What's cool is that they want to see a movie almost sixty years old. One with no cursing or shootouts and not a cell phone in sight."

# CHAPTER 18

A bell rang, and a cultured voice announced, "Ladies and gentlemen …."

We all turned as a man dressed in an elaborate tuxedo complete with tie and tails addressed the crowd.

"…please take your seats. The film will start in six minutes."

He then bowed and extended a white-gloved hand toward the entrance into the theatre proper.

People crowded past him excitedly; we followed them into the theatre with its plush red velvet-lined seats before a wide Broadway stage on which hung red velvet curtains.

Abrams led us to two seats in the center of a middle row. There was a cord across the seats, and hanging on the cord were two white cards that read: Reserved. He picked up the cards, pulled up the ropes, and we sat down in two of the best seats in the house.

"How did you manage this?"

"A friend knows I love classic cinema and had these reserved."

As the stage curtain rose, reveling bit-by-bit the huge, life-less, white movie screen, the crowd clapped and hooted their approval. The lights dimmed, and everyone quieted as Audrey Hepburn, accompanied by the music of Burt Bachrach, appeared in early morning New York wearing an evening dress. Abrams took my hand and entwined his fingers with mine.

Two hours and ten minutes later, the movie ended. We lingered in our seats as the other moviegoers clapped during the end credits before filing happily out of the theatre. When most of the other patrons had exited and the screen was dark, we got to our feet and walked out into the lobby without speaking.

Reaching the street, Abrams turned to me, "How about some dinner? G.G. Carlson's is only a block down, and they have great tapas if you like those."

"I do. Let's go."

As we started down Fulton, Abrams crossed behind so that he could walk on the outside near the street. His protectiveness warmed me. We strolled through the night alongside other strolling New Yorkers.

As we walked, we talked about other movies we'd seen lately. Abrams said he'd seen a Martin Scorsese film called Silence on Netflix that he highly recommended. I told him I'd seen everything starring Kate Winslet and loved her work. We talked about music and found to our mutual delight that we were both connoisseurs of old-school hip-hop: Snoop Dogg, of course. And Tupac, forever. Before we knew it, we were chanting the words to 'Dear Mama', and when we finished, we grinned happily at each other.

When we arrived at the restaurant, it was packed. G.G. Carlson's was a four-star supper club with some of the best food in the city and usually took reservations a month in advance. I thought we would have to wait at least an hour or more at their lavish and well-stocked bar before they would even consider seating us for a meal. But I was wrong.

Inside, as we walked up to the maître-d's podium, the man was on a cellphone and was repeatedly saying 'no' while his eyes ran over numbers in a book in front of him. He glanced up at us; then back down as his mouth dropped open before he abruptly disconnected the line. He came from around the stand.

"Abrams, nice of you to join us."

"On a lovely night at this, Raoul; G.G.'s the only place I'd be."

The man, who was tall and thin as a rail, boomed out a delight-ed laugh, "You got it. I knew you had it, just like her. Let's get you a table. Marco will be happy to see you."

Abrams put a warm hand on my arm, "This is Jesse."

Raoul made a slight, effortless bow before sweeping an arm before us, "This way, please."

We moved into the restaurant proper, which was beautifully decorated and filled with enticing smells of ginger, pepper, and baking bread. Every table was occupied beneath soft glowing lights while the sound of Ravi Shankar rhythms floated through the room, counterpointing the steady sounds of the patrons. There was a party atmosphere in the restaurant, which only enhanced its popularity.

Raoul stopped at a perfectly placed table next to the floor-to-ceiling windows and partially cut off by a waist-level, white parti-tioned wall. There were two other tables in the area, but because there were at least six feet between each one, it gave the illusion of total privacy.

The maître d' pulled out a chair for me, and I sat down at the already set table, complete with filled water glasses. Abrams took the chair across from me.

"Again, we're delighted to have you here with us," Raoul said. "Our tapas are extra wonderful tonight, made fresh, of course. But if you want something else, name it, Marco will prepare it for you. I'll send someone for your order right away, and in the meantime, what would you like to drink?"

"A glass of red wine," I said.

"I'll have the same," Abrams held out a hand to the man, and they shook. "Thank you, Raoul. You didn't have to do this. Take time away from your work."

Raoul's face flushed all the way down his slim neck, "It was no trouble; I wanted to do it, to let you know how proud I'm - we all are of -"

"Thank you," Abrams said again, gently cutting him off. "I'll be sure to tell her."

With a slightly embarrassed nod, Raoul turned to me, "Nice meeting you, Jesse. You have a good guy here."

"I'm beginning to suspect that too."

After the maître had left, I looked at Abrams, "Her? Is that your sister, aunt, mother, friend?"

"Mother. You'll have to meet her someday."

"Yes, and the same goes for your meeting my parents. As a matter of fact; I'm going to visit them this weekend. I try and see them at least once a month."

We looked up as the waiter was suddenly there, a young, dark-haired man who looked as if he'd stepped out of an issue of Esquire Magazine. He held a silver tray with a bottle of expensive wine a top of it.

Behind him stood another young man, this one blond, also holding a silver tray which held two crystal wine glasses. Both men gave us brief, self-possessed nods before putting down their offerings. The blond walked away as the other picked up the wine bottle and presented it to us before pouring each of us a glass.

"What do you think?" Abrams asked as we both took sips.

"It tastes of summertime."

"Then it's ours," Abrams smiled across at me. He looked at the waiter, who was hovering expectantly. "We'll have the tapas with the marinated chicken."

Without writing anything down, the man disappeared, leaving Abrams's full attention to fall on me.

"Since I met you," he began as the dreamy tones of Frank Sinatra wafted through the room, crooning 'It Had To Be You.' "I've been very cognizant of water lately and its faultlessness."

"Faultlessness?"

"Clean, clear, and pure at its best. Can you think of anything more perfect than maybe a newborn baby?"

"I call it a blessing."

He thoughtfully took in my words, then nodded," Yes, I guess there's a spiritual aspect to it too. After all, people are baptized in water. The water to wine story is a miracle. As a matter of fact, one of our new clients is the Advent Conservatory Group. One of their many interests is water conservation."

"I know them," I said, delighted by his news. "We did a presentation with them at the U.N. last year. Rand Peabody heads it, right?

"An interesting guy. Smart, intense, committed to reversing climate change."

"Another Bloomberg for the city, is that it? Maybe with more money - if that's possible."

"New York's full of them," Abrams said as if he'd met them all. "It's going to be great working with Peabody and his team. We're going to do all we can to portray them as one of the city's most honest, viable, and responsible companies."

"Portray them? What does that take?"

"Well, we -" Abrams broke off, staring at me. "Why are we talking about Peabody? We should be talking about you. How kind you are and a good listener too."

"Don't all guys want a woman who listens well? Because they love talking about themselves."

Abrams grinned, "That has not only dropped me down a peg or two, Jesse; it's dropped me into the basement. Here I was, thinking I'm a better man when I'm only a guy."

I sat my elbow on the table, my forearm up to cup my chin as I stared at him, "But you're some guy, Abrams."

He threw back his head and roared with laughter as the waiter arrived with our food, wheeling it on a tall, narrow cart. The plates were covered with silver tops though I could see the steam piping out around their edges. The waiter removed the tops and set the plates in front of us with a flourish. The food looked and smelled wonderful.

"It looks great," Abrams said.

"Enjoy," the waiter said and wheeled the cart away.

"You first," Abrams nodded toward my dish.

Picking up my water glass, I took a healthy swallow of the cool liquid, "To cleanse the palate."

I then picked up my steaming, rich, delicately looking tapas with succulent chicken and vegetables, placed them in my mouth, and groaned in pleasure. Abrams was right; it tasted like a piece of heaven.

We chatted as we ate our way through one of the best meals in town.

"So, did you like the movie?" he asked between bites.

"Yes, even though it's been a long time since I've seen it."

"That part with Mickey Rooney pretending to be Japanese," Abrams's lips downturned in disapproval, "It was stupid as hell."

"Absolutely, stupid as hell," I agreed. "But white people playing other races was the norm back then. A caucasian Mickey Rooney playing a person of Japanese descent didn't raise any eyebrows regardless of the fact that he played it as a caricature that was, at worst, racist. You see how New York was portrayed? Beautifully white. Everyone, everything was white. And Audrey Hepburn was the epitome of that beauty with her perfectly white skin. She was just dark-haired instead of blonde."

"Blonde?" Abrams stared at me as he took a sip of the excellent wine. "Is there something about having blond hair you don't like?"

"No," I took a sip of my wine, "I wanted to be a blonde so badly when I was fourteen, I tried dying my own hair."

"You have lovely hair. What happened?"

"It was awful," I said, remembering it now with a little less horror. "I looked as if somebody had frightened me to death. The chemicals - which I didn't properly mix - stripped it almost white, the texture of dried straw, and it stood out in all directions."

"Sounds terrible."

"It was."

"Why'd you think you needed to change your hair?"

"Oh, to assimilate, so I wouldn't feel different or be ostracized because I didn't look like everyone else," I shrugged. "To be accepted into the broader culture. The most dominant one, I guess."

I put down my fork after taking more bites of the succulent chicken. "You have to understand where I grew up, Nantucket. It's an all-white enclave and the only thing I knew. I was the one different from everyone else. Other. Foreign."

"I used to go to an Asian cultural school, and we would gather and sing songs from China and Eastern Asia to show our adopted parents how much we were learning. There was a viewing area where they would stand and look down on us. Anyway, I would watch them watch us. All these mostly white faces were staring at all these little darker faces. I used to think it was as if they were staring at animals in a zoo or from another planet. Does that sound bitter to you?" I asked, catching Abrams's frown. "It was how I felt."

"You never thought they were looking at their kids with unconditional love instead? Like most parents do."

"Of course, they loved us. Yet, sometimes I would catch a glimpse of the look underneath from some of them," I stared beyond Abrams, not seeing him but the past. "It didn't remind me of love but ownership."

"I'm sorry to hear that, Jesse."

"But was it any worse than what my friend Loosha and I used to call ourselves? Bananas. Yellow on the outside and white on the inside." I gave a brittle laugh, more sad than funny. "Just about everybody I knew, who I came in contact with was white: my family, school friends, relatives; I hated being so different, looking so different. On forms, I would check my race as Caucasian; at least I used to."

"I understand."

"Do you, Abrams?" I asked him seriously, staring at him. "Can you? How? I bet you've never ever gone anywhere, been in any situation where you weren't accepted. The ultimate white guy."

"I don't take anything for granted, Jesse; believe me. I believe that everyone has the same rights and privileges as I do."

"But they don't, Abrams, because other people do all they can to keep them from participating fully in the so-called American Dream."

"Who are the other people?" he asked. "The 'dominant culture' as it's called? Which is not so dominant anymore. Everyone is demanding their place at the table, and rightly so."

"While those at the table are fighting right and left to keep them back. Especially the right."

"True, they don't want to share," Abrams looked at me evenly. "But I do. Do you mind if I ask you another personal question?"

"If I can ask you one in return."

He nodded, "It's only fair. Do you date only white boys?"

# CHAPTER 19

I sat calmly back in my seat, deciding uneasily to accept the question as only a question and not a rebuke of my character.

"I don't date boys. I date men I have something in common, whom I find attractive. And if they happen to be white, it's the way it is. What about you?"

"I only date women with whom I have something in common I find attractive. A nice woman from Kenya. A young lady in college from Puerto Rico who relocated to California after graduation."

"So, you're the United Nations of dating. African, Puerto Rican, Chinese."

"No," he shook his head. "I'm here for only one reason: you." He reached over and gently ran his thumb over the knuckles of my right hand. His touch made my belly quiver. His dark eyes searched mine gravely, "I like you, Jesse. Everyone else fades beside you. I enjoy being with you because you're passionate about your mission; you visit your parents regularly, and you don't mind old-timey movies. And I hope to get to know more of you."

"I feel the same," I said simply. Abrams was beyond charming; he was real, sexy, and utterly desirable.

"Good," he grasped my hand briefly, tightly then let go as my attention was caught by a small commotion. A short man in a butcher's white apron was moving among the tables. He was stopping here and there, conversing briefly with some of the patrons though I could tell he was purposely making his way toward us.

"The chef is coming," I said.

"Is he?" Abrams didn't look around.

The chef, Alexander Marcos, who owned six four-star restaurants in the states and two in Europe and was one of the most inventive chefs on the East Coast, arrived at our table with a wide smile on his round face.

Abrams stood up, and the famous man took him into his arms in a tight bear hug that Abrams returned.

"Alexander, nice to see you." He turned to me, "Meet Jesse."

"Jesse," Marcos came around the table and brought me to my feet in a hug. "You're so sweet," he said, the accent on his words Spanish tinted. "You enjoy the tapas?"

"I did; they were wonderful."

He turned to Abrams, "Tell her we're behind her all the way."

"I will, and she appreciates everything you've done."

"Good," Marcos hugged Abrams again. "Go ahead, sit and finish. See you both again, yes?"

"Soon," Abrams said.

And with a pat on Abrams's back, Marcos moved off to the next table, where he was greeted by applause and air kisses.

"A nice man," I said and looked at Abrams closely, "Are you famous or something, and I'm the only person in New York who doesn't know it?"

"Of course, I'm not famous, just one of too many start-up guys. Hey, speaking of nice…it's a beautiful night. How about going for another walk if you're finished eating? Or would you like dessert? The flam here is excellent."

"A walk, definitely."

Without waiting for a bill, Abrams reached into his pocket, pulled out a sheaf of notes, placing two one-hundred-dollar bills onto the table before taking my hand. He led me through the restaurant and onto the street, where he put an arm around my shoulders, pulling me close.

It was a lovely night for New York City. Everyone seemed to be falling in love and enjoying themselves while at it. I felt an immense kinship with the people we passed by. Everybody was feeling wonderful. I felt wonderful too, happy and in love with this man.

We passed a florist shop closed for the night, and Abrams pulled me into its semi-darkened doorway.

He took my face gently between his hands and softly whispered, "You still in love with me?"

Staring up into his large, steady dark eyes, I could only whisper back the truth, "Yes." My hands came up to cover his.

"Good," he said, and bending his head, he kissed me, really, deeply kissed me for the very first time.

His lips, soft and gentle, opened mine. His arms went around my waist, pulling me close, then closer. His tongue touched mine, a brush of exploration, then another until the heat caused me to entwine my arms around his neck as our bodies tightened against each other. We stayed entwined, pressing hard, our bodies unbelievably aroused until we couldn't breathe. We pulled away, a breath apart, breathing in the heated air between us.

"Do you want to catch the next ferry home?" he asked, taking breaths almost harshly. "You can stay –"

"No, I have to go," I said, wanting never to leave his side yet afraid to stay. "I have to catch the early train to Boston."

He nodded, then ran his hands down the length of my back, underneath the weighty darkness of my hair, before taking me into his arms again for one long, last thirsty kiss. I felt his touch from the top of my head to my toes and in between, including the solidness of his erection and the rapid beating of his heart counterpointing the pounding of mine.

It felt as if we were the only two people in the world as we stood cocooned in the doorway, unmindful of the people passing by, the traffic in the street, and the sounds of the city.

Finally pulling back from me, Abrams leaned back against the doorway wall, "You overwhelm me."

"In a good way, right?"

"Absolutely," he grinned, taking my hand. "Let's, get a cab."

At the ferry, Abrams again took me into his arms for a brief but intense kiss, "You have to go, so I won't keep you. Though I want nothing but." He gently pulled away from me, "I'll call you in an hour to make sure you got home safely." You sure you can't -"

"I can't. At least not this time."

Reluctantly, I backed away from him up the ramp and slipped, almost losing my footing. Abrams was there; he caught my arm and steadied me.

"You saved me again. You're always saving me."

"It's my pleasure." As I headed up, he said, "I'll call."

The lights on the dock outlined his figure. On the deck, I watched him until he was only a speck in the distance.

At home, I settled myself onto the couch, wrapping my arms around myself, deliriously happy at that brief moment in time. I lay there until I remembered I needed to pack the small bag I always took for weekends to my parents.

I stood, took a few steps toward my bedroom, and stopped as a feeling, darkly opposite of what I'd felt only seconds ago, stole over me. My sweet happiness was gone and replaced with dread and tragedy. A veil of sadness and loss overwhelmed me so much that I sank to the floor. Was it against some law of the universe to feel good and for it to last? Wasn't I meant to be truly happy? Was the answer: no? I shivered at the thought.

I got up slowly off the floor. Maybe I was coming down with something; that had to be it. I'd take a couple of Advil before going to bed and would be fine in the morning. After packing, I showered so I wouldn't have to do it in the morning, cleaned my teeth, and went to bed though sleep was a long time coming.

# CHAPTER 20

The next morning, I awoke from a dream about Abrams, about a wedding and babies that looked like us. I dressed and ferried into Manhattan an hour and a half before time to catch the Acela train to Boston so that I could buy gifts for my parents. I always brought them presents when I visited. Loren once asked why I bothered.

'It isn't as if our parents need or want anything,' she'd say and laugh with an edge of sarcasm that frayed my nerves. 'You act as if they won't let you inside the old homestead unless you entice them with gifts.'

It wasn't true. I didn't need to bribe our parents into welcoming me back into the fold, back into their lives once a month. I was their daughter, after all. I enjoyed giving them a small present when I visited, letting them know I was thinking about them and appreciated all they'd done for me. I wanted to be as generous to them as they'd always been to me; that was all there was to it.

I took a cab over to Fifth Avenue, to the shops at Saks, and bought my mother a small bottle of perfume called, A Midsummer's Dream. It smelled wonderful and cost half a paycheck; she would be impressed. For my father, I got a Champagne Day summer tie by Tom Ford and even had time to have them gift-wrapped before heading over to Penn Station.

The Acela was on time, and since I'd purchased my ticket online, I boarded right away when the train's number was called.

Ten minutes later, we slowly left the station, picking up speed as I watched the world stream by. Instead of grabbing for my phone or the Rolling Stone Magazine with presidential candidate Camile Harrington on the cover, I stared out and let my mind amuse itself by wondering what Abrams was doing at this moment.

I checked the time on the throwback Swatch watch on my wrist; it was ten twenty-seven. Was he thinking about me? I chuckled a beat to myself. Why would he be thinking about me? Abrams was a busy and successful man. He was great-looking and, more importantly, didn't act it. And even though we'd met only a few times, in my heart, there was no doubt he was a good person. He'd shown me how gracious and caring he was, the kind of man easy to love.

As the train rounded a bend, I realized it was almost full, which wasn't a surprise; this line was well-traveled. With a hand over my mouth, I yawned hugely and readied myself to take a brief nap when my phone beeped. Taking it out of my purse, I saw it was Loren and didn't answer; I would see her soon anyway. A few minutes later, there was another beep, this time a text from Abrams: 'Have a safe trip and we'll get together again.' I sent back: 'Yes. Take care, Abrams.'

I put my phone away and stared back at the passing scenery, the passing lives, wondering if those people looking at this train wondered about us passengers, our lives and where they would end up.

My phone rang again, I sighed deeply knowing it was Loren again. She wouldn't go away. An extremely determined woman was my sister.

I answered, "Yes, Loren, I'm on my way. What do you need?

"Something's come up," she sounded a little breathless. "I won't be there until tomorrow morning, in time for Dad's famous waffles."

"What's wrong? Where are you?"

It wasn't like Loren to cut her visit short; she was already going to stay just the one day when she usually stayed a day or two longer than I did.

"Nothing really," she said vaguely. "Work. A meeting, "she sounded nervous and very unlike Loren, "I need to be here."

"You sure? Can't you have one of your assistants handle it?"

"I have to take care of it, no one else."

"Okay, you do what you have to; we'll see you in the morning."

"Alright," she hung up without saying good-bye.

Uhm, I mused, they must be having a problem with the Katy Perry project; only a top client would keep Loren from our scheduled visit to Nantucket. I was going to be home alone with them for the first time in ages.

Yet, more often now than at any other time in our lives, it seemed as if there was something between Loren and me, not exactly a wall but an invisible barrier, like the one in Stephen King's novel, The Dome. The folks in Chester's Mills could see the people on the other side but couldn't get to them.

There was something between Loren and me, too; just as invisible and unfathomable, and only God knew what it was and where it had come from because I didn't. I'd once tried to talk with Loren about this subtle estrangement between us, and she'd waved me off, telling me I'd imagined things, and for a while, I believed her until I didn't. Despite our seeming unity, there was a form of alienation between us I deeply felt though I couldn't explain, and it troubled me.

Slouching down in my seat, I propped my head and promptly dozed for a bit. After a brief nap, I went to the snack car and bought an over-priced croissant and a luke-warm cup of black tea that tasted nothing like tea.

Back in my seat, I read a few online articles until I saw we were heading into Boston's South Station and quickly gathered my things. I had only seven minutes to reach the train for Hyannis; there, I'd catch the ferry to Nantucket.

I caught my train with only two minutes to spare. It would be a two-hour trip to Hyannis. I would do some work on this leg of the trip to ready myself for the upcoming week. I checked my phone for messages, and as I did so, a picture popped up, and I was delighted at who it was and immediately answered, "Auntie Erin, how are you?" I asked my favorite relative.

"You sound chipper this morning. On your way to the island then?" She asked rhetorically; knowing when we visited the folks.

"Yep. How're you and Sam doing?"

"Fine, he's on his way to the market and says 'hello.'"

"Hello back," I said, picturing my aunt's partner gathering the large wicker baskets he took with him. He eschewed those reusable bags on the premise that they too were made of some kind of plastic, making them just as bad for the environment. He'd often expound on how in the 'old country' where his great, great grandparents had been born, they'd used baskets and net sacks to carry their purchases, and those things had lasted forever.

"Is there something special we can get the anniversary couple? Though it's not as if my sister doesn't have everything in the world she could want," my aunt said. "She has Chagall's for chrissakes. Still, there might be something they want and just haven't bought for themselves. Clue me in, darling girl."

"Auntie, you don't need to give them anything; your being there will be enough." I paused, "You two haven't seen each other in six months."

"My God Jesse," she laughed, a deep melodious sound I remember hearing first as a kid; a kind of throaty, heated chuckle when she thought something was hilarious. "You make six months sound like six years. Your mother and I are not like you and Loren, practically in each other's hip pockets. We don't need to see, let alone talk to each other all the time. We get along better when there's space between us."

"But it's not right."

"Jesse," she dismissed my protestation. "It's sweet of you to try and make something out of nothing. Seriously, we are too different from each other; we always have been and always will be, and it has nothing to do with my lifestyle versus hers. We were never close, and as we got older, we finally owned up to it, that's all."

"It saddens me, always has."

"It's the way it is," my aunt said abruptly, ending that part of the conversation. "So, what should we get? Whatever it is, it's going to be from Sam too. I wouldn't embarrass my correct-in-all-things sister by showing up at her thirty-fifth wedding anniversary with just my ball face hanging out. Lillian won't say anything; she's too polite. Instead, she'll give me 'that look. You of course know the one I'm talking about, don't you, Jesse?"

I laughed, knowing it very well, her: I'm-horribly disappoint-ed-in-you-but-I'd-never-say-it-out-loud look. I'd tried my best to avoid it at all costs all my life.

"Okay," I said ruminating for a few long seconds, then, "What about golf clubs?

"Golf?" she sputtered. "For Lillian?"

I understand her having trouble picturing my very proper mother striding across green and unnaturally bright fairways, sweating, and lugging heavy iron sticks around. Yet my mother, both my parents really, had come around to the idea of playing golf. It was a pastime many of their friends had taken it up and not just on the island's small but popular course but at some of the best courses in the world.

"They've been considering it for the last year. Dad got himself a set of used clubs a few months ago and is busy trying to retool them in an effort to make them more aerodynamically sounded."

"That sounds like your old man," she laughed. "Alright, that's what we'll get them. Won't she be surprised?"

And we said in unison, "Not."

"Nothing ever seems to surprise your mom. Okay, I'll let you go. Thanks sweetie for the info. Text me when you get home, so I know you got there safely. Can't wait to see you next week, love."

"Me too, auntie. Love you."

"Love you back. Bye." Then, "Wait, how's your sister?"

"Fine, working hard on the big event."

"Not a surprise. Tell them all I said hello. Bye for real." And she was gone

Aunt Erin and my sister were not as close as I hoped they'd be. They loved each other; there was no doubt about that, yet; it was a tainted love. I figured it had to do with the example of our mother's life. She'd managed to find love with one person, marry and stay that way for thirty-five years. My Aunt, Erin, didn't have the same thing, and hadn't wanted it. And my mother didn't understand it or pretended not to, and this 'misunderstanding' had colored my mother's attitude toward her sister, colored it cold. Loren had picked this up from the beginning, she'd become like our mother toward our aunt, and it saddened me.

Settling back in my seat, I watched a young woman coming down the aisle with a baby in her arms. The baby was chunky cute and dressed in a pink tutu, and she was smiling and patting her mother's cheek affectionately as the mother held her tightly while doing her best to keep her balance as the train rolled along. A man was behind them, carrying a large diaper bag over one shoulder and two backpacks over the other. As they passed by, I pictured Abrams and me, with a happy baby between us. Our family.

I pulled out the magazine began reading the article on Camile Harrington. She'd been a former senator and attorney general for the state of Washington. She had decided it was time for there to be a woman president of the United States, and she would do everything in her power to be that woman. I heartily agreed with her; I thought she'd make a great president, so-much-so I'd contributed a thousand dollars to her campaign and vowed to give more.

I'd heard her speak at New York University last year to a standing-room-only crowd, and she'd riveted the entire room. Her topic had been on climate change, and she'd said that until every American recognized its devastating effects and pledged to do whatever they could to mitigate it for their families, neighbors, and fellow Americans, we would face a country galloping toward disaster.

Mrs. Harrington had continued speaking even in the face of ranting and screams of protest from some in the audience. Instead of backing down, she'd out yelled, outspoken, and out maneuvered her detractors until they'd had no choice but to be quiet and listen.

She'd been relentless in getting her point across and, at the end of her talk, had received a roar of approval and a standing ovation; I'd never forgotten it; even thinking about it now gave me a thrill. She would be president of the United States.

# CHAPTER 21

When we finally arrived in Hyannis, I immediately felt the temperature change; it was ten degrees cooler which, of course, had to do with being fully on the ocean. A light breeze blew, yet, the sun was warm and bright, the sky a brilliant blue as seagulls glided over the ocean. A perfect New England summer day.

I caught the waiting ferry and sat above deck as I usually did so I could watch Nantucket approach as the boat chugged toward it. No matter how often I visited, I loved seeing the island first appear.

As a child, I'd walked those cobblestoned streets, ran on the beach, played hide and seek among the dunes, and ate ice cream with my friends on the wharf as we watched the tourist arrive. Many memories, thank goodness many of them were good ones.

It took less than an hour to get from Hyannis to Nantucket, and as the boat pulled into the dock, I saw my father standing outside the terminal. His head was bent low, he was not looking toward the approaching boat or out to sea, or at his phone but scribbling something into the small black notebook he carried with him everywhere. I'd named the book and all its former iterations his 'idea book' while he called it the 'because-I'm-forgetful-I-have-to-write-crap-down' notebook. As one of the foremost designers of sculling and rowing boats in the world, living on the island near the water was essential.

As we docked, only then did he look up and see me standing

on deck. He put the book away before waving at me. I waved back before gathering my things and exiting the ship with the other people that I noticed were all tourists. I was the only 'islander' aboard this trip.

When I reached my father, he took my bags, sat them down, and gave me a hug. "There's my Golden Girl," he said, bussing me on the cheek before picking up my packages and overnight bag.

"Hi Dad, how're you?" I asked, giving him the once over as I took my bag from him.

He was a tall man with lean, ropey muscles toughened up by years of handling sculling and rowing boats in and out of waters from the raging Colorado River to the quiet meandering byways of the Amazon. He had thinning, still-dark hair, bushy eyebrows over sharp brown eyes in a bony weathered face.

"Fine, the same as when I saw you last month," he grinned at me; his smile transformed that thoughtful, even fey expression usually on his face to one of mischievous playfulness. "Though you look a bit different this time, Jesse."

We had reached his car, a green fifteen-year-old Saab he'd converted from all gas to an electric vehicle hybrid that used minimum gas.

He assessed me for a few long seconds before he started the car and drove off, "You look more settled than you did last time I saw you. Work going better?"

I stared out the window at the familiar scenery: the streets with their clapboard houses and boat docks out back, "It's the same; putting out fires here and there so our field operators can work their magic."

"That's my Golden Girl; taking care of things."

"Trying to, Dad."

I wondered why I hadn't asked him years ago to stop calling me 'Golden Girl' after all these years. He was the only one who did; who'd I allow to call me something so ridiculous when it came right down to it.

He'd started calling me Golden Girl when I was twelve or thirteen. I'd been hanging out with Kerry Thomlinson, it was funny how I hadn't thought about her in years. We'd been in my room Googling movies we were considering seeing that afternoon, either Roll Bounce or Into the Blue when she'd said, "Let's go to your sister's room."

"Why?" I'd stared at her as she headed for the door.

"Because she has the nicest clothes and always looks good in them. I would die to see her wardrobe, and now's my chance. She's out with your Mom, right?"

"Yeah," I said, following her out into the hall, "but she doesn't like people messing in her stuff."

Kerry threw me an irritated glance as she practically marched down the hall and across it to Loren's bedroom, "We won't mess anything up. Anyway, you're her sister, aren't you? She won't care if you're in her things while I'll just be going along for fun."

Loren's door was closed and with a quick peek both ways down the hall making sure no one was coming; Kerry had pushed the door open and stepped inside. I stood outside my sister's room for a few seconds, unsure what to do. But then Kerry was my guest, so I was responsible for her and needed to ensure she didn't mess with any of Loren's prize possessions.

Inside, Kerry stood in the middle of the floor, staring around mesmerized. Loren's bedroom was large, the largest room in the house, with a wide bay window that looked out toward the back of the house and the ocean. White silk curtains were on the windows, held back by golden yellow silk ties. The two other windows had plush window seats where Loren's stuffed animals she'd had since babyhood sat; floor-to-knee bookcases were built beneath the window seats. Her white chest of drawers was half opened and crammed to bursting with clothes.

Loren's bed was queen-sized, with a white canopy and white bedspread; golden-yellow pillowcases covered the four feather-downed pillows that rested against the white, heart-shaped headboard. The four-poster rested on a fluffy white carpet.

"Just as I pictured it," Kerry said, awe in her voice.

"Now that you've seen it," I said nervously, my ears frightfully attuned to the sound of the front door opening or footsteps coming down the hall. "We have to go before they comes back."

Kerry had darted to Loren's closet, which was the walk-in variety that ran the length of one wall. Before I could stop her, she had waded through Loren's clothes, grabbing at shirts and dresses and exclaiming over pieces she pulled forward to look at and touch.

"Oh my God, these are Revelation jeans," Kerry had screeched. "They cost two hundred dollars a pair, and she's got eight pairs; I can't believe it! Yes, I can. Loren has everything." Pawing through silk-hangered pants, sweaters and jackets tucked tight against each other, she pulled out a jade green tank top and held it up against her chest before quickly putting it back and rummaging some more.

"Holy crow, she could wear a new outfit every day and not wear the same thing in a year. Lordy, here's a Stella McCarthy sweater - two of them!"

Kerry pulled one out, it was a rich, inky blue. "I want one of these so badly," Kerry had said.

Moving up to the mirror, she'd taken the sweater off its hanger and pulled the delicate fabric over her head, "She wears the coolest colors. I could never look as good in these as your sister does even if I did look like her."

I'd watched uneasily as Kerry donned the sweater. She was right, I thought; she could never look as good in it as Loren did because Kerry looked like me. Kerry had also born in China and adopted when she was six months old. She was a friend whose family lived in Weymouth.

"I can look like her though," Kerry had said.

She'd then gone over to the bed, taken off one of the golden yellow pillowcases, and to my astonishment, tucked her hair inside its opening and picking up a couple of Loren's barrettes, clipped it onto her hair.

Stepping back, she'd gazed admiringly at herself in the sweater and pillow case, "Look at me, I'm beautiful." She'd tossed her cased-in hair left to right, giggling at the picture she made.

"Don't I look awesome, Jesse? The same as those girls in New York Fashion week." She'd strutted up and down Loren's carpet as if she were on an imaginary catwalk. "With my long blonde hair flowing out. I look as cool and sophisticated as everyone else."

I'd felt a blazing touch of envy at her easy manner when touching Loren's possessions, something I would never have done without asking her first. I'd suddenly run over, grabbed one of the other pillowcases, stuffed in my hair, and pinned it on. I'd pulled a shirt out of Loren's closet, one I'd admired when she bought it and pulled it over my head.

I'd stood looking at myself in the mirror and was soon joined by Kerry. We'd stared at ourselves and each other, and I'd realized how I looked more like her sister than Loren's. No matter what we did, how many pieces of her clothes we wore, how many yellow pillowcases we hid our dark hair behind, we would never be like my sister, never fit in as she did at school, with her friends, with this town. She was born and bred here, and we were not.

Yes, I was growing up in the town and might even die there; yet I would never fully, totally be an 'islander' no matter how much I wished it or pretended I was. I would never be someone fully accepted, a true American, because of where I'd come from and how I looked, which was what mattered. If it hadn't mattered, Kerry and I wouldn't have been there trying to be someone else.

I remember my father calling me, first from my room then coming down the hall toward Loren's, "Girls, lunch is -"

He'd stopped in the doorway, looked at us, and said nothing. The expression on his face had at first been puzzled, then gone to neutral as if he'd clamped down on his thoughts, keeping them from his face.

"Lunch is ready," he'd said quietly. "When you're done, don't forget to put the pillowcases back; they're your mother's best ones."

He'd retreated out the doorway and back down the hall.

When Kerry had gone home, and we were cleaning up the dishes, my father, who'd been quiet during the meal, had taken the plate I'd been drying and sat it carefully on the draining board before turning my face up to look at him.

"Jesse," he'd said earnestly, making me swallow back tears that had popped into my throat for no reason. He'd pushed a long strand of hair back behind my right ear. "You know we love you just the way you are. We love 'who' you are and never want you to be, look or act like anyone else in the world but you. You're my golden light, my Golden Girl. We're blessed to have found you. You'll always remember that, won't you?"

Unable to speak, I'd nodded and thrown my arms around him, hugging him tight until my mother and Loren had come through the front door shouting for us to help with the shopping bags.

I know he'd never told my mother about us messing around in Loren's room or about the pillowcases because if he had, she would have come for me with 'that look' and given me a stern talking to about trespassing in my sister's room.

"Why do you bring gifts every time?" my father asked, bringing me back to the present.

"They're just to prove I've been thinking of you."

"No need to prove anything," he glanced at me with a slight frown, his bushy eyebrows raised. "Save your money, sweetheart. Your mother and I don't need a thing. You remember Kyra Lyndstadt, don't you?"

"Didn't she move to Colorado or someplace out West?" I asked, picturing a chunky girl with a small port-wine birthmark on the right side of her neck.

"New Mexico. I ran into her father at the hardware store last week and he told me, she hadn't visited in two years, and didn't want them to visit her. Isn't that sad? Not seeing your child for three whole years. Having you visit us is more than enough."

"Okay, but I think Mom likes the presents," I said as we idled in the traffic that picked up ten-fold in tourist season.

The cobblestoned roadway was thick with bumper-to-bumper high-end Range Rovers, Mercedes SUVs, and Tesla roadsters. The well-heeled tooled around the small town in their cars, not minding the hefty price charged to bring them onto the island.

"How's the new project going?" I asked, changing the subject.

He shrugged, "Alright, I'll have the prototype ready in a couple of weeks."

We drove the rest of the way home in companionable silence. The picturesque seaside town with its astronomically priced properties and quaint but expensive shops looked picture-postcard beautiful. Nantucket had become the haunt of not just the rich and famous but the mega-rich. A haven for billionaires getting away from it all.

My father turned down our road, Halcyon Way, with its large rambling houses and boat docks tied down with sleek watercraft and small, sturdy yachts that bobbed gently in the water.

"Loren texted your mother this morning. She won't be here until tomorrow. Short notice on her part."

"You know how it is with RJC and their work."

"Yes," my father sighed. He pulled up into the driveway and stopped the car. "How she can stand being around that circus day-in, day-out…" he shook his head in wonder, "I'll never understand."

"Loren effortlessly keeps her boss's life on track which keeps him in high demand."

# CHAPTER 22

I got out of the car, retrieved my bags and packages from the back seat before going round back of the house.

A small section of the lawn had been turned into my mother's prize-winning garden. It was a bountiful array of blooming flowers, from sweet yellow roses the color of a canary's wing to pink and purple carnations so bright they looked unreal; the garden was her pride and joy.

I watched my mother walk through the kitchen and out through the sliding glass doors which made up the back of the house. She was dressed in white pleated boating pants, a sleeveless white blouse, and black ballet slippers. She was a petite woman in her late fifties with pixie short, expertly colored white-blond hair, large grey eyes Loren had inherited, and delicate features in a face lightly-lined but regal in its intensity.

She was wearing light make-up as usual and lipstick that was a delicate shade of peach. I'd often thought, if the late Jacqueline Kennedy Onassis had a BFF, she would have looked exactly like my mother.

She saw me, "Jesse sweetie, you're on time," she greeted and gave me a brief hug and kiss before stepping back. "You look fine. Maybe a little tired around the eyes, but I'll put that down to your working too much. You and your sister work, work, work."

"So, Rihanna says."

"Who?" she asked then, "Let's go inside."

We went back the way she'd come as my father came into the kitchen, "Jesse, why are you still holding your things?"

"I was talking to Mom."

"She's brought more presents, Lil," he said to my mother with a touch of surliness. "I told her it wasn't necessary."

"Your father's right," my mother trailed after me toward my room. "We don't need more presents." She followed me inside, it was as I'd left it the previous month though I knew my mother had it cleaned every other week. "New York is outrageously expensive; you need all your money to live."

"Mom, I'm not destitute." Changing the subject, I held out the gift bag. "It makes me happy to do this tiny thing for you and Dad."

She studied me carefully, not taking the package, "Is this to prove you're a good daughter?"

"To show you I love you."

"We already know that, so gifts aren't necessary, Jesse."

"Then why are you making such a big deal out of such a little thing?" I asked, feeling a hot spurt of angry exasperation at them both and at Loren, who'd also given me a hard time over these small tokens. "It's small, Mom, please." I pushed the package toward her.

She took it, albeit reluctantly.

"Perfume," she sniffed the air delicately. "Very pretty. Thank you, I'll open it later. Are you hungry?" She turned from me, "I'll go set the table." At the door, she said over her shoulder, "On your way in, get your father; he's in his study by now going over whatever he's working on."

"Alright," I said, suddenly flashing at the sight of her tossing the box into the garbage bin. No, that was wrong-headed; she'd never do such a thing. "What're we having?"

"Chicken Italia and kale salad; you'll love it."

I'd forgotten about her Italian phase. She'd taken a twelve-week Italian cooking course in Boston and mastered every dish. Loren was like her; they both mastered anything they tried, making it look easy.

I found my father sitting one of his deep armchairs, reading a manual about motorcycle engines, an iPad balanced precariously on one of chair arms. At the same time, a golf game played silently on television set above the fireplace.

"Lunch is ready, Dad."

He looked up, his gaze far away until his thoughts shifted back to the now, "Okay, honey. I'll be a minute. I'm going to…," he broke off and went to the iPad where he scrolled through whatever was on the screen.

Giving him a few minutes, I strolled around the room looking at his awards, honors, and citations, which were mixed in with the ones won by Loren and me for soccer, track and field, and volleyball. On the mantle were pictures of us at various ages and stages of life. Comparing us two, I was struck hard by how I was so different from everyone. Why did I see this so clearly now after having looked at these pictures countless times without a bother? Why was I now hyper-sensitive to the fact I looked nothing like any of them?

Loren favored our mother with her coloring, especially the eyes; they had the same grey eyes though her face was the shape of our father's. And then there was me. I hadn't realized how I stood out, alone, even in a family portrait.

My mother stuck her head into the room, "Lunch is getting cold."

We followed her out and into the kitchen, where our meal was already waiting on the table. The kitchen was large and sunny with vases of my mother's flowers sitting on the wide island, the table, and work-stations.

Also adding color to the room were four side-by-side shelves holding brightly colored diaries, no 'journals.' My mother kept journals, not diaries like some heart-sick teen mooning over her idolization of blue-eyed Paul Newman; she always said. She'd kept them since she was ten years old. There were over two hundred, the oldest ones she kept in storage bins in a climate-controlled shed on the property.

We sat at the table while my mother fussed over the pots and pans at the stove in between putting platters of food in front of us.

"It looks delicious, Mom."

"Your mother takes her cooking to heart."

"You bet I do," she said, stirring a pot. "Look at your Dad; I need to fatten him up."

"That'll never happen," my father said. "Not only do my jeans say skinny-old-man, so do my genes."

Rolling my eyes, "That's hilarious, Dad."

"You've been quiet on your last few visits," he said, studying me narrowly. "I thought it had to do with work. Or is it something else?"

"Do you think my quietness has something to do with my being Chinese?"

"Not funny," my father said unsmiling, "I don't want to hear you say anything like that ever again. You have a strong streak of steel in you, Jesse, hidden behind a beautiful kindness. Yet, you still see yourself in a lesser light."

"I'm the dark sister remember?"

He opened his mouth to tell me to cut it out, but I got there first. "Just kidding."

My father had always been the one who'd seen things realistically. He saw behind the false smiles; the 'everything's fine; the 'school is fine.' He saw the name-calling instead, the pulling up to 'slanty eyes', the 'you look like no one in your family. He knew the miseries I'd like to forget but would never forget. He'd always tried to make it better and succeeded more often than not.

"They're no major problems with work or anything else," I assured him.

"If you say so," he smiled, a rare full one that transformed his often dour, preoccupied countenance. Loren had his smile; another one of the things I envied her for.

Finally, sitting down at the table, my mother passed around plates of food, "It's the kale salad to start, and that's Italian chicken with tomatoes and a touch of a sweet vinaigrette sauce. For dessert, we're having fruit sorbet."

I bit into my chicken; it was juicy, succulent, and as good as she'd said it would be, though I hadn't doubted her for a second.

"Auntie Erin called; she said 'hello'."

"I don't understand why she doesn't call me, or at the very least, text me herself more often," my mother said, taking a small piece of chicken onto her plate.

She was perpetually watching her weight though she weighed less than ninety pounds.

"I'm almost always free to talk to her, to catch up. Even though she usually wants to talk only about that, Sam."

"Sam is her partner, Mom," I reminded her again the umpteenth time. "They're very happy together."

My mother threw me a skeptical look, "I'm just surprised at her, Jesse; letting herself be so effortlessly controlled by another person; especially someone young enough to be her son. The Erin I grew up with wouldn't tolerate half of what's happening in that supposed relationship."

"Now, Lil," my father lightly admonished. "That's Erin's life and her business."

"I'm just saying," my mother opened her eyes wide in forced innocence. "I want her to be happy, but not as a doormat for anyone, especially someone not worthy of her and half her age."

She picked up a basket of wheat rolls and placed one on our plates without asking; she'd done the same thing when I was a child.

"Your sister will be here on the morning 's first ferry" she nudged the roll toward me with a perfectly manicured nail. "Eat some of the bread, Jesse; it's gluten-free, and you're getting too thin."

"I'll have an extra helping of the sorbet."

"She wanted to come out tonight, but there's some sort of luncheon today she can't miss."

"She didn't mention it to me," I said, reflecting on our earlier conversation. Loren hadn't said exactly what she'd had to do; as-a-matter of fact, she'd sounded vague and had hurriedly ended the call.

"It's a small fundraiser - if you can call $10,000 a plate, small - for Senator Harrington. Hosted by..." my mother tapped a nail on the table in an effort to remember. "Amal Clooney, that's right, I wrote it in my journal so I wouldn't forget. Richard was invited, and he's taking Loren along as his escort."

"Good for her," my father said and sat his fork beside his empty plate. He always devoured whatever my mother cooked; I suspected it was so not to hurt her feelings because she took her cooking so seriously, though I wondered how much it might occasionally hurt his stomach. "She'll be the first in our family to meet a president."

"She's not the president yet," my mother said with dry realism.

"She's close," my father countered before rubbing his hands together. "What kind of sorbet are we having? I hope it's peach-mango."

After helping my mother clean up the lunch dishes, I stepped onto the flagstone patio and took a deep breath of Nantucket. It was nice to be home, away from the enclosed caginess of the city.

In front of me lay my mother's color-filled flower beds, with its profusion of roses, petunias, chrysanthemums and hydrangeas. It met the green and verdant lawn which sloped down to the ocean's edge. I walked down the flagstone path running my hand across the soft petals as I moved along. Their sweet summery fragrance mixed with the smell of the ocean brought my childhood back to me in full force.

Down a small patch of land that was our beach, I took the two steps up to our short dock, where I discovered my father had installed an old-fashioned two-seater bench with soft cushions instead of the old and rickety Adirondack chairs that had been there forever and she'd asked him to replace with something more comfortable.

Sitting down, I looked out over the vast ocean, a gently swaying greyish-blue. The waves reflected the sky while a soft breeze pushed up whitecaps. Sailboats dotted here and there while motorboats sliced through the water, towing, shouting, and waving water skiers delighted by the day.

It was strange how I still lived near the water, crossing it daily into work. Yet, I didn't feel the same for that part of the Atlantic as I did for the open waters of this island. But why would I? This place was truly home, where I grew up, where my touchstones were and where my life had really begun.

I checked my messages. There were three, none from Abrams. I missed him and wanted to hear his voice, to know he was alright. I typed: 'Hi Abrams. Made it safe and sound. Hope your day is going well.' I added a sappy, happy-faced emoji, then hit send.

Laying the phone down, I stared out again at the sailboats moving lazily along. A few minutes later a message beeped in from him: 'Are you having a good time? Hope your parents are well. Call me if you need me and as soon as you get back to town. Miss you.'

I read it once more. Did he mean it? That he cared about me? We'd been on maybe one and a half dates if they could officially be called dates. We still didn't know much about each other. Yet regardless of that fact, I knew I was in love with him and for now; it was enough.

# CHAPTER 23

The next morning, there was a knock on my bedroom door, rousing me from a deep sleep. It was pushed open, and my mother stood in the doorway.

"It's eight-twenty," she announced. "Almost eight-thirty."

"Not for ten more minutes," I said, sitting up in bed. "Why so early, Mom?"

She was dressed casually but expensively in light pink pants and a sleeveless silky white tunic blouse with tiny yellow sunflowers stitched here and there. Her make-up was flawless even first thing in the morning.

"Your sister's ferry will be here at eight forty-five, and I thought it would be nice for you to pick her up."

"Alright, Mom," I stretched. "I'll get dressed."

"I'll have coffee ready when you get back. Your Dad will get breakfast once he's finished whatever he's doing."

She stepped further into the room and quickly fluffed the pillow in my armchair before placing a book back on the shelf. She then turned to face me with a slightly sheepish look on her face that surprised me. My mother was never embarrassed about what she considered 'being honest and above board', so I wondered what had brought this on.

"Jesse, you know I don't mean to be negative about your aunt, I know how fond you are of each other. She and I are just too different, that's all. As I said, I want her to be happy just as I want you and your sister to be happy." She looked at me quizzically, "How about you, honey? Is there anyone special in your life? It's been a long time since Stephen."

Opening my mouth, I started to tell her again about Abrams even though I wasn't wholly sure of him and how he felt about me, but she spoke again before I could.

"I think your sister has really found someone this time." A small, knowing smile flickered across her peach-tinted lips, "She's been acting so coy lately, almost flustered and off-kilter, not like your sister at all and I believe it's because she's in love." She gave a long dramatic sigh. "Finally. Has she mentioned anything to you?"

"Not a word," I said truthfully.

She was wrong about Loren. If my sister were in love, she would have told me, I was sure of it. Mom was only guessing anyway; there was no substance to her suspicions. She wanted Loren to be in love that's all, to find someone who deserved her, a man that was her equal in all things; preferably someone so outstanding he'd fit right in with the crowd of billionaires who inhabited the island every summer.

"Too bad," she looked disappointed. "She'll tell us when she's ready." She turned away, "You'd better go; she'll be here soon," she said on her way out.

I knew my mother, like most mothers, dreamed of elaborate weddings and cuddly grandbabies, and the person she pictured giving her those treasures first was Loren. Of course, she wished those things for me, too; but Loren was her firstborn. Loren reminded her of herself. Plus, many of those faces in the bridal magazines, on honeymoon brochures, and in baby catalogs looked like Loren's: all blushing, blonde, and beautiful as they fulfilled the dreams of marriage and motherhood.

Shrugging off my thoughts, which made me feel inadequate anyway, I got out of bed and picked up my phone. My stomach somersaulted in delight at the message from Abrams: 'Good morning, Jesse. Thinking of you right this second.' I typed back: 'Same here.' I hesitated only a moment before typing: 'I love you.' Full out. No shortened 'u' version but 'you' Abrams Harrington. It was the first time I'd written it outside my journal. I hit send. Not waiting for a reply, I put the phone gently down onto the bed and headed for the shower.

Arriving at the wharf early, I watched the ferry cruise into its slip and hook up to the dock as the passengers waited to disembark.

Loren, as usual, was the first one off the boat. At her side was a young man with a scruffy beard and tousled blond hair, dressed in jeans and a blue chambray shirt. He talked and laughed with Loren as they walked through the crowd of arrivals. He had a backpack over one shoulder, and his full attention was on my sister.

When Loren saw me, she waved. She said something to the young man who dug a card out of a side pocket of his backpack along with an ink pen. He wrote something on it before handing it to Loren who threw him a gorgeous smile. The man stared at her star-struck before waving back at her as she finger-waved her goodbye and headed toward me.

## CHAPTER 24

"Who was that?" I asked, taking hold of the oversized Burberry overnight bag she always brought along with her.

She gave me a one-armed hug which I gave warmly back. On her other arm hung a Louis Vuitton traveling bag that was almost as large as she was. She wore a pair of distressed jeans, a Ralph Lauren sailor blouse, and white Alexander McQueen sneakers. Her hair, which had turned a white-blonde from the sun the same as our mother's used to, was tied back with a blue suede ribbon. Her flawless skin glowed, as did her gray eyes. Loren was effortlessly beautiful.

"He's the Chief Creative Officer for Visual Show and Pictures. The group behind special effects for major Hollywood movies, from what he told me more than once."

"Seriously?" I stared after the young man. "His company has been nominated for an Oscar for the last three years."

Loren shrugged, "I'd never heard of them." She put her free arm through one of mine as we headed for the car. "He's here visiting Steven Spielberg. You should have seen how he looked at me when he dropped the name," she smirked. "I guess he thought I'd drool or faint or something. He said the Spielberg's have a house on Stormy Shore Point. I told him they vacation here every other summer."

"He wants you to call him right?"

"Yeah, well, I'm not. I'm around enough conceited name-droppers working for Richard; I don't want to be around one while I'm here. And anyway, "she glanced back once, and when she turned around, there was a cold, dismissive look on her face. "He's not good enough for me and I mean it." She flushed at the taken-aback look on my face and tightened her hold on my arm. "I'm being discerning and honest that's all."

"Okay," I said hesitantly, surprised at her being so dismissive of someone she'd only met.

"Your hair is growing out," she pulled a few strands of my hair through her fingers. "I didn't notice the last time I saw you. Why don't you have Collette give you a trim."

"Collette's too pricey, and it takes too long to get an appointment."

"Don't worry about it; I'll message her and she'll take you. I'm starving, by the way. The stuff sold on the boat can hardly be called food. Let's put the bag in the car and get some coffee before we leave."

"Mom will have some ready."

"Yeah, but I want to breathe a minute before I see her," she said as we reached the car. I opened the back door and watched as she placed her bag on the back seat. "Let's go over to the Beaumont."

We strolled downtown, taking our time. The heart of Nantucket was teeming with early morning tourists and some residents. The city's center was lovely, with quaint facades of distressed ocean-winded wood and glass-fronted shops and boutiques along its cobblestone streets that have been the village's foundation for centuries. The island, once a prominent and thriving whaling community, was now the summer home of some of the wealthiest people in the world.

As we entered the restaurant, someone called Loren's name. We turned as a woman hurried up to us; she looked almost like Loren except she was a few inches shorter and had wide corn-flower blue eyes. I knew her immediately, Patsy Scott. No, not just Scott anymore; she was now Patsy Scott – Grier. She'd been in Loren's class.

Patsy had been a popular, athletic girl in school and was now a successful trendsetter and online influencer with thousands of followers for her skilled room designs and organizational motifs.

"I thought that was you two," she stopped in front of us and gave Loren air kisses on each cheek. "The light and dark sisters."

Patsy stepped back and gave Loren a razor-sharp once over from the ribbon in her hair to her designer sneakers. I noticed Patsy was in designer gear, too: a blue summer sleeveless dress from the Tom Ford collection I'd seen in one of his catalogs. She'd complimented it with sky-blue Louboutin heels and a white Lemaire tote that cost a month of my salary. Patsy looked polished and wealthy, exactly what she wanted the world to see.

"You look wonderful like you did at the iHeart Gala. My parents were there. They saw you but didn't get the chance to say hello; my mom told me celebrities surrounded you. We were with the Valentinos at their house on San Cristobel. You remember Michael Valentino from school?"

Loren didn't answer as Patsy continued speeding on, not stopping to take a breath. "They redid their entire place last year with help from me, I might add. Next time, you should go with Ron and me; they'd love to have you. We could --"

"I'll have to see," Loren cut in quickly. "Jesse and I are on the way in for coffee."

"I thought so," Patsy patted Loren on the arm before her gaze shifted to me for the first time; it was critical and dismissive, the same as it had been when we were younger. "Hi, Jesse."

It wasn't as if Patsy and the girls who'd been part of her clique disliked me; they hadn't; to them, I was a non-person; seen only when she wanted to make me feel insignificant, less than, nothing. While at other times, I was treated with total indifference as another symbol of my family's financial success and security, like their sailboat. I was my sister's adopted Chinese sibling, not a real person with significant feelings and dreams.

I hadn't minded at first because I hadn't known any better. I'd become used to it, ignored it even when she and her group had said things aloud like: 'They smell funny'; 'When is she going back to where she came from?'; 'Does she tan?' 'She should be grateful to be in this country.' And those were their nicest comments.

"Is your number still the same?" Patsy asked my sister, who nodded. "Great. Then I'll text you the next time we're going; the Valentinos would love to see you. Well," she patted her bag. "I have to go; a busy day ahead starting with a nail appointment in fifteen minutes, then reviewing a new line of area rugs I'm considering for my line." With more air kisses to Loren's cheeks and a final wave, she was gone.

The cafe featured the best coffee and pastries on the island. The rest of the Beaumont was an upscale hotel where the clientele paid upwards of two thousand dollars a night for accommodations. Luckily, a couple was just leaving, enabling us to take their table by the broad windows that looked out onto a garden and the constant ocean view.

The waitress appeared, "Thank you for joining us today," she said in British accented English. "How may I help you?"

There was a menu on the table between two decorative napkin holders, it was the size of a greeting card, and its choices hadn't changed in ten years. We didn't need a menu; we knew exactly what we wanted.

"May we have two hibiscus teas and a pomegranate streusel with tiny sprinkles of brown sugar."

"Of course," the waitress said evenly. "Anything else?"

"A glass of tap water for me," I added. Then to Loren as I got to my feet, "Back in a minute."

In the nicely appointed restroom with its basket of flowers (roses, of course) and stacks of brown and white hand towels; I was using one of those on my washed hands when the door to the stall behind me opened, and Patsy stepped out, smoothing down her dress before catching sight of me. She paused for a second before joining me at the vanity.

"You don't talk much, do you, Jesse," she stated, staring at me in the mirror as she washed her hands, her blue eyes avid with tainted curiosity. "From what I remember, you were a silent, tiny mouse following behind your sister. Or is that a silent Chinese geisha?" she gave a tart laugh as she smoothed her hair that didn't need smoothing.

After drying my hands, I deposited the towel in the receptacle, turned to leave then thought better of it. What was I walking away when I didn't have to take her crap anymore? I was better than that; my life was better and her days of bullying me were over.

Stepping back to her, "A geisha is Japanese, Patsy. You need to get your culture's straight, you nasty thing you."

I left her staring open-mouthed after me. Later I'd tell the story to Loosha, who'd howl with laughter and say, "You should've called her 'you nasty, ignorant bitch thing. It was what she deserved after what she put you through for years."

When I got back to the table, Loren was rearranging our China saucers, plates, and silverware while she waited.

"You only do that when you're nervous. Why are you? You can't be worried about the party; you have it totally under control."

The waitress appeared with a silver tray topped with our tea, lemon, sugar, my glass of water, and our pastries. She carefully sat everything down before departing with a small smile.

I sipped the red tea, immediately feeling revived, "So what's up, sis?"

Loren leaned forward, her beautiful face still and serious, she said in a low tone, "I've met someone."

"Someone?" my tone was off-hand. "You're always meeting someone, usually famous or infamous. Are you talking about someone bigger than Katy Perry? A movie star? Ryan Gosling?" My eyes opened wide, and I pretended to swoon, "Don't tell me, Tom Hardy?"

"Don't be funny, Jess."

"Who's left? There's no one bigger or sexier than him in my book."

"No, not an actor. A normal guy – well, maybe not so normal."

She suddenly blushed, which made me sit up straighter. My sister was really serious because it took a lot to make her redden. She'd been around too much weirdness and crazy strangeness working for RJC that she was now jaded and couldn't be surprised by much.

"He's not like anyone else," she said. "He's smart, beautiful, loving. Every terrific adjective you can think of fits him."

I stared at her; this was extraordinary. She'd met someone, and so had I. I thought how ironic, us being sisters and meeting great guys at the same time.

"It is serious? Are you sure? Is he?"

"Yes, I am," Loren took a sip of her steaming tea. "Of course, I'm not one-hundred percent sure he feels the same, but I think he's coming around about me. Or soon will."

"Did you just meet him?"

"No," she shook her head. "I was introduced to him by the Mobleys.' Remember them? They gave the four-million dollars to the Guggenheim last year. Anyway, I met him again at a few other functions. At one of those, while we were talking, I realized: he's the one."

This sounded dubious to me, not like my sister, "Have you gone out with him?"

"We both attended a showing of Amy Sherald's paintings last year at the National Museum of African-American History. We were on the same flight to D.C. and talked there. We exchanged numbers but were so busy we couldn't connect when we got home."

"He's a New Yorker then?"

She nodded, cutting into the streusel and putting a piece on my plate then on hers," Uhm, this is always nice and fresh."

"Come on, Loren, go on."

"Well, he travels pretty extensively, has a great family, and he's extremely generous to them."

"Oh my God," I said horrified. "He's married."

She laughed. "He's not married, and I'm not going to tell you his name. I want to keep what I know about him to myself until the times right."

"Is he with the CIA or Secret Service? You sound so undercover and mysterious."

Loren looked at me squarely, "You're trying to be funny again, and you're not."

I gazed soberly back at her, "You're not giving me much information to go on here, so what'd you expect?"

"It's complicated for now, Jess. All questions will be answered soon enough." She suddenly reached across the table and grabbed my right wrist. Her fingers were cold and thin on my skin. The look in her eyes was tense and revealing.

"Promise me you won't mention him to the parents. I don't want them bombarding me with questions, pestering me for information, especially her. Not until I'm ready, we're ready, to go public."

I nodded, realizing she wasn't playing around here. No joking, not being funny; she meant what she'd said about this man.

She released me and sat back, the intense light in her eyes dulled to a bright gleam of unusual weariness, "It's time for me to be serious about someone. I'll be thirty-three in December, and I'm still alone –"

"A lot of people are alone."

"Most not by choice," she tossed right back at me. "Many of the girls I went to school with are married with families. Look at Patsy; she's my age and has been married for two years."

"So what? That's Patsy, and what's to say hers is a happy marriage? That woman is all lies and show anyway."

Loren made a face, "Yeah, she is. You should see her Instagram and Twitter accounts; they're full of pictures of their trips to Paris,

Rome, and St. Moritz. The showbiz people she parties within the Hamptons."

"There you go then, all show. This is not the fifties, Loren. There's no timetable you need to follow where you have to be married by a certain time or age; not these days."

"True," she waved my words aside. "But it doesn't change how I feel, Jess. I've been feeling this… this…" her fist clenched in frustration as she tried to find the right words. I remained silent because Loren was hardly ever speechless.

"… discontentment. Dissatisfaction with my life for far too long. I'm tired of fetching and carrying for Richard. Don't get me wrong, I love him and my job. And it's not because I need more money or more success. I didn't fully realize how deep my feelings were until I laid eyes on him. And when I got to know him better, I saw what I was missing: the person I wanted to spend the rest of my life with."

"You love him?"

"I think so," she then gave a small, decisive nod. "Yes, he's the right one."

I took her hand across the table and squeezed it, "Then I can't wait to meet him."

My phone beeped, and a few seconds later, so did Loren's and we said simultaneously, "Mom."

My sister finished her tea while I ensured she didn't want anything other than to find out what was taking us so long to get home.

Driving there, we spoke little, each wrapped in our own thoughts. Should I have told Loren I'd found someone too? That I'd fallen head over heels in love with Abrams? But what else could I tell her about him? He lived in Manhattan, had a sister, and was an entrepreneur with his start-up; that was about it. What else did I know? Not much else. I wanted to know everything about him, and until I did, I wouldn't mention him to Loren.

Loren and I were close, maybe not as close as sisters could be though it wasn't because of anything on my part. For now, Abrams was my secret, and I wanted to keep it, him, close to my heart, at least for a while longer too.

Pulling into the drive, the front door opened, and my mother greeted us. Loren jumped out, and our mother enveloped her in a tight hug. Feeling the start of it as I usually did when we three were together, what can only be called a 'light tension', tightening my throat. I watched them embrace; watched my mother hug her daughter, her real child, and I thought the same thing I always did: how much they favored each other; they were the ones who looked more like sisters. And who acted - it nearly floored me as the thought struck - more like friends; they were friends and the truth sank deep into my heart; that was something our mother and I would never be.

Watching them enter the house together, I got out of the car, took out Loren's bag, and followed them inside. In the kitchen, our father was making breakfast.

Our mother was the family chef, but our father's only culinary skill was breakfast. He made the best waffles in the world and delighted in making them for 'his girls' as he called us. Standing out of the way so he could greet Loren, I sat her bag down. He kissed her on the cheek and then twirled her around before standing her on her feet to look at her properly and give her the compliment she was due.

"You look terrific, honey. As you can see," breakfast is ready." He glanced at me, "I have fresh strawberries from Cal's for you, Jesse."

"Thanks, Dad."

"Anything special for me, Dad?" Loren asked.

"Freshly squeezed orange juice, of course, icy cold the way you like it. Let's all sit," he said, pulling out the chair for our mother.

The house phone rang, and she went immediately to answer it. We waited for her; we wouldn't start until all of us were at the table. She spoke for a few minutes before coming back and taking her place.

"It was Gretchen calling to tell me the tickets to the Randolph exhibit sold out within an hour. I already knew that; Celia Townsend called a few minutes before you arrived and gave me the news."

"Sorry, Mom," Loren said, "we knew how much you wanted to go, it being the event of the year and also because he might be showing 'Us By The Seashore."

"It's fine. I'll try and catch his show in the city. Let's eat. Dad's waffles are getting cold."

We started in on the food.

"We received two offers this month," my mother said, perking up as she passed around the pitcher of orange juice.

"Down from the three last month, right?" Loren stated.

"Only one down?" I asked, trying not to sound already bored.

Real estate, owning property was at the top of the list for any Nantucket landowner with property worth having. The offers made by billionaires to buy their land for astronomical prices and build mega-mansions were, for them, endlessly fascinating.

"Yes, but both were double last month's offers."

"Sound like they're getting desperate," I said.

"They're insane," my father chimed in. "Millions for a house that'll only be used three months out of the year, if that. When the money could be used to build affordable housing on the mainland where it's needed."

"Right, Dad," Loren was the one who now sounded bored as she ate a couple of blueberries. "Do we have to go into it again? Why don't you have Arnold vet these offers? It's what you pay him for."

"I don't mind," Mom said, cutting a strawberry into two sections. "It's fun to see how high they'll go, and it gives me something to talk about at the club." Brightening, she turned to Loren, "How was the luncheon?"

"It was fabulous. Afterward, we met Mrs. Harrington."

"What was she like? What was she wearing?"

My father and I glanced at each other and shook our heads. Usually, when we were together as a family, we didn't need to add much to the conversation. They dominated and we let them.

"She's going to be the best president we ever had if you ask me," Loren cut into a piece of turkey bacon and popped it into her mouth with relish. "I didn't realize how hungry I was," she said, not mentioning the streusel we had earlier.

"She was wearing a dress made by this up-and-coming designer named Elissa San Ruiz. Mrs. Harrington promotes up-and-coming designers like Michelle Obama did when she was the first lady. You're going to vote for her, aren't you?" she glanced from one parent to the other.

"Of course, we are," my mother nodded confidently toward my father. "Because we should have a woman president this time around."

"She was so poised," Loren said dreamily, "very intelligent. You can immediately tell she understands who she is, what she's doing and how our country should be run so that everyone has a chance."

"You were very impressed then?" Dad said, forking the waffle into his mouth.

"I was impressed by the entire family," Loren said bemusedly.

Later, while we were cleaning the kitchen, she said, "Did you see the new seat down by the jetty?"

"Oh, yeah, it's Dad's cool new touch."

"Don't leave Loren's bag on the kitchen floor, Jesse," my mother pointed as she exited the room.

"It's okay, Mom, I'll get it," Loren picked it up before turning to me. "I'll meet you outside."

"Okay," I said, then called down the hall. "Mom, Dad, do you need anything else?"

"No," my father stuck his head out of his study. "Go spend time with your sister."

<h1 style="text-align:center">CHAPTER 25</h1>

Leaving the house by the sliding doors, I walked down to the jetty and sat on the bench, pulling my legs up beneath me and wrapping my arms around them as I held my face up to the sun. I thought about Abrams and hoped he was okay. I missed him and couldn't wait to see him.

I heard hurrying feet, turned, and watched Loren approach. She was carrying a leather-bound notebook. It was one of our mother's journals. Loren liked to read about her early life as a schoolgirl, what she was like in college and her beginning life with Dad. I used to believe it was an affectation to please our mother; now, I believe Loren just enjoyed all those old stories.

"You got Dad to finally replace those splintery boards," Loren said and patted the seat cushion before settling on it. "It's even waterproof. You get to spend your quality time with him before I got here?" she asked. "Because you two have so much in common," her voice robotically bored.

"We both make our livelihoods from water."

"A boring fact if I ever heard one, Golden Girl," she laughed at the shuttered look that came over my face. Although she'd only called me that once or twice, she knew I didn't like it because I felt as if she was trying to be funny or as I suspected; to make fun of me.

"Okay, no more joking around," Loren opened the notebook on her lap and pulled out a starched piece of paper. "Thanks for your list of RSVPs. I received a reply from the Jones and the Minelli's yesterday; they were the last. Here's the menu," she handed me a manila card that was half-filled with writing.

"Loren," I sighed dramatically, "have you taken a breath and looked at the day? The water? The sky?"

"Later," she said brusquely. "Jesse, you're too sentimental."

"What're you then?"

"I consider myself a romantic realist."

"What does that mean?"

"Romantic when it suits me, a realist when it counts."

"I'm the same then."

Deep and loud, she laughed, a real belly laugh, that confused me. What had I said that was so funny?

"On most things, Jesse," she finally got herself under control. "True. At your job, for instance, you're completely level-headed, but when it comes to love, you pile on sentimentality, it's fate to you and that's crap. "

"While you see it as some cold, heartless business deal right?"

"Because it is, Jesse; it's the business of security, lifestyle, peace of mind."

Loren stared at me, her gray eyes storm dark and resolute. The breeze blew strands of her hair around her face.

"Don't you want what Mom and Dad have? I do. A stable marriage with all their wants and needs financially met. Sure, they're compatible and enjoy their life, but it took them being the right kind of people who got together at the right time to make it all happen."

She let up a bit at the horror on my face.

"I'm sorry, sis. I don't mean to burst your bubble; your belief in romance, that giddy feeling, true love, happiness, whatever. I can't go along with that, I need to have my eyes open to understand what I don't want and what I do. And what I have to do to get it."

Now, I wasn't just horrified; I was appalled by her words and their clinical nature.

"You make me sound dense, Loren. A love-lorn wretch who'd fall for any joker who looks her way."

"Really, Jess," Loren rolled her eyes. "Remember Joe Forrester -?"

I raised my hand in a stopping motion, not wanting to hear anymore as my mind's eye flashed embarrassingly on the handsome face of Joe Forrester, who'd looked like Paul Walker of Fast and Furious fame. Back then, I'd thought there was no one else in the world for me but him.

"You were so hooked on that guy it was pathetic," Loren shrugged. "He was good-looking as hell I give him that."

"That wasn't the only reason I liked him: he was a good athlete, in the honor society, was funny."

She threw me a hard glance, "Yeah, so funny he went around telling his friends, 'I got me a chink chick.'"

"We were all in the cafeteria when you hit him right in the face with that soccer ball, bloodying his nose."

"I wasn't going to let that jerk get away with talking about you. If I'd had the chance, I'd ripped his head off."

"I know, I know," I soothed, calming her down, letting her know I got that she'd done what she thought was best for me. I was doing my job on her like I always did. "I don't think I even thanked you. I got mad at you instead."

"You couldn't help it; you liked the jerk and he hurt you." She patted my arm soothingly before changing the subject. "You think we're going to have enough to eat?"

I looked at the card in my hand, the menu: steak, lamb, baked salmon, lobster, and chicken marsala. A variety of salads, including quinoa, kale, and fruit. Fresh string beans, brown rice, and corn on the cob. Two pasta dishes, baked rolls, a chocolate cake, and a cassata cake; our mother's favorite. There was enough food to feed a family in Bangladesh for a month. So much food, and most of it would go to waste, I knew.

"Other than a roasted pig on a spit, we're covered."

"What did Julie say about the decorating?"

"She messaged me about it on Monday. Icariss and Company promised it would take them an hour, two at the most, including putting up the tent. Oh, I also ordered more champagne in case the guests want to take a bottle home with them. It'll have a little card around its neck with their names and thirty-fifth-anniversary celebration inscribed on it in silver leaf."

"Excellent," Loren looked out at sea for the first time. "It's going to be a wonderful time."

## CHAPTER 26

That evening we had family game night which consisted of playing: Monopoly, Pictionary and Scrabble while laughing all the while.

After watching a PBS special on the Civil Rights Movement with my father, my mother having already gone to bed with a Ruth Rendell novel; I kissed him goodnight and headed for my room. I felt pleasantly tired, though not ready for sleep and lay on my bed thinking about Abrams. Like some goofy, love-bound teenager, I hadn't yet looked at my phone; my bravery having deserted me at the thought of what he may have or not, written back.

Picking up my phone off the pillow, I messaged him: 'Hello, hope you had a good day. Hope to see you soon.'

I re-read it. Were those two 'hopes' overdoing it? It sounded stupid sappy. So what? It was how I felt. I tapped the 'send' button before I could agonize further over those twelve little words.

A few moments later, it rang, "Hello," I answered.

"Hey, you," Abrams said back and chuckled" I couldn't help myself; I needed to hear your voice".

My door opened, and Loren stepped inside.

"Hey," I said into the phone, sitting up on the bed. "I have to go."

"Okay, I'll definitely see you when you get home."

"Yes," I disconnected.

"Who was that?" Loren stood in the middle of the floor, adjusting the towel wrapped around her hair.

"What do you want? I don't ask who you talk to on the phone."

"True, but I'm nosey. Do you have some Paul Mitchell? I ran out."

"There's a bottle of conditioner in the cabinet under the sink."

Loren moved toward the bathroom, unwrapping the towel from her hair and letting it cascade to her shoulders. As I watched her, I remembered how I loved playing with it when we were small; its color and softness seemed so rich and alive compared to my midnight, straight locks.

All my favorite Barbie dolls had been blond-haired, even though my mother had bought me dolls of all colors and kinds of styled hair. Yet, I'd ignored them, preferring the blond dolls; I'd liked those best because they'd looked nothing like what I saw in my mirror.

I took in who I lived with and what it seemed the world preferred on television, in the movies, in magazines, online, everywhere; or so it seemed to me. As an impressionable young girl who wanted to fit in with her new family, country, and world, I bought into it all, right down to the blond-haired, blue-eyed Barbie doll as the most desirable.

It took years for me to come into my own and realize who I was and how I looked was fine. Being best friends with Loosha helped too. She made sure I knew I was Chinese-American, so I'd better damn well embrace it. When I'd turned fifteen, we'd burned all my blonde Barbie dolls in a funeral pyre. A teenage rebellion I'd tried to hold up in the real world.

Loren came out of the bathroom and leaned against the door, jamb yawning hugely and covering her mouth at the last possible second before asking, "You going to sleep now?"

I yawned helplessly, imitating her, "Might as well. I think I'll take the afternoon ferry and get home in enough time to get ready for back-to-work on Tuesday."

"Fine. Then I'll wrap- up any last-minute details before I leave Tuesday afternoon." She moved toward the door, "They're going to be shocked and overwhelmed at what we've done."

"Greatly surprised and happy," I said. "Goodnight, sis."

With a hand on the doorknob, she turned back to me, "They have been very happy together - still are, I mean, even after all these years. It's what I want too, Jess," she said, the expression on her face one of surety and determination. "I want it badly enough, I'll wait for just the right person, and when I find him, I'll never give him up."

"I believe you, Loren," I said and meant it.

She stepped out of the room closing the door, "Goodnight, Jess."

Turning off my bedside lamp, I lay on my side. I did believe her. Loren was the most determined person on the planet. She hadn't succeeded as manager for one of the world's wealthiest and most famous photographers by being timid, not standing out, and giving in and giving up. Loren was a force of nature when she wanted to be.

I understood much of her confidence, bravery and boldness came from being white, intelligent, and privileged of course; topped off by being beautiful to boot. This combination opened doors for her that were closed to others. Loren got callbacks when others didn't. She was given more chances when someone else would be given only one. Those who knew her background went out of their way to help her. Success, in almost everything, her inherent certainty; her privilege, a part of the deeply ingrained sense of entitlement, was part of her DNA. It was just the way the world worked.

It would never cross Loren's mind that she wouldn't get whatever she wanted in life. Add to the fact she would fight for it; down and dirty, I didn't doubt; made my sister one formidable woman. But then, wasn't I the same? Even though we didn't have the same genes and weren't born to the same parents, we grew up together.

So, wasn't I just as confident, smart, and emboldened as she was? Wasn't I? On that question, I fell asleep and didn't find the answer in my dreams.

The next morning, I left the island, my parents and Loren seeing me off as they always did. "See you soon," Loren whispered before I boarded.

"You bet," I whispered back before walking up the ramp and calling to my parents, "Bye, see you next month. Love you."

They waved as we pulled away from the dock and out to sea. Traveling back to New York was uneventful. It was raining when I arrived home, and as I drove the few minutes to my house, it rained harder.

As I got out of the car, I fumbled my keys and overnight bag and was soaked in seconds. Inside, I locked the door, dropped everything, and went immediately to the bathroom, where I stripped out of my wet clothes and ran the hottest shower I could stand.

My phone rang, and I closed my eyes in weary annoyance. I should just let it ring to voicemail, I thought. Whoever it was would text me anyway when I didn't answer. But what if it was important? Something might have happened to a Rutherford field worker.

"Dammit," I said aloud, hopping out of the tub and out of the bathroom.

I got my phone; it was Abrams.

"I saw it was raining," he said immediately.

"Bucked. I got in only ten minutes ago."

"Can you be free on Wednesday? Why don't we disregard tradition and get together in the middle of the week."

"Be bold and unconventional you mean," I laughed the spur of the moment idea sounding wonderful.

"How about an early lunch, then go from there."

"Hold a sec," I checked my calendar for any meetings or conflicts and saw none. "I'm good to go."

"I'll see you then." And he was gone.

Smiling to myself, I walked back into the bathroom. Standing under the shower, feeling the water cascade over me, my mind suffused itself with the thoughts of Abrams. I felt the day of travel, the rainy wetness, and the cold wash out of me as my mind conjured up his handsome face. The way he'd looked at me in Mandalay. His voice, his eyes. The way his hands held me touched me.

My hands slipped over my body as my thoughts, consumed by him, caused a quickening of my pulse as my hands slid wetly over my thighs, stomach, and breasts. My breath quickened as my fingers slid between my thighs, where I was already wet. My eyes closed on Abrams; he was right there with me, his breath mingled with mine, and his soft lips slipped across mine.

I adjusted my stance and stroked slow, then faster as he kissed me harder; our tongues tasted, the kiss deepened, and at its peak; an orgasm rocked over and through me, causing me to stagger slightly in its intensity as my breath, that had strained with me, burst out in a heated rush.

Taking a few moments to gather myself, I stepped out of the shower, dried off, found pajamas, and got into bed. How long had it been since I'd had sex? I wondered in the dark. Quite a while, I figured from that episode in the shower.

Stephen and I had made love a couple of days before we'd broken up, and that had been two long years ago. I hadn't felt much of a sexual need or even desire after he'd gone. I'd dated two other men since him, but the dates hadn't led to sex because I hadn't wanted it to; I hadn't felt the kind of attraction that heralded the physical need for either one of them. Abrams had now reawakened my physical desires. I couldn't wait to see him.

The shower scene had taken the edge off, but now was time for the real thing, not just a fantasy but Abrams in the flesh. Turning onto my side, I grasped my pillow tightly and prayed Abrams would be in my life permanently and I fell asleep on that prayer.

## CHAPTER 27

On Monday, I worked feverishly, not leaving the office until after seven. Tuesday was the same, except for a two o' clock meeting I had outside the office. I was glad to go even though it was drizzling out, it had been raining for two days causing people to complain and hurry to get where they were going.

Earlier, I'd received a cryptic message from Loren: 'Come by the gallery, I have something to show you. For the parents.'

I'd stared at her message, unsure what she meant and asked back: 'What for the parents? You're giving them another present?' She'd messaged back: 'DUH.' I'd wondered at her change of tune. I gave them presents all the time, and she sneered at my doing so, and now she was giving them more along with the grand party.

I took the train to Thirty–Third and crossed the street to the Ruschler Building near Bryant Park. I'd take my business meeting first, I was leery for some reason at having to see my sister. I met with the owners of a company that made biodegradable water filters that could be shipped around the globe and even though I was the Rutherford's logistics specialist, I'd sometimes evaluate companies whose products would work in the field.

After twenty minutes of their presentation, I knew as soon as I got back to the office, I'd send an email to Weber and the other board members, letting them know how effective the filters would be in saving lives.

Leaving the Ruschler, I took a shortcut through the park to Sixth Avenue. There were people in the park despite the rainy weather. A few sat on benches alone underneath black umbrellas while a few strolled here and there, faces closed to the rain. Others hurried as I did, taking a shortcut to their destination.

Loren's office was in one of the few stand-alone buildings on the street. It resembled a miniature castle, except it was built of glossy black stone and glass. I pushed open one of the double glass doors and walked into the front section of the building. The place was not only an office but a gallery where Richard displayed his photography work, the work of his team and that of the up-and-coming new talent he cultivated.

The receptionist stood behind a stark white platform and greeted me with a stiff nod which I returned, trying not to laugh aloud as I always did on the few occasions I'd visited the place.

It was all hush-hush, soft-shoes and whispers as if the building was a holy temple when, in truth, it was only a temple to money. Some of the works in the place, including a few of Richard's rare paintings, started at twenty thousand dollars and went up from there.

Walking through the silent gallery to get to the offices, I saw RJC standing next to an easel covered in a sheet. I heard a door open on my left, expected to see Loren coming toward me, and instead I saw, or thought I saw, someone exiting the room. I froze at a flash of dark hair and lean shoulders. A swift tilt of déjà vu came over me, and I closed my eyes.

"Jesse, what took you so long?" I opened my eyes and saw Loren coming toward me.

She looked flushed and excited, "Wait until you see what I have?"

I glanced once back over my shoulder, but the feeling of 'knowing' was ebbing away as she took my arm and led me over to where RJC stood.

He took both my hands in his and kissed me on both cheeks. He was wearing a tailored dark blue Givenchy suit on his athletic frame. With his suave features and loosely flowing dreadlocks tumbling down his back, he looked the epitome of a successful businessman.

"Nice to see you, Jesse. You're always welcome here."

He had a soft, melodious voice he used well to get his photography subjects to pose for him at their best and, sometimes, most outrageous.

"Hello, Richard."

"I'll leave you two alone," he looked at Loren. "Before I forget: Mrs. Carter messaged me this morning: she won't be available anytime in August and will see what can be arranged in September."

"One of her assistants could have emailed me," Loren said with a fleeting touch of annoyance. "Instead of involving you."

"It was fine," he started away. "Anyway, she wanted to say 'hello.'"

"He did not mean Beyonce?" I asked in awe after Richard had disappeared into his office.

"You got it, Sherlock; it's some kind of running joke with them." My sister turned to the sheet-covered easel. "This is what I got for them, for Mom."

"Something covered in a white sheet," I said drily.

"Loren pulled the sheet off in a flourish. "Ta-Da. Isn't it wonderful, Jess?" She grinned at me gleefully. "She's going to freak out when she sees it."

I stared as I caught my breath. It was the painting, 'Us By The Seashore'; the one painting in the world my mother had coveted for as long as I could remember.

It was a pastel watercolor painted by Michael Liam Randolph. A painting of three figures. A woman was sitting on a bench in the sun. Flowers, trees, and tall sea grass swaying behind her. She was in profile, her face half-shadowed by her summer hat. There was a book or a journal in her left hand and a pen in her right, poised over the book.

She was bent slightly forward, watching her two small daughters at the water's edge, creating sandcastles together. You couldn't tell if the small smile on her face was of pleasure, sadness, or regret, and because you couldn't tell, it made you stare at it almost hypnotized by her visage.

The colors and the scene itself evoked instant nostalgia and bittersweet melancholy. This made me and anyone who saw it, want to sit with it for a long time and feel the day, the passage of time, and love so sweet and pure that it brought tears to your eyes.

Yet, I found it disturbing too. It was the two girls, both with light hair so long it half-obscured the face of the smaller girl. They were sisters, you could easily tell that fact. But what did that matter? It was just two little girls loved by their mother among the swirl of summer colors and warm, nostalgic tones. I was positive these qualities made my mother want this painting so badly.

And Loren had bought it for her, the one thing our mother truly wanted in the world. This made every gift I'd ever given her instantly worthless.

"How?" I barely got out.

"It wasn't easy, believe me," Loren said with delight. "I'm going to have it specially delivered the night of the party."

I tried again, "Why didn't you tell me?"

"I wanted to, but wasn't sure I would get it."

"How'd you get it then? Randolph hardly ever shows it."

"I heard it would be one of the pieces featured in a private auction. I made all the inquiries but couldn't get in on it, so Richard called a few people he knew and I was able to bid." She lowered her voice conspiratorially, "At a lower price. Don't tell her, by the way."

"No…" I said absently, still staring at the painting, feeling its vibrancy, the sheer beauty of its sense of place; one I was familiar with, had been a part of many times, at the beach with our mother, wonderful times. "…I won't."

Now Loren had been able to secure those moments, that innocence in a work our mother loved. This would, without a doubt, be the best gift our mother had ever received and Loren had given it to her.

"I hope you're not upset by my giving her this painting," she watched my face.

"No, you got it for her and deserve the credit. She's going to love it," I said quietly. "Listen, I have to get back to work."

She pulled the sheet gently back over the painting and walked me to the door, where we said our goodbyes. It had stopped drizzling though now there was a high breeze that pushed against me. I didn't mind; I felt pushed and pummeled.

I'd lied; I was bothered by Loren's gift to our mother, even dismayed by it. I'd nothing to compete with it. Our mother would adore the picture, had wanted it for as long as I could remember, and now it was hers. And Loren hadn't told me a thing about it. But then why should she? It wasn't her fault I was making too big of a deal out of it as if she'd done it on purpose to hurt me, which was ridiculous. As long as our mother was happy on her anniversary, that was all that mattered, wasn't it?

## CHAPTER 28

By Wednesday, I'd only worked through half of the emails waiting for me when I'd gotten back from visiting my parents. I answered some and discarded the rest, which took up time. I met again with Mr. Weber, we discussed the last couple of weeks and how best to go forward and improve security if we could.

After my meeting with Weber, I attended a full staff meeting and before I realized it, lunch time had come around. My cell rang; it was Abrams.

"I'm downstairs. I have a cab waiting."

"I'll be right there."

"You have your passport with you?"

"I told you I always carry it."

"Good, see you in a minute."

Tamping down my curiosity and growing excitement, I quickly turned off my computer, and grabbed my purse.

There was an abrupt knock at my door before it was pushed open, and Clarence stuck his head inside. He opened his mouth as I held up a halting hand.

"Can it wait till tomorrow?"

"Yeah, but not really. It's about the pumps being held up in Nigeria."

"Tomorrow, I won't be back today," Ignoring the look of surprise on his face, I pushed past him and left him staring after me.

I understood the look on his face. Most days, I was the last out of the office, staying so late that sometimes I missed the last ferry and ended up sleeping on the couch in the lounge. So, for me letting wait for what could potentially be a big problem was something I'd never do. Yet, I was, running during the middle of the day to meet a man.

The elevator was taking too long, so I took the stairs. Abrams was standing on the sidewalk, his hands in his pockets as he watched the entrance. A cab stood idling at the curb.

He saw me, and a wide smile hit his face. He beguiles me, I thought, realizing the truth of that one word when it came to him. I was beguiled by Abrams.

As I walked up to him, he reached for me. He pulled me into his arms and bestowed a kiss first on both cheeks and then lingeringly on my lips before looking into my eyes.

"Lets go, we can't be late."

Abrams pushed me gently into the cab and got in after me.

"Late for what?"

"La Guardia," he told the driver and settled into the seat with an arm around me.

"Late for what, Abrams?"

"Lunch, what else?" His deep dark eyes swept over me before he took my hand and threaded our fingers together. "Tell me about your morning."

I told him, watching him as he watched me. His smooth, expressive face was animated as I told him a hilarious story from the day before. I loved the feel of him against my side; the warmth of his body permeated my skin as we sat close. He was dressed in a summer-weight light gray suit and open-throated white shirt which displayed his strong, tanned neck.

At the airport, Abrams hurried me out of the cab and into the busy, thriving terminal bustling with people from every place on the planet. We made our way to one of the escalators and took it down to an elevator which took us several floors up.

As the elevator stopped and the doors opened, Abrams checked his watch, "We're right on time."

"Stop," I pushed the button, holding the doors wide. "Abrams, what is this all about? Why're we here?"

He looked at me patiently, "If you'll step out, we'll be right where we should be and it'll explain everything."

"You sure? I'm starting to get worried."

"Come on, Jesse; there's nothing to worry about, I promise."

"Okay you promised," I said and stepped out of the elevator into a corridor.

We walked a few steps to a set of glass double doors. Behind those doors was a large glassed-fronted lounge, and beyond the glass, a black tarmac where sat three idling private jets.

We entered the lounge, where I saw, standing at the bottom stairwell of the plane closest to sliding exit doors, a pretty, dark-haired young woman dressed in a green summer dress. As I watched, she walked quickly toward the building, the doors opening at her approach.

"Good afternoon, Mr. Allen. The pilot is on board, ready to take off."

"Thank you, Marla."

Abrams turned to me as the woman walked back out and to the plane. I looked toward it as the baking heat from the tarmac sent waves wiggling the air.

"You first, Jesse," he stepped back and let me precede him out of the cool lounge and onto the tarmac toward the waiting plane.

Halfway there I stopped in my tracks, unwilling to go any farther.

"Do you trust me?" Abrams asked quietly from behind me.

I didn't turn around, "Any reason I shouldn't?"

"So far, have I given you a reason not to?"

"No, but we're just getting to know each other well."

"But we're not there yet," he said. "I'll try my best not to do anything to frighten you or ever hurt you. We're only going to lunch."

Only, I thought, what could be the harm? I walked the rest of the way to the plane and took the stairs up with him following close behind. I stepped onto a thick, plushy white carpeted space occupied by six buttery yellow leather chairs, two seats facing each other with white lacquered tables between them.

A long white couch sat off to the right, opposite it, a mahogany bar with leather stools. Above the bar was a large flat-screen television set. But what caught my attention was the fireplace loaded with birch logs that looked ready to be set ablaze. There was a partially open door at the other end of the room.

We sat in the chairs as I sighed in pleasure at its softness. Marla entered through the door at the other end, smiling professionally as she moved toward us.

"Captain Southern will be here in a minute to have a word before takeoff. Would you like anything to drink or eat while you wait?"

"Lemonade," I said.

"The same," Abrams said.

When Marla had gone, I threw my arm around his neck. I kissed his face with butterfly kisses, making him laugh as he pretended to fend me off before soundly kissing me back.

He pulled back only a little as Marla reappeared, wheeling a silver cart topped with crystal decanters of lemonade and water, a set of crystal glasses along with plates of fruit, vegetables, and cheeses. There were also linen napkins and china serving plates.

A few seconds later, the jet taxed down the runway and lifted smoothly into the air. We were off, and I was mesmerized by all of it. At least so far.

We drank and sampled some of the food but mostly talked about everything and anything while enjoying each other's company. I looked out the window once at the blue sky we were traveling under, then down at the bluest ocean we were traveling over.

Abrams's cell phone rang. I'd put mine on vibrate after receiving a message from Loren. I'd automatically started to text her back, then decided not to; she could wait. I'd also received a couple of texts from the office and decided those could wait too.

Abrams's phone trilled again. His ring tone was that of a bygone ringing telephone. He took it out of his pocket and checked the screen.

"I'm sorry," he glanced at me. "I'll make this fast."

He stood and moved toward the other end of the cabin, the phone at his ear. Even as I tried not to listen, I could still hear some of his conversations.

"…she'll keep telling you that until she's beaten you down. Don't let your guard down, Jackson, or she'll walk right over you."

I watched him and noticed how his voice had dropped, become deeply commanding to the point of demanding. I wondered briefly who he was talking with and what about. I hadn't heard this side of him before.

Abrams turned back to me, his eyes on mine as he spoke, "I'm going to be unavailable until tomorrow. If something crazier than usual jumps off, get in touch with Van Zandt."

The door at the other end of the room opened and a man came through, bending his head under the door's overhang to keep from bumping into it. He was dressed in a white shirt with epaulets on the sleeves, a dark tie, and pants. He stopped in front of us as Abrams stood and held out his hand, which the man shook warmly.

"Abrams, how nice to have you on board."

"Nice to see you, Brian. Everything okay?"

"Yes, and I promise you a continued, relaxing flight. The weather is clear and sunny. An easy ride to Cuba. Sit back and enjoy." He turned to me, a smile on his sad-sack-looking face, "Brian Howard at your service." He glanced at Abrams, "Our thoughts and prayers are with her - with your family."

"Thank you, Brian."

The pilot left, and I turned to Abrams, shock on my face, in my voice, "We're going to Cuba? Cuba!"

He grinned at me. "I'll have you back sometime tonight." As he finished, he looked at me seriously, "If you don't mind."

"You really do know how to show a girl a good time."

Later, the fasten-your-seatbelt sign discreetly housed in a niche under the window came to life.

"We'll be descending to Havana Airport in eight minutes," the pilot's voice came through a few seconds later, pleasurable and professional over a small overhead speaker. "Please make sure your seatbelt is securely fastened."

"Cuba," I turned to Abrams. "I can't believe it."

As the plane banked and then descended, I looked out the window at the approaching land with its waving palm trees. I heard then felt the wheels drop seconds before they hit the ground, jerking us in our seats before smoothing out and speeding us down the runway. We were literally on Cuban soil. A part of the world I'd only heard about and never dreamed I'd visit. A couple of minutes later, we were descending the stairs to the land of sugar and smoke.

# CHAPTER 29

The air that hit me was tropical and tantalizing. The sun seemed different to me, fuller, more radiant as it beamed down on us. I guessed it was seeing and feeling it over the ocean and not surrounded by, at times, oppressive skyscrapers.

A car waited at the bottom of the stairway; the kind of car that made my mouth drop open. It was candy apple red and first built when Eisenhower was president. It was a Cadillac Coupe De Ville and gleamed like a beacon. Its chrome was spotless and radiant as if it had just rolled off the assembly line. Its shark fin wings were as sharp as razors, its body smooth as silk; it shone.

"Beautiful," I said helplessly.

A smartly dressed man in a yellow summer suit and red shirt stood next to the passenger door. He was of medium height, dark brown-skinned with jet black hair and straight-edged sideburns touched with silver. He flashed a carefree smile as we approached.

"Javier," Abrams said and extended his hand.

"Buenos Dias, mi amigo," Javier said, taking Abrams's hand in both of his.

"Thank you for meeting me," Abrams said in effortless Spanish before turning and introducing me in English, "This is Jesse."

"Buenos Dias," I replied and shook Javier's hand.

"Welcome to Havana," Javier replied in thinly accented English.

He removed two post-sized cards from his pocket, "Your visas," and handed them to Abrams, who pocketed them.

Javier opened the back passenger door, and I slid onto the soft, snow-white leather seats, which were plush, sturdy, and felt new. The interior also had that new car smell, even though the car must have been more than sixty years old.

Abrams followed me inside. Javier closed the door on us before getting into the driver's seat and starting the car. The air conditioner came alive, sending cool, then cold, air toward us as we drove smoothly out of the airport.

Looking up at us in the rearview mirror, "Where would you like to go first?" Javier asked.

"The Sabado."

"Habana Viejo it is."

"What's Sabado?" I asked, snuggling into Abrams, who sat with one arm around me.

"It's one of the best restaurants in Havana. I hope you'll like it; the food is terrific."

"I'm sure I will."

It was another world. Not like the other Spanish-speaking countries I'd visited: Mexico, Spain, Brazil, not even Miami. As we headed into the Habana Viejo neighborhoods, I stared at its narrow streets, its side-by-side dwellings painted in different rainbow colors, and its residents walking and talking under the blazing sun.

It also reminded me of a by-gone era I couldn't possibly have lived. Yet, passing along the streets with their aged buildings and automobiles, I felt as if I'd gone back in time; while at the same time moving forward to a life with this man by my side.

Javier drove us down a quiet, narrow, street I hadn't caught the name of. This was one of the things I'd noticed about Havana; there weren't many street signs, not much signage of any kind. It was weird compared to what I was used to at home, where it was everywhere; to catch the eye and clog it even briefly.

He parked in front of an elegant building with a black, wrought-iron fence in front it and got out. Javier opened the car door for us as people of all shades of brown passed by, mixing with small crowds of other people wearing brightly colored clothes and holding their camera phones, tourist I realized. There were many of them in the streets, sitting in cafes, bargaining at outdoor markets; more tourist that I would have imagined; Cuba had become a destination country.

We walked down a short walkway and up an ornate brick stairway into the restaurant, which was a large, open-planned room surrounded by windows on one side and an open veranda and seating area on the other. On the left side was a small but sturdy-looking bar. At this time of day, only a few tables were occupied, and those diners seemed to be in no hurry to leave.

"Would you like to sit outside?" Abrams asked.

I nodded, and before we moved off, I stopped him with a hand on his arm, "This is unbelievable."

He lifted his right hand and briefly caressed the side of my neck, "It's wonderful being here with you."

We moved out to the veranda, where a short green lawn led down to a wall, and beyond the wall, the deep blue sea. As we seated ourselves side-by-side, close together, we stared out at the gently rolling ocean. A few minutes later, a waiter appeared holding colorful dining ware. Wow, I thought; in New York, they were on you as soon as you stepped inside.

The dark-haired, bronze-skinned man quickly set the table before speaking in rapid Spanish.

Abrams turned to me, "What would you like to drink?"

"Some kind of fruit juice, papaya or orange."

Abrams spoke to the young man, his Spanish just as fluid and rapid before turning back to me, "Ever had Ropa Vieja? It's made with chicken. We can try it for lunch if you like."

"Sounds great," I said.

I'd gone along with everything else so far, why stop now? I understood I was easy as pie in this man's hands and couldn't help myself because of it.

After taking the order, the young man strolled leisurely away only to appear seconds later with a bowl of lush fruit and one of warm flatbread he sat on the table between us.

"You minored in languages in college," I said, "so Spanish was a no-brainer."

Abrams shrugged, "I actually learned it in grade school. My parents insisted because, and I quote my mother: 'It's common sense, millions of people speak it every day and so should you.'

"A lot of people believe that when you come to America, you should learn and speak English as your first language no matter what country you come from. I did, knowing only Mandarin, much of which I'd already forgotten before middle school."

"But you re-learned it at your club because it's part of your cultural heritage. For me, it's unrealistic not to know Spanish. People from every corner of America speak it and so many other languages, and to communicate with them effectively, or at least attempt to, knowing their language can be key."

"You sound like a politician; you also make it sound easy."

He gave me a rueful look, "Believe me, it's not."

I started to ask what he meant when he said, "Thank you, Jesse, for trusting me enough to come with me today."

"Well, you asked nicely," I said before narrowing my gaze on him. "How many other girls have you brought to Cuba?"

"Too far to go on an average date."

"I'm not average then?"

"You're amazing; one of the kindest people I've ever met. You're generous, smart, sweet —"

"- stop it," I waved his complements away.

"- open-minded and real."

"You need a drink; you have heat stroke."

"I wish I'd met you sooner," he said with a wistfulness that surprised me.

"We met at the right time. You saved my life, Abrams. An old Chinese proverb says, 'He who saves a life is responsible for that life.' Forever. I do want you in my life, forever, Abrams."

"Together forever," he reached over and kissed me lightly on the nose. Then, "Here comes our lunch."

The young man arrived with a huge tray of wonderful-looking Roja Vieja's and fresh slices of vegetables: tomatoes, squash, radishes, and peppers, along with fried plantains the color of the sun. There was also more flatbread still hot from the oven.

We dived into our rich and spicy meal. It was the best food I'd ever eaten in my entire life. Or maybe it was being take to another country in the middle of the week by someone you loved.

After our meal, we sat quietly, holding hands.

"I have a surprise for you," Abrams said.

"You don't think bringing me to Cuba for lunch was enough of a surprise."

"This was only the beginning; there's more to see and do. Ready to go?

He motioned over to the waiter and handed him a stack of American bills without looking at them. The waiter did look, and the grin that fell on his face was almost beatific.

When we reached the street, Javier was waiting at the car; Abrams spoke to him, "We'll walk down to the shop."

"I'll be parked out front when you're done."

Abrams took my hand, and we started walking, "Our destination is up half a block."

"Where are we going?"

"To make magic," Abrams said cryptically.

"I don't think my heart can take any more surprises," I said, half-laughing, half-serious.

"It can because these are nice surprises. The fun kind. The best kind. A visit to Los Sentidos."

"In English?"

"The Senses."

As we walked, we side-stepped around other couples, young people, and old people with carts of groceries or selling fruit in baskets. We passed by men sitting on chairs, smoking hand-rolled cigars and reading newspapers.

I smelled our destination before I saw it and thought at first we were heading toward a grand open-air market. I could smell vanilla, lilies, saffron, cinnamon, rosehips, and so much more that my sense of smell was tested and overwhelmed even before we reached the place. Where were we going, I wondered; a flower emporium? A huge spice shop?

We stopped in front of a non-descript building wedged tightly between a warehouse on one side and a ceramic factory on the other. The front of the building was a narrow glass door with a green shade pulled down on the other side so that you couldn't see through into the interior. Yet, that didn't matter; the smells emanating from inside were indescribably wonderful.

"What is this place?"

"You'll see."

Abrams pushed open the door.

# CHAPTER 30

I entered a world that, at first, blinded me with a cascade of color. I had to blink to focus because the sunlight reflected off hundreds - maybe even thousands- of bottles, jars, and glasses of every size, shape, and color imaginable. The bottles were everywhere, from floor to ceiling, on shelves, on rows of racks, and even along the baseboards.

I realized then we were in a world geared toward one sense: smell. The air was redolent with odors, perfumes, incenses, and so much more it was beyond description.

Standing amid this swirl of smell, in this world of glass; behind a desk that was as bare as a white sheet of unlined paper, was a short, wide man in a grey business suit-wearing rimless eyeglasses and a calm smile on his round face.

"Welcome to The Senses," he said in English as we approached. His voice was musical and soothing at the same time. He looked from me to Abrams, then back to me.

"Here is all about your senses," he indicated the room with a sweep of his long, supple hands. "Your sensibilities. It's how we make you, who is already special, a fragrance for you alone. That is alone: you."

He took two steps backward and pushed open a door I hadn't noticed and crooked a finger at us, "Come, let's get started; I'm Professor Ruby, by the way."

We entered and halted at the noise: the swishing and the bur-bling of things being mixed, added, and sampled. Three people wearing white lab coats, gloves and protective googles were mixing and adding ingredients to tumblers, centrifuges, test tubes, and bottles.

Professor Ruby moved behind a long table swathed down the middle by a blue velvet cloth. On top of the cloth sat bowls, glass tubes, different size bottles of liquid, fresh and dried flowers, and small boxes of what I thought were spices.

The short man adjusted his glasses and gave me a long, access-ing look, so long I began to feel uncomfortable. After a while, he closed his eyes, took a long, deep breath, and held it for such a long time; it alarmed me enough I reached out for Abrams's hand. The professor finally released the air in a long, hissing stream before opening his eyes.

He reached for a liquid that smelled of ginger and poured a couple of drops into a bowl before adding two fresh rose petals; he then swirled the liquid around. He held out a vial of slightly viscous liquid, "What does that smell like to you?"

I took a whiff, "It reminds me... of the ocean on a summer day." I took another whiff, "First thing in the morning when the air is cool and clean."

He nodded, "Exactly," and added it to the bowl.

For the next fifteen minutes, Mr. Ruby measured, poured, sniffed, and added more dried flower petals, bits of scent and spices I didn't recognize, and even tiny pieces of a crushed apple to the concoction. He let me take a whiff now and again, but that was all. Later, he sent me to the front of the shop to choose the perfect bottle for my scent.

I returned a while later(the choice of bottles seemed endless) with one in the shape of a butterfly, the glass thin and so light-weight, I felt as if I were actually holding a live butterfly in the palm of my hand. Mr. Ruby took it from me and held it up to the light.

"This will hold your essential essence," he said softly. I was raptly attentive to his steady, sonorous voice. I realized that Mr. Ruby was a showman as well as a purveyor of scent.

"What we've created here is all about you, Jesse; how people will come to know you, your uniqueness. This scent is one of a kind because you're one of a kind; there's no one in the world like you. This belongs to no one in the world but you."

He took what looked like a nasal aspirator except longer and thinner and placed it in the bowl. He squeezed the instrument lightly and pulled out all the bowl's contents. He picked up my butterfly and filled it with the perfume, the scent wafting outwards. It smelled wonderful, heavenly, and tempting; it smelled like treasure. I closed my eyes and breathed it in, understanding I was breathing in me.

Mr. Ruby put a tiny, glass stopper into the top of the bottle. Opening a drawer, he took out a dark, ruby red velvet box with a small white silk pillow inside and placed my perfume on its bed. Closing the lid, he handed it to me with a small bow.

"Would you like a bag to carry it in?" he asked.

"Yes, and thank you, Mr. Ruby; this is one of the most wonderful things that's ever been done for me."

"It was your partner's pleasure," he nodded toward Abrams.

Mr. Ruby found a silk, ruby-red wrist purse for me and placed my box inside before handing it to me.

"Come again," Mr. Ruby said.

"One more stop," Abrams led me out of the shop and onto the street before I could get him to stand still.

We were out onto the street before I could get Abrams to stand still.

"Stop right this minute."

"Javier's waiting."

"He's going to have to wait," I wrapped my arms around Abram's waist and stared into his face, feeling a rush of tears in my throat. "No one has ever done for me what you have."

"No, don't," Abrams cupped my face with his fingers before fanning them through my hair and gently cupping the back of my head. "This is not a day for tears - of any kind; come on," he tugged me to the car. "One last stop."

Javier opened the door for us, and we got in. When Javier had settled himself behind the wheel, Abrams said, "The Jardin de Gales."

As we drove along, I laid my head on Abrams's shoulder, my perfume bottle on my lap. I caught a glimpse of a lone sign which read: The Plaza de San Francisco.

Abrams leaned forward and spoke rapidly to Javier before turning to me, "Close your eyes," he said.

"Really?"

"Yes, for the last surprise. You'll enjoy this even more than Mr. Ruby's."

"I don't see how," I said but closed my eyes in willing anticipation.

We rode in silence for a few more minutes before I felt the car glide to a halt.

"Wait a second," Abrams said. "I'll come around and get you."

I waited and heard Abrams's door open, then mine a second later. He reached in and caught my hand, "Careful," he helped me out, putting a protective hand on my head as I cleared the car and stepped onto the sidewalk.

He came up behind me and lightly gripped my shoulders.

"Alright, open your eyes."

I did, and they went wide as my fingers went helplessly to my mouth in stunned disbelief.

"What? What – is…" I stumbled over my words, "is this?"

"As you can see," Abrams held his arms open wide. "Another park."

"Oh my God, it's amazing."

"Jardin Diana de Gales. Havana's memorial to Princess Diana of Wales; her tribute garden."

I stared at the delicate black wrought iron entrance gate attached to golden pillars and a small, golden crown atop it.

"How beautiful. Can we go in?"

"Your wish is my command."

Abrams pushed the gate open, and we stepped through into a lush, beautiful world. We walked slowly among tropical green leaves, waving palms, and flowering plants of pink, purple, and orange, seemingly all colors of the rainbow. Birds and bees flitted among the plants as a fountain quietly burbled in the park's center.

We strolled down slate walkways, our footfalls a quiet, subtle accompaniment. The garden was a peaceful sanctuary. We stopped in front of a marble pedestaled sundial; its gold gnomon glittered in the sun as it marked time.

"It represents light triumphing over evil," Abrams said.

"It's a wonderful homage to Princess Diana. Let's sit for a few minutes."

We sat on a bench near the fountain and didn't speak, only sat and enjoyed this lovely world with its trilling birdsong and royal beauty.

After a while, Abrams turned to me and said quietly, with a touch of regret in his voice, "We'd better go; it's going to be late when we get back to New York."

"Can we make one more stop, the Malecon sea wall?"

A short while later, we stood at a section of the Malecon, one of the most famous sea walls in the world. I ran my fingers along its cool, damp stone as Abram watched, the sun behind his shoulder throwing his face half in shadow, half in light, and as the water lapped at the rocks below us, it was a picture of him I'd never forget.

# CHAPTER 31

When we arrived back in New York, I insisted Abrams drop me at Whitehall.

"I'll catch the last ride home," I said, pleasantly exhausted, barely able to believe what had happened to me. No one else would believe it either.

"No, it's too late. I'll drive you home."

I laughed, "All the way to Staten Island." I shook my head, "Too far. Better yet, I'll stay with you tonight if you don't mind. We won't have to worry about going all that way."

He laughed, "Less worry is always a plus; let's go."

We didn't say anything else until we got halfway to his apartment.

"I'm at Forty-Fourth Street and Ninth; we'll be there in a minute."

I didn't say anything, only held on a little tighter to my perfume box. I'd admit I was a little nervous, but I was not going to let that dissuade me.

The car pulled up in front of his building, and before the driver could get out and open the door, Abrams did it for us with a hasty goodnight to the driver. He led me through glass doors into his building. As we stood by the elevator, we wrapped our arms around each other and kissed until Abrams picked me up, and I wrapped my legs tightly around his waist as our mouths fused together again, again, and again before pulling reluctantly apart.

Abrams set me on my feet as the elevator arrived, and we stepped inside, close to each other. He took strands of my hair and rubbed them across his lips before we kissed again. His lips left mine only to slide down my neck. The feel of Abrams's mouth on my skin was an experience that made me want to wrap myself around him again.

We ascended smoothly to the fourteenth floor onto a long corridor. We walked to a set of blond-wood doors at the end of the corridor. Abrams keyed one open and allowed me inside. There was a short set of stairs, and we hurried up them to another corridor thickly carpeted with doors on both sides.

He pushed open one door, and we stepped through into a large bedroom where one wall was of glass fronting a view of the river. In the center of the room was a queen-sized bed with a dark, teak wood headboard carved with designs of birds. I ran my hand over the headboard, which was hard, smooth, and cool.

Abrams took me into his arms. We kissed deeply, holding each other tightly as our tongues tangled and entwined. We pulled apart, and Abrams rained tiny kisses all over my face as if sipping me. I returned the favor feeling my excitement and passion for him overwhelm me so that I greedily began unbuttoning his shirt, pulling at the middle one so hard it flew off, making us laugh.

I pushed the shirt down his smooth, muscled shoulders as Abrams unbuttoned my blouse, revealing my plain white bra, which appeared whiter against my lightly tanned, heated skin.

"You're beautiful," he said and ran his fingers over the skin of my chest and throat above the bra.

"So are you," I whispered.

He shook his head, laughing as he took a few strands of my hair and ran them over his lips again.

"No more words," he whispered back.

Our hands collided and fumbled together as we reached for each other's pants, pushing them down the other's hips and legs.

Abrams picked me up and laid me on the bed; our lips sealed as he sank between my legs.

The weight and warmth of him forced me to breathe faster, almost hyperventilating. I could feel every muscle, line, and inch of him, which caused my heart to beat so hard I could feel it in tandem with his, pounding fast.

Wrapping my legs around him, feeling his erection as he felt my wetness, I moaned in pleasure. Our hands glided over each other, our lips following the same path. I touched his face and ran a finger over his forehead, down his nose to his lips.

"Thank you for us," he said, his passion-filled face above mine.

We kissed deeply again, tongues tangling, skin-sticking-to-skin. He tasted wonderful, so much so I needed to taste more of him and pushed him over onto his back.

"I'm going to taste my fill," I said and ran my tongue around his right nipple, tasting sweat and him.

Abrams's hands never left my body. He touched everywhere, missing none of me; over my back, my neck, squeezing my breasts and my butt, pressing my stomach, caressing down my arms and legs over and over until all I could do was moan at the wonder of my feelings.

I learned the terrain of his chest and his stomach with kisses and with the tip of my tongue, dipping into the hollow of his belly button as his body was feathered with the long skeins of my hair. As I moved farther down, his stomach flattened with excited anticipation as my lips felt the light coarseness of the hair surrounding his penis, which was dark with its rush of blood, one drop of semen at its tip, which caused me to smile.

I licked off the wet pearl causing him to groan and his hands to tighten almost painfully in my hair. I opened my mouth and slid him inside, as much of him as I could take, and sucked deeply, my throat working along with my hands which were gently squeezing his testicles. I felt him stiffen even more, and suddenly he pulled me up to his body.

"Together," he said, the word a rasp of pained pleasure.

His hand slipped between my legs, and I was there only with a brush of his fingers. An orgasm that hit me took over my body in a wave of pleasure so intense it caused the world to rotate on its axis as Abrams shifted me beneath him, his body raised against mine, my hips there to meet his thrust. The explosion this caused ran so loudly through our joined bodies; I felt it not just inside me, but in the room, in the universe, even as our bodies pounded against each other.

It took me a few moments to realize the sound was not in our bodies but an actual sound beyond us. Someone was pounding hard at the front door. We abruptly stopped moving and stared at each other, realizing at the same instant that his phone was beeping incessantly somewhere in our pile of clothing.

With a groan of what sounded like physical, biological pain, Abrams dropped his forehead down onto mine, his eyes closed, "Some asshole is at the door." He opened his eyes, "Don't you move."

With another groan, he levered away from me, got off the bed, grabbed up his pants, and stepped into them even as he moved out of the room.

I pulled the duvet around me, left the bed, and hurried over to the door. Opening it a little, I peeked out and watched Abrams glance through the front door's spy hole before opening up. He stepped back and allowed two dark-suited men to enter the hall.

One of them spoke in low tones, so I couldn't hear his words, yet whatever the man said, it rocked Abrams back a step, the color dropping from his face.

He turned abruptly away from the men and hurried toward me, an expression of controlled panic in his eyes. It made my heart, settled down from its sexual excitement speed up again, this time with fright.

"What is it?" I asked. "What's happened? Another attack?"

Abrams passed by me and picked up his phone that had landed on the floor. He tapped a number and, when it was answered, asked one question, "Is she alive?"

The answer he received was enough to cause his body to sag briefly with what could only be a relief. He moved toward a small flat-screen television half-hidden behind a stack of books, picked up a remote, and turned it on; CNN filled the screen.

"I don't see anything yet," he said into the phone, "that's good. Say nothing until you have to – tell her team as well."

I turned away, picked up my clothes, and quickly dressed as a sudden sick rush came over me, a transitory feeling of loss, here then gone.

"What's happened?" I asked again. "What's going on?"

"Family emergency," Abrams said, then listened intently to the other end of the line, "No, I'll call my sister. You call her private physician, Thomas Ash. He'll be on the list. I'm on my way to the hospital right now."

My God, hospital. Had someone died? I slipped on my shoes, "Do you want me to go with you?"

Abrams was still listening to whomever he was talking to, "Have him meet us there. Hold on a minute," he looked at me.

"You have to go. I can wait here for you if you want. Is it your mother?"

"I don't know much of anything right now," Abrams plowed an agitated hand through his hair. "No, you go home, and I'll call you later. The car will be waiting downstairs. I'm sorry about all this, Jesse."

"Just let me know what's happened as soon as you can."

His phone beeped again, "Hold it a second, Frank; I have to answer this." He tapped on again, "Jean. No, listen to me: her medical records are available, but I can tell you no allergies or medical problems. Her doctor will be there as soon as possible. What? No, she's not allergic to latex, from what I know, or anything else. Isn't she talking?"

I lingered for a few unnoticed seconds longer before leaving the room. I could hear him answering yet another call. The two men who'd arrived earlier still stood by the front door, their faces blank and unemotional. Without a word, one of them opened the door for me, and as soon as I exited, the door closed soundlessly behind me.

# CHAPTER 32

The car was waiting and took me home. I slept fitfully and woke early the next morning to breaking news: Presidential Candidate Camile Harrington had been rushed to Columbia Hospital with a suspected case of anthrax poisoning.

"Oh no, my God," my stomach lurched in panic. I turned on the television and switched from one channel to another for the latest updates.

I caught Anderson Cooper standing in front of Mrs. Harrington's political headquarters on one station. A somber-looking reporter stood in front of Manhattan City Hospital, one hand pushing an earpiece into her right ear as she stared at the camera, "We have just been informed that one of the victims, a Jennifer Selwyn, a young campaign volunteer, has died."

I sat on my couch, trying to piece together all that had gone on. Abrams had broken off right in the middle of us. But he'd had no choice because those two men had come for him, to tell him there was some kind of emergency. At the same time, presidential candidate Harrington had been the victim of an assassination attempt though the news had yet to corroborate it was an attempt on her life. Still, I couldn't believe it would be anything else.

Maybe it was all just a coincidence; I was hoping. I was making connections where there wasn't any proof, jumping to conclusions I had no right to jump to. No, I was all wrong about this - whatever this was. He would have told me, right? I mean something so important. So, earth-shattering. Yet, would he have told me? Told me what? How would I know? What do I know about him in the first place? Other than the one fact that I was in love with him.

Looking at my phone again, I tapped up Abrams Allen instead of tapping in on the news. Pausing for a second, I added: Harrington. A list of articles appeared along with pictures. The articles I would read later it was the pictures I wanted to see.

I thumbed on the first one titled, "First Day of Work for Abrams Allen Harrington at Shusett, Kennedy, and Shusett."

It was a picture of a young man pulling open a glass office door. He wasn't looking at the camera, and he was wearing sunglasses. I couldn't tell what he looked like, so I wasn't sure it was the Abrams I knew.

Swiping left to the next blurb, it was another picture; this one was titled, 'Abrams Harrington our favorite son volunteers.'

It was a picture of him carting a crate of oranges on one shoulder, his unsmiling face partially obscured by the box.

The next was titled, 'Our next president's only son. Does he have political ambitions?' It was a long shot picture of two men shaking hands on a flag-dropped stage.

Feeling rattled, I tapped to the next picture, and this one caused my heart, already hammering with sick fear to stutter to a painful halt. It was Abrams; it was him, no doubt about it. His full face was exposed as he entered the back of a limousine. Holding the phone close to my face to be sure of what I was seeing: it was him alright.

The phone dropped from my nerveless fingers onto the carpet. I didn't want to look at his face anymore. He. Abrams. The man who took me to parks and to the movies. To Cuba. He'd had a perfume made especially for me. He is the country's most famous son for chrissakes and I had no goddamn clue.

I picked up my phone, tapped it, and when I heard the voice at the other end say, "Hey, girl. What's up?"

I burst into loud sobs.

"What the hell? Jess, what's wrong?" Loosha asked, alarmed. "Are you at work? What's the matter?"

Unable to answer through my tears, finally managing only, "I --he --" then more sobs.

"I'm coming over right now," she urgently said.

"Don't, I can't -"

"I'm going to my car," I could hear moving motions, and something hit the floor. "I'll be there as soon as I can. Remember the wine I brought over last week? Have a glass."

I nodded, realizing she couldn't' see my nod, and said through a mouth of tears, "Okay."

I dropped the phone to the floor and went to get the wine.

By the time Loosha arrived at my house all the way from Brooklyn, I'd drank half the bottle of wine by ten in the morning and felt fine. I'd left the front door unlocked and retreated to the lounger in my small backyard, slouching there with a glass in one hand and the wine bottle on my lap.

She looked frantic as she hurried toward me, her hair all over the place, no make-up on, in jeans and a sweatshirt, wearing one black high-top Chuck Taylor and the other blue.

"What the fuck is going on?" She stood over me, her face a study in angry relief, "You're not bleeding. You don't look as if you need to go to the hospital. You're not running around the street naked and screaming. What is it then? I don't know what I thought -but all of it was bad."

"Wanna drink?" I held up the bottle of wine.

"Too early even for me," she dropped down on the chair across from me, "I want to know what's up with you? I race over here because you sounded crazy."

"I can't tell you," I said miserably. "I don't think I can get it out."

"What?" she screeched, "I narrowly missed getting into a pile-up on The Narrows rushing to you."

I straightened and clutched my stomach," I'm going to be -,"
I staggered inside and barely made it to the toilet before the wine
that had gone down so easily came galloping back up in a fruity
bitter, uncontrollable rush that brought me to my knees.

When I could finally get my face out of the toilet, Loosha stood
beside me with a wet wash cloth in her hand. Bending to me, she
wiped my face, clucking soothingly as she did. She poured me out
some Listerine, and I cleaned my mouth. Helping me to my feet,
we moved into the living room where I lay on the couch; on my
back, one arm thrown over my eyes, still feeling weak and sick.

Loosha went into the kitchen and returned a few minutes later
with toast and orange juice.

"You can't drink this early on an empty stomach," Loosha said
quietly. "Eat, then tell me, Jesse."

I ate a piece of toast and took a swallow of juice before beginning: "Remember last week when I didn't meet you for the drink?
I met this guy instead."

"I figured it was a date. So what?"

Uncovering my eyes, I looked up at her, "The guy saved my
life."

"Saved your -- what? How?"

She dropped crossed-legged onto the floor in front of me as if
she was sitting in front of a storyteller at a campfire.

"I was in Walker Park when some boys knocked me down and
started attacking me."

"Jeezus christ, Jesse!"

"But before it worsened, he came along and pulled them off
me. He chased after them, but they got away."

"You call the police?" Loosha's face was a mask of disbelief and
outrage.

"It was over so fast," I explained. "Anyway, he helped me up;
I filed a report at the precinct house, then we went over to Mr.
Kirby's. He looked after me there, ensured I wasn't badly hurt and

applied ice to my bruises. And one minute he's sitting in front of me, icing my face, and the next I'm in love with him and told him so right then and there."

"Oh, my, God," Loosha's fingers went to her mouth as if holding in astonished, disbelieving laughter as she stared at me wide-eyed. "Who was this guy? Captain America and Mr. Marvelous all rolled into one? A mystery-man, then. Enough so that you told him you loved him, Jesse? Right there? Out loud?"

"To his face Loosha," I said glumly.

"Wow, wow, wow," she gaped at me. "Those assholes must have hit you in the head and scrambled your brain for you actually to say that to a total stranger."

"I didn't hit my head."

"Well, it was a crazy, emotional situation no matter what," she insisted. "Hell, you could have been killed. And this guy comes along and rescues you, so it's probably a matter, of course, you'll fall for him," she pointed a finger at me." "The Stockholm Syndrome or some form of it," she said triumphantly. "It's not love, Jesse, it's gratefulness, that's it. He's just some dude who happened to be in the right place, at the right time. For all you know, he could be a criminal, married, or con-man."

"He's not a criminal. I know exactly who he is," I reached down for the phone, flicked through my browsing history then held out to her.

Loosha squinted then her mouth dropped open. I watched a string of spittle lengthen and then pop loose between her top and bottom teeth. She pointed at the screen.

"Abrams-fucking-Harrington. That's the guy?"

"Yes," I sighed wearily and sank back onto the couch. "They keep playing this clip of him going inside the hospital where they're treating his mother."

"Wait, let me get this straight," Loosha held out her hands in a 'whoa' gesture. "You're in love with the Abrams Harrington?"

"Allen. He told me his last name was Allen."

"Abrams Allen Harrington then. And you didn't know?"

"Not until a couple of hours ago."

She dropped on the couch beside me, "Oh, this is priceless." She gripped both my hands in hers, "Tell me all of it, leave out nothing."

I told her everything. Almost. The J. Walker rescue, Breakfast at Tiffany's, the trip to Cuba, right up until she came in at the wine and toilet.

Loosha, to her credit, didn't interrupt once. When I finally stopped, feeling wiped out, she asked, "Where's your iPad?"

I pointed to my bookshelf, where it sat gathering dust near a vase of pink carnations.

"You never looked him up because you knew something was up with him, from the very first, even if it was unconsciously. Everybody's everything is out there for the world to see, and he has; I don't know how many freak'in sites dedicated to him. There are piles of information out there on almost every aspect of his life."

She scrambled through one site after another, "Your Abrams Allen doesn't have his own Twitter, Instagram or Facebook page; he doesn't need one. His so-called fans have created all those for him. They call themselves Abrams Acolytes, by the way."

I laughed; I couldn't help it, "Are you serious?"

"It's true. Look," she held up the IPad and scrolled through the pages dedicated to seemingly every aspect of Abrams's life.

"His every move since he was a kid has been recorded, tweeted, featured in magazines, and on social media pages. Everything anyone wants to know about Abrams, mostly made up, I figure, is out here. And you'd never heard of him," Loosha stopped scrolling and pointed to a picture of Abrams on a soccer field with a bunch of other athletic-looking men.

She tapped at the screen, "You see this guy here? Ricki Silvestri. His entire page is about Abrams. He follows his every move. And I don't see even a hint of you on his page - at least not yet. Mr. Allen Carrington is keeping you well-hidden."

"Silvestri's latest," she read aloud: 'Abrams Harrington hasn't left the hospital but is staying by his mother's side. We'll pray for them'. She stared at me, "You're one-hundred percent sure this is the guy, Jess?" she asked earnestly. "The so-called, "America's Prince"

"Yes," I said, the ring of truth etched in my words.

She took a turn around the room, "He's one of the world's most eligible bachelors, Jesse." She stopped directly in front of me, "And you didn't know."

"I honestly didn't, maybe because I didn't want to; he seemed so normal." I massaged my forehead, which felt hot and achy. "America's most famous son. One of the world's most eligible bachelors. Are you sure, Loosha? "

"Hell, I'm not sure anymore myself," she sounded confused. "You don't just meet fucking Prince Charming on the breeze like in some fairy story. It doesn't happen, especially not to people like us.

What kind of people were we other than good citizens and kind souls? We paid our taxes, had nice careers, and had good families. We were women who deserved to be loved just like anyone else. So, why couldn't there be a Prince Charming for us too?

"But it did happen, Loosha."

"You'd be more sure if you hadn't been too afraid to check him out."

"I wasn't afraid."

"Rachel Maddow interviewed him a few months ago and asked if he wanted to be president someday. And he hadn't said no, Jesse."

She returned to the iPad and read silently for a few minutes, "They're saying she's out of danger." She flipped the screen to face me. It was Abrams, looking exhausted and relieved at the same time. He needed a shave but was more handsome than ever as he gave a brief press conference. A man who could have any woman in the world, I thought, and he'd been with me.

"I need to talk to him," I reached for my phone.

"Why now?"

"Because he needs me. Look at him, Loosha," I gestured at the picture of Abrams looking worried and forlorn. "And I need him."

"What makes you think he feels the same about you?" She asked softly, "A guy who dated supermodels and actresses like Jennifer Lawrence and Scarlett Johansson."

"It doesn't matter."

"The hell it doesn't," hands on hips, her face taunt. "He's bigger than any celebrity. He has Jay-Z and Tim Cook calling him. And the added fact his mother is going to be our next president; the first female president of the United States, and he'll be by her side; they're damn near larger than life."

"The man, Loosha, that's who I'm worried about. I love the man. The one who loves classic movies and parks; I don't care about the rest."

"You'll have to whether you like it or not. If you don't let this thing go now – let him go – you'll regret it. Don't you get it?" She put a hand on my arm, halting my exploration for my phone. "He's not for you and never will be. It's impossible."

She continued, "Right now, he's being groomed for future political office regardless of the fact he's working in some start-up. It's inevitable. I bet he never mentioned that to you, did he?" I didn't say anything. "Did he tell you he loves you too?"

"In not so many words -"

"Which words then?"

"He's in love with me too."

Though I'd listened to Loosha and felt my heart wanting to crumble, I wouldn't let it happen. Abrams had asked me to trust him, and I would.

The look on Loosha's face was one of high skepticism. She

didn't believe me. She's just jealous; the thought immediately seized my mind. I'd finally fallen in love with a wonderful man -someone she had nothing to do with - and she was jealous.

"He can't be," she stated flatly.

"Why not?" I asked, confused by her statement which sounded so sure.

"Because you're not white."

A bark of laughter shot out of me, "What does that have to do with anything? This is not the nineteenth-century Loosha,"

"Bullshit, it doesn't. He's American royalty, and they go for their own. Has Prince Charles or Prince Harry married anybody who looks like me or you, Jesse? Abrams Harrington is no different."

"Allen," I said off-handedly then. "Why are we talking about any of this? I didn't say anything about marriage."

"It's what you're picturing, though, isn't it? A life with him? But then, how could you not? White framed house and babies. I bet every woman who meets him fantasizes about a fairy tale life with him," she pointed a finger at me. "Remember, I know you; he doesn't. He's not for you, not even close, and the sooner you incorporate that fact into your thinking, Jess, the sooner you'll get over him and get back to the real world. All I'm saying is: it's impossible, and I'm saying it for your good. You're my best friend, and I don't want to see you badly hurt."

My phone rang, making us both jump. I let it ring for a few seconds, and we both looked at it as it sat on the cushion; the screen lit up. It was Abrams.

Turning my back to Loosha, I picked it up and answered, "How are you? I've been so worried. Are you alright?"

"Not too bad," he said tiredly. "Can we get together, Jess? As soon as possible. I can come out to the island to see you for a few minutes. We need to talk."

"I'll meet you at the terminal."

"I have a few things to do - but I'll be there in about an hour."

"Alright."

I disconnected as Loosha stared at me.

"Why don't you call him back, Jess," she said quietly, "and tell him no. Because being involved with him is a bad idea. He's the wrong guy for you."

"No, you're the one that's wrong."

I suddenly threw my arms around her in a hug she didn't return, "It's going to be alright, Loosha; I promise you." Pulling back, I looked into her unhappy face. "You'd better go now; he'll be here soon."

She picked up her bag and slowly walked toward the door. Her hand was on the knob when she turned back to me, the expression on her face solemn but steady.

"No matter what happens, I'll always be here for you."

She left without another word.

# CHAPTER 33

An hour later, I walked into the terminal and was standing there waiting when the ferry arrived. It pulled into the dock; the ramp came down, a crewman opened the gates, and out walked Abrams, followed by the two men who'd come to his apartment. There were no other passengers. He'd commandeered a ferry that usually held up to five-hundred people and rode it here alone, other than the two men and the ferry crew. Something like that took influence, power, and connections, I thought, something I knew nothing about and wasn't sure I wanted to.

He came through the sliding doors where I stood waiting. He looked slightly disheveled, his suit wrinkled, his face world-weary. He stopped in front of me while the two dark-suited men stood a few feet away, glancing around and in at the terminal proper where people were gathering for the next ferry.

Before I could do or say anything, Abrams threw his arms around me in a tight, life-saving hug. He flexed his fingers tightly around my middle, so I could barely breathe as he buried his face into the hair at the side of my neck.

"She's going to be alright," I whispered, smoothing my hands down his back, gentling him.

He nodded before pulling back from me; his arms loosened but didn't let go. He smoothed the hair away from my face and stared down at me, "I dreamed about you."

"That's a nightmare," I said, wanting to make him laugh, but he didn't. "Have you gotten any rest?"

"Some, I've been mostly at my mother's bedside."

"I was so worried about you and your mom, too," I stared into his lovely dark eyes and felt the anxiety, doubt, and panic that had suffused me at Loosha's words and at all that had happened fall away. The way he looked at me with what I knew was a mixture of need, love, and wanting; made me love him even more.

"She's leaving the hospital tomorrow and returning to the campaign trail."

I pulled away from him, causing him to completely release me, "Why didn't you tell me who you were?"

"You didn't seem aware or even care about that part of my life. You got the real me," he gave a self-deprecating shake of his head. "And you accepted me anyway."

"I know all about being accepted or not."

We didn't say anything for a moment, then I said, "They call you 'America's Prince.'"

He made a disgusted face, "Don't believe that crap; they know nothing about me, not really. It's only to sell ads or whatever the hell they do and none of it is important next to me and you." He moved closer, "Us."

He planted small kisses at my right ear and whispered again, "Us."

"Us," I softly repeated.

"I'm going along with my mother for the first forty-eight hours of her campaign."

I nodded, understanding he was that kind of son.

"She doesn't want Apollonia or me there with her; she says it's too dangerous, which is why I'm going."

"To protect her, save her too."

"Like I can stop anything," he said, "but just being near will make me feel better. I'll call you when I can, message you."

"What about your company?"

"We'll string a few accounts along. I have a commitment I promised to make in person, so I can't be gone long anyway."

"I'll miss you."

"Me too. Kiss me again."

I did, deeply. I watched him get back on the boat, his two guards right behind him. The ferryman closed the gate, and they set off. We didn't wave at each other this time. I watched him until they were out of sight.

# CHAPTER 34

Back in the car, my phone was ringing. I hadn't taken it into the terminal with me because I didn't want my time with Abrams to be interrupted. It was Loren on the line.

"I've been trying to get you forever," she sounded peeved. "What's the matter with you? What's going on?"

"I left the phone in the car by mistake."

"Where are you?"

"Out shopping. What is it, Loren? What's so urgent?"

"Could you call Samson's? They left me a message they were out of white roses and could they substitute yellow. I don't want yellow, and I'm not calling to talk to some assistant; if I call, I talk to Pierre and he wouldn't be thrilled with the conversation. Tell them it's the white, or cancel the order, and we'll get Reeds, who'll get our business and RJC's from now on."

"It might be too late."

"If they want to get paid and a nice bonus, it's never too late. Get it done, Jess. I'm taking care of everything else, so you -"

"Alright, Loren," I said shortly, feeling hounded by her. "I didn't say I wouldn't handle it, did I?"

"What's the matter with you?"

"Nothing's wrong," I said tightly. "Is there anything else?"

She was quiet for a few seconds, and I could picture her running a pen down her lists.

"That's it. We get there, you take them out, the guests will arrive, you come back and the party starts. It's all up to you, Jess."

"Thanks, Loren. I'll try and not screw it up."

"You'd better not," the snap in her tone was unmistakable; I'd heard that same tone from our mother and laughed shortly. "I have to go," she said, "I'm expecting Richard back from a meeting any minute; we're preparing for the Oprah Winfrey shoot."

"Alright, talk to you later."

She hung up, and I sighed. I had enough on my mind with Abrams, and combined with making sure our parent's anniversary was a success, the stress of it all made me drop my head weakly to the steering wheel.

Abrams would be back in Manhattan in a couple of days. His mother was safe, for now. The fact that he was the son of the soon-to-be first female president of the United States freaked me out even as I wondered about us. Jesus, how selfish could I be? I drove home and inside, dropped into bed.

At seven-forty, I woke having slept the night through though I still felt groggy, and even a shower didn't help, though two large cups of coffee did. At work, I checked my phone for the first time that morning: there were two messages from Loren asking if I'd contacted the Samsons yet. For the love of water, she was relentless.

"Shit," I said aloud, I'd forgotten.

I called them immediately and was assured there would be more than enough white roses for the event. Right then and there, I vowed to concentrate on nothing else but making sure my parent's celebration went off without a hitch. I also had plenty of office work to do, and between those two obligations, I'd force myself not to think about or read anything about Abrams, his family, or the campaign.

The rest of the morning was business-as-usual; I checked on our water workers and how they were fairing in their respective countries, spoke to embassy officials, and signed off on the paperwork.

It was after two when there was a knock at my door. I'd been closeted in my office all day and hadn't seen anyone.

"Come in," I said, not looking up.

The door opened, and a brown paper bag with the words: Harlem Shake in black ink was shoved through first followed by Loosha's round face with a tentative smile on her lips.

"A turkey burger for you and a big American beef patty for me. Please, no lecture on how much water it takes to create a burger.

"It takes 660 gallons for one burger," I went to the door and opened it wide.

She stepped inside, "A peace offering."

"You went all the way to Uptown," taking the bag with one hand, I kissed her on the cheek. "You were only doing what you thought was right."

"Which only turned out to be wrong," she sat in a chair in front of the desk. "I can't deal with hurting you."

I sat back down, "It's over." I put our treat out before us, "Let's eat. The best burgers up or downtown."

"No doubt the best in the Five B's," she said with a mouth full of greasy, salty French fries topped with one of the restaurant's famous sauces.

"Mrs. Harrington gave an interview to Bloomberg television this morning," she said.

I remained silent. "She expressed how sad and grief-stricken she felt over the death of her staffer, whom she called 'sweet and kind' and those still in critical condition from what she called an 'attack on democracy. She said it wouldn't stop her from running for president, and she was committed to putting the perpetrators behind bars. Everyone in the studio was cheering her on by the end of the interview."

"I don't want to talk about it, I want to enjoy my burger."

She watched me under her lashes, "I didn't see her son, he must have been behind the scenes."

I finished half the sandwich. "That hit the spot; I've never had bad food from there."

Loosha wouldn't be sidetracked, "You heard from him today?"

"Please, don't start."

She held up a placating hand, "I was only wondering, and I won't do it anymore; it's your business, your life. From here on, I won't say another word about the Harrington's."

"Good."

"Unless I can't help myself."

"Loosha."

"I'm done," she laughed. "I forgot to tell you, the official invitation for your parent's party came." She frowned playfully, "Why would your sister waste stamps and a ten-dollar invitation on me when you already told me about it weeks ago?"

"You know Loren, she likes everything just so."

"She's a pain in the ass," my friend finished her burger and put the wrappings in the bag. "I'm surprised she didn't write in the invitation: Loosha, behave. Act like a lady at my big to-do, you slanty-eyed kook."

"My God, Loosha," I said, genuinely horrified. "Loren would never say anything like that, let alone think it."

"Right," she rolled her eyes. "Keep up that pretty fantasy all you want. Your sister's ruthless; you know it as well as I do." She got to her feet, "Gots to go."

She held up her purse, a gold brown satchel the size of a small suitcase. "A fake LV," she grinned. "Can't tell it from the real, can you? Got it on 39th, right outside the wig joint."

"If you like it, I love it. Thanks for lunch."

"What are friends for? I'm meeting Zhu tonight for cocktails at Mitchum's. He's thinking about going to China with me."

"I thought he gave up on the idea of finding his birth parents."

"He's still on the fence and changes his mind from day to day," she made a face and went to the door. "What can you do? Okay, girlfriend. If you can make it tonight, it'll be cool."

She left, closing the door after her. I worked until a little after seven, and only then did I decide to join Loosha and Zhu at the Platt Street restaurant. It would be much better than sitting at home and brooding over Abrams.

# CHAPTER 35

Mitchums listed itself on Facebook and Twitter as a premium bar. In reality, it was only a dive bar though a popular one. It featured plush booths, six tables, and a center-round bar manned by a drink-slinger famous for his potent cocktails. The place's other prize possession was a beautiful, regal-looking Wurlitzer jukebox. The bar owner, Eddie McNamara, was somehow able to get all the vinyl records he needed, not just balladeers from the golden oldies but the likes of Mary J Blige, Sam Smith and Kendrick Lamar, all on vinyl discs. Loosha figured he made them in the basement.

When I arrived, the place was filling up, no surprise; it was usually packed. Loosha, Zhu, and a couple I hadn't met before; had taken a booth near the middle of the room. They were of Asian descent, and as I approached, the men stood with quick bows. As I took a seat, I realized I'd interrupted the young woman's story.

"Jesse, meet Caroline and Li Yang," Loosha introduced us. "They're newlyweds. A round of drinks," she called to the waitress.

"A pineapple juice for me, hi Zhu," I said, brushing my lips across the cheek of the young man sitting next to Loosha, whom I'd known almost as long as I'd known her. "Are you going to China or not?"

Zhu nodded his head. He was a thin, small-boned man with dark hair and a small, neat goatee.

"I'm going, albeit reluctantly. Even if I find them, I'm not sure

I want to meet them. It'll change my entire life, and I'm not sure if that's something I want. But if I don't try, I'll regret it forever. It's a conundrum."

"It's a mess," Loosha quipped.

"It would've been a lot easier if I'd been adopted in China by a Chinese family," he said.

"Then you wouldn't have met me," she countered.

Loosha's on a role, I thought as the drinks came, and we all took sips.

Loosha drained her cocktail and motioned for another before she said, "Anyway, if you'd been one of the black children, it wouldn't matter."

"For godsakes, Loosha," I looked around, hoping no one else had heard her. It sounded racist even to my ears, though the term had nothing to do with skin color.

"Heihaizi then."

"An out-of-plan birth," Caroline succinctly defined the term. "A child born without permission; I feel ridiculous saying it aloud. My mother told me it's what they called her brother's second child, a girl."

Loosha said with supreme confidence, "I was forcibly taken from my mother's arms, and she's been looking for me ever since."

I'd heard this one too many times to count. My friend never for a moment doubted she'd find her birth parents, 'her people' as she called them, so she didn't understand (or tried not to) what Zhu was grappling with.

Despite all the evidence she'd been willfully abandoned, Loosha still made up elaborate stories to justify their decision: 'I was kidnapped and placed in an orphanage.' 'Out of all their children, they chose to give me a better life'; 'I was the only child who'd survived a famine, and they wanted to make sure I lived.'

I'd never confronted her on these imaginings; it was how she coped with being the 'different one' in her family; I even saluted her for it. I just couldn't commiserate with her actions, with her wanting to go back to China and search for people who hadn't wanted her in the first place.

I'd come in as Caroline was telling a story about her travel business, "Please, finish," I said, "it sounds interesting."

"Well, there's money out there; tons of it, and people are willing to spend it on adventure tours all over the world."

"Giving Disney World the finger," Zhu said, and we laughed.

"You mean sky diving into the Grand Canyon, that sort of thing," I said.

"It's illegal to parachute into the canyon though it's been done," Caroline said evenly. "My tours are totally above board."

She was a very pretty woman with a fragile face and even features beneath long, dark, curly-edged hair.

"I book things like swimming underwater in the state's Lake of Venus or hiking Mount Tevar, a semi-dormant volcano in Papua New Guinea; we went there on our honeymoon."

"Had a great time," Li said, his voice lightly accented and clear.

"You met Li on one of those tours, didn't you?" Loosha asked Caroline, who smiled and took her husband's hand.

Suddenly, I felt envious and lonely looking at them, something I hadn't felt in quite a while. I missed Abrams.

"You've been married; how long?" I asked.

"Sixteen months and very happy," Li said.

"Especially for me," Caroline handed over her glass as the waitress brought fresh drinks. "This is my second marriage, and I'm only twenty-nine."

"You got married too young the first time," Loosha said picking up her martini with pinky finger out.

"Too true," Caroline agreed and squeezed her husband's arm affectionately. "It was not the right time, the right match; not the right anything."

"He wasn't Chinese –American," Loosha said.

"Asian-American," I corrected automatically.

"Still a white boy," she tossed out as she tossed back her drink.

Caroline colored prettily, "No, that wasn't it. Well, maybe ten percent of it, but there was more to it. We weren't right for each other, that's all."

"In what way?" I asked, and by the look on Loosha's face, she was enjoying my curiosity.

"He - Wyatt - came from a Southern Baptist family out of Alabama."

"Whoa," Zhu said. "And you got out alive?"

"Yeah, but when he first showed up with me, they weren't too thrilled. Not that they weren't nice and gracious with their southern hospitality and all; they couldn't get over the fact I wasn't Baptist," Caroline suddenly grinned. "Let alone Buddhist and Asian to boot."

Everyone at the table laughed again.

"They tried their best to look past my race. After all, they were nice people and knew it was the twenty-first century. They wanted to embrace me as much as their ancestry, place in the community, and their Republican politics will allow."

"Where's your ex now?" Zhu asked. "If you don't mind me asking."

"Wyatt's doing fine. Why wouldn't he be? He lives in Chelsea. He's an investment banker and engaged to an editor at Doubleday. But that's the past," Caroline said, her arms going around her husband. "I'm the one who got the best out of the situation; I got Li."

Loosha glanced at me from underneath her lashes, and right then, at that precise moment, I realized the real reason she'd asked me out; it wasn't for drinks or to hang out with friends but to show me how wrong Abrams was for me.

Caroline and this unknown Wyatt had been the living-breathing example of a mismatched couple who had no choice but to divorce because they were from different worlds, one white, the other Asian. Now, they were both satisfied with 'their own kind.'

Bullshit. That was not going to be me. Abrams and I were different, our lives were different, but race, ancestry, and position would not stop us. We were made for each other, and I wanted to scream it across the table, into her face; scream it throughout the room, the world. Instead, I quietly finished my drink, pulled twenty dollars out of my wallet and laid it on the table.

"It's getting late, and I have to get home."

"Can't you stay longer?" Loosha grasped my arm. "We're going to order Margaritas with a side of burritos."

"No, thanks," I got to my feet and looked at Caroline and Li. "Nice to have met you both, and congratulations. Bye, Zhu."

I walked away as a chorus of nice-to-meet-you-too; followed my exit. On the street, I stood unsure which way to go or what to do, swamped by my anger at my best friend.

Her not-so-subtle betrayal of what I'd told her about Abrams. She twisted and turned my love for him into something wrong by parading that married Asian couple in front of me as if to say: this is what I should settle for instead of a life with Abrams. How dare that bitch do that to me?

Starting up the street, I turned abruptly back; I was going the wrong way. I'd taken a few steps pass the bar when my name was called, and Loosha came hurrying after me. I turned to face her.

"Are you mad?" she stopped; her face tight with guilt.

"Why the hell shouldn't I be?"

We ignored the people bypassing us; New Yorkers were used to maneuvering around sidewalk obstacles, street arguments, and scuffles.

"You brought me here under false pretenses to parade those two as some kind of warning, didn't you? If I stick to my race, I'd been happy, and if I don't, I'll be sorry."

"I don't want to see you not just hurt, but gutted, Jess, and that's exactly what'll happen if you keep chasing the guy."

"You keep saying that," I shouted. "Who says I'll be gutted? You don't read tea leaves, Loosha. You don't have anybody; you're more alone than I am, yet you have the damn nerve to give advice when you haven't a clue what you're talking about."

"I care about what's happening here, to you. You don't care because you're white worshipping."

I stared at her shocked speechless, "I'm not – ", I tripped over my words. "Never have – "

"You only date white men, you always have. Look at Siyu, he's great but you didn't give him a second look."

"I wasn't interested that's all."

"Of course you weren't," sarcasm edged her words. "Because you think you've got a fucking prince. But if you really knew, you wouldn't – "

"Wouldn't what? Love him? Not going to stop, Loosha."

"Cause you're stuck so deep, you can't see your way out, and I'm heartedly sorry. And for you."

Her words were devastating and mournful, making me hesitate over my next ones, yet they had to be said.

"I don't need you to feel sorry; I only wanted you to feel thrilled I found someone to love." I backed away from her, "I'm not giving him up."

# CHAPTER 36

Turning away, I saw a taxi coming my way and waved it down. I got in and didn't look back but left my best friend standing alone, that mournful look still on her face.

That night I had a terrible nightmare about Abrams; it was so bad that I woke to a scream and was barely able to recall any of it the next day except that it had been back-dropped by a snow-covered, cannibalized world where everyone was dead. Though the details escaped me, the feeling stayed with me, ones of loss, fear, and heartbreak.

Over the next few days, there were no calls or messages from Abrams. I wasn't alarmed by this; he was busy taking care of his mother, that's all.

I did my best to keep away from posts on how Candidate Harrington was doing during the campaign, and health-wise, though, it wasn't easy. Her every move was breathlessly reported.

My only saving grace was that I could see the finish line at completing the preparations for the big event, and with Loren blowing up my phone every hour, it seemed it was the best distraction I could ask for. And anyway, I wanted our folk's anniversary to be something they'd never forget.

# CHAPTER 37

I arrived on the island a little after noon the day before the festivities. I'd called my parents, telling them I'd be arriving a day ahead of schedule because of an appointment in town. Loren and I finalized the last details on my way in, making sure the decorators and caterers would arrive on time.

I was responsible for the most important part of the plan, getting the parents away from the house long enough for the guests to arrive. Loren had managed to procure tickets for us to the island's most prestigious art exhibit of the year being held at the newly built Ferreira Arts Center and to which my mother was dying to go.

The featured artist, Michael Liam Randolph, would be present on opening day, and the summer residents who believed they were somebody-among-a-bunch-of-somebodies were going to be present.

My father again met me at the dock with a kiss on the top of my head before saying resignedly, "You've brought more with you this time than the last."

I didn't answer right away, just kept hold of the large, close-lidded box that held an array of items popular in the world the day they were married, June 26th, 1986. Inside were posters, music, current events, plastic food items, and even a blow-up doll of Harrison Ford from the eighty's movie era. I knew my parents would be thrilled when they saw the stuff.

"Remember my friend Ami? She needs these things for a film project she's working on."

I didn't look at him as I spoke; I hated lying to him, even for a good cause. We stored everything away and drove home, where my mother waited with breakfast ready.

"Better not be more presents," she gestured toward the boxes and bags. "Don't leave it all over the place, Jesse."

"It's for Ami," my father said.

"What're we having?" I intercepted any questions from my mother.

My phone pinged, I fumbled at my purse pulling it out.

A message from Abrams; 'On my way home.'

A wave of relief shot through me, ""I'll take this stuff up right now, Mom."

I started the countdown in my head and heart, I'd be seeing him soon. At that precise second, I was at my happiest, not realizing it would be the last time I would ever be happy again.

After lunch, I left to meet Ami and Jack, two life-long high school friends who still lived on island. In high school we had been not been popular kids, more like outcasts and because of it; we'd gravitated to each other. We met at the only Starbucks. The coffee house was located in a discreet historic building between an upscale jewelry shop and a hair salon. Many of the full-time residents hadn't wanted the ubiquitous coffee giant to come, but the billionaires who'd wanted a Starbucks within walking distance, got their way.

Our lattes and blueberry scones sat untouched as we checked off each accomplished task on our phones. Ami and Jack were our emissaries on the island who took care of what we couldn't because we didn't live there full-time.

"The Charming has a van," Jack said, "for picking up its guests from the ferry. I also booked two Escalade SUVs for anyone who needs a ride after the festivities: a.k.a falling down drunk folks."

"Hey, no falling down," I said.

"With all the top-shelf booze that's going to be flowing all night?" Ami said. "Don't get your hopes up."

She was a tiny, elfin woman with light green eyes who favored spikey auburn hair and diamond-studded piercings through her nose, ears, and top of her lip, making her look as if she'd been sprinkled with fairy dust.

I asked, "Is there an official total on how many guests have booked into the Charming? Last check, it was twenty-three, or was it twenty -four?"

"Officially thirty-seven as of eleven-oh-six this morning," Jack said. He was a small, ginger-haired man with a wispy mustache and beard that still didn't make him look older than twelve years old. "A number of the guests will be piloting their boats and should have no problem in the harbor. Anyone else can get a berth for the night or a couple of days if they want."

"It's going to cost them," Ami said, then shrugged. "But, if they have their own boat, they can afford it."

"Most will be flying in any way," I added then. "Thank you two for all you've done."

"We have no problem helping you," Ami said, her eyebrows raised on the 'you'. "Loren's the one who treats us like servants."

"Not true," I automatically countered.

"Believe what you want."

We were silent for a few moments.

"Don't forget to get your wife her coffee with soy milk," I told Jack.

"I'll get it before we leave."

"I'm not apologizing for my snide remark about Loren," Ami said.

"You never do."

"She never will, "Jack added.

"I just hate when she bullies you."

"She doesn't -"

"While you barely stand up for yourself."

"Come on, Ami; Loren and I have a different kind of relationship, a different kind of closeness, that's all."

She barked an abrupt bitter laugh, "So close; you can't see it's not true; but an illusion in your mind, Jesse, though, not in your sister's believe me."

I said nothing else. We'd been friends a long time, my only two true friends on the island, and they knew how complex was my relationship with my sister. They'd never liked Loren despite the overtures of friendship she'd extended over the years; but for some reason, she rubbed them the wrong way.

"So, we're done," I stood. "Everything checked off and put away."

We moved to the front counter, where Jack got his wife's coffee before we walked out onto the street.

"I'll see you both tomorrow at seven," I said.

"Dressed to the nines, wifey and me," with a wave, Jack headed up the street.

"What's next?" Ami asked. "You going home?"

"I have one more thing to do. What about you?"

"Nothing, so can I come along?" she asked, the sun glittering off the diamonds on her face. "I have a free afternoon. Unless it's a secret. What're you up to?"

Her words caught me off guard for a second, making me think instantly of Abrams, "No, I'm going over to Autumn Day."

"Whoa, my girl is going to do it up right then," she raised her fist, and we bumped knuckles.

"Right and proper. Come along if you want to see it first."

We talked companionably along the way, moving leisurely down the cobblestoned centered streets, speaking to neighbors we both knew, passing by the tourist and summer rich. Nantucket is more of a village than a small town. Even though it's similar to other New England hamlets, it was special. Even though I'd grown up there and seen its dark underbelly; even been a victim of its racism, elitism, and narrow-mindedness, I couldn't help but love it.

At Autumn's Day, we stopped in front of its large, bowed display window, that displayed only one item, a gown. It was the color of midnight blue and looked like something worn by the most beautiful person in the world.

"I've never been inside," Ami said, gazing at the gown. "Never could afford it."

"Neither can I, but this is a special occasion."

I opened the door causing the bell overhead to jingle prettily as we stepped into a world of sublime sophistication; it smelled of roses and the subtle scent of money.

There were no racks of clothing on display except for one or two pieces draped on a couple of mannequins. There was a tea table between two Victorian chairs, all of which sat on an Aubusson rug. A woman in her late fifties with long, all-white hair, wearing a sky-blue jumpsuit on her lean frame, sat in one of the chairs. A set of gold curtains back dropped her. As we approached, the curtains parted, an elegant woman of indeterminable age appeared. She had a beautifully designed white dress draped across one arm.

"Hello," she smiled politely at us. "Ramona will be right with you."

She held the dress out to the white-haired woman, "As you can see, Ms. Monahan, the color is as pure as snow. A bias-cut so that it will drape wonderfully and effortlessly on your frame, leaving you with no worries, only the look and feel of immeasurable elegance."

Ms. Monahan reached out a hand where a large, squared diamond sparkled, "The quality is exquisite. I give you that. But it must be in pink; I want it in pink."

"Jesse," a voice called from an alcove to my left. "Right on time."

"Hi Ramona," I smiled at the lovely woman with her smooth brown skin and long, dark hair, silvered at the temples. She was more than six feet tall and still had the swaying elegance of the fashion model she'd once been.

"Is it ready?"

"I finished it yesterday."

Ramona's parents were from the Dominican Republic and had come to Nantucket as domestic servants: her father, a handyman for over thirty years on some of the largest estates on the island; her mother, a housekeeper on those same estates.

They'd raised seven children here, with most having moved off except for a brother and Ramona. She'd modeled extensively all over the world and when her career was over, she'd eventually opened the shop designing many of the clothes she sold.

Ramona knew what kind of women vacationed on the island. She'd grown up helping clean their homes, cooking their food, and watching their lives. She was smart enough to use that knowledge to create a place that catered to their vanity and wallets.

"This is Ami," I introduced them. "She's here to give me moral support."

"You won't need it," Ramona's sharply accessing gaze ran over my face and figure. "The dress was made for you. I'll be right back with our creation."

She disappeared behind the golden curtain.

Ami turned to me, "Our creation? Sounds kinda Zen."

"It's more basic than that: I told her what I wanted, and she did the rest."

"Brave of you," Ami played with a row of scarves, running the silk through her fingers like cool water. "I couldn't trust a stranger to tell me what looks good on me."

"I trust Ramona."

"That's one of your hang-ups: being too much of a trusting soul."

The curtain parted again, and Ramona was there, her arms cradling the dress of my dreams. She held it up: it was the color of a twirling green sea tossed with cerulean blue sky in whisper soft confection.

"Wow, you call that basic?" Ami ran a hand down the material in what could only be called a caress. "It feels unreal, hardly even there."

"You outdid yourself, Ramona," I said, not yet touching the dress.

"Don't go there yet, "she said shortly. "You haven't tried it on."

I followed her to the dressing rooms, and as we passed by, Ms. Monahan got to her feet, swinging her Hermes bag up on her shoulder, "I'll take the two Sinanese originals, in pink and white." She held out a black credit card to the woman, "Please contact me when the Ashler design is ready; I'll want two of those in pink and white as well, no matter the cost."

Ramona opened the door onto a room with wrap-around mirrors. I stepped inside, and she followed, carefully hanging the dress on a stand.

"Take your time, Jesse. Make sure it's what you want," she added and exited quietly closing the door behind her.

With my back to the mirrors, I carefully took up the dress and slipped it over my head before turning back to the mirrors.

I stared, shocked at the sight of me. The swirls of luminous green and blue were magnificent. Did I see thin strands of gold in there too? The dress shone against my lightly tanned skin, made it glow, and turned my black hair, obsidian. The front V was quaint, almost puritanical; yet it enhanced the delicateness of my neck while the daring dip in the back, ran nearly to my waist in a pure jolt of sexiness. It made me feel both beautiful and wanton. It flowed to the ground and trailed in the back to a long, feathery wisp.

"Are you coming out?" Ami called impatiently.

"In a second," I called back, still staring at my reflection. I didn't look like myself but someone out of a dream.

I opened the door and stepped out where Ramona and Ami waited, they stared at me.

"Oh, wow," Ami said. "And wow again."

Still bemused myself, "It's something ha?"

"You look…" Ami walked around me. "There is no clichéd word in the world good enough to describe how you look. You'll give Loren a run for her money at this soiree."

"That's not what I'm trying to do."

She looked at me somberly, "You started competing with Loren five minutes after your parents brought you home."

I ignored her, having heard similar statements from her. I turned to Ramona, who was studying me critically, her eyes sharp on the lines of the dress.

"It's gorgeous," she said, admiring her work then, "You make it gorgeous, Jesse.

"It's the dress," I said and smoothed my hands down my sides; the material felt other worldly.

"What material is this?" Ami asked as she stroked both sides of my waist.

Ramona adjusted the hem and straightened the neckline, "A cotton and silk-blend, mostly silk; that's why it falls against Jesse so well. I have earrings that'll set the dress off even more, I'll be right back."

She hurried away.

"Who's making Loren's dress? Ramona?" Ami picked up the hem and fluttered it as if it were a fan. "This feels cool and warm at the same time."

"No, Jason Wu," I twirled the dress around my legs; it moved as if made of feathers.

"Why am I not surprised?" Ami threw up her hands. "The same man who dresses Michelle Obama would, of course, design a gown for Loren. Your sister has to try and top you on absolutely everything."

I stopped moving and turned on her, "Ami, no more, please. You've said more than enough today – enough for a lifetime."

"Is that why you bend over backward to please them - even when they tell you not to? And Loren doesn't have to?"

"She doesn't have to because she's their daughter."

"You're their daughter too."

"Why are we having this conversation?" I asked, exasperated by Ami's harping.

"Why are you always defending her?"

"I don't - I'm not."

"Bull," Ami waved me off. "She's going to be at the party taking all the credit, drawing all the attention to herself, walking around as if she has a stick up her butt."

"This is for our parents, and we want them to enjoy every minute of it."

"It's not what you want that matters is it, Jesse? Only what Loren wants."

"I get it; you've always hated my sister."

Ami shook her head, looking like a disgruntled pixie, "Hate's too strong a word. Dislike maybe. She's manipulative and secretive, and I don't trust her as far as I can throw her. The only saving grace is that one day you'll stand up to her, just go off on her, explode, and won't that be a sight to see."

"And since we were kids, you've had a crazy imagination."

Ramona returned with platinum and diamond earrings the size of small sparkling pearls and handed them to me.

"These will compliment you and the dress. I'll put them in a box for you. When you get home, lay the dress down flat, and it'll be perfect when you put it on."

I turned back to the mirror, still taken aback by the fact that pieces of silk and cotton are sewn together could make me into another person. A fairytale princess. Cinderella finally goes to the ball, which already has her prince. Maybe not perfect, I thought, but damn good.

# CHAPTER 38

After telling my parents I was exhausted from the travel and hanging out with friends, I went to my room. In bed, I checked my phone, and there was another message from Abrams: 'I love you. I miss you.'

'I love you too. Can't wait to see.'

I went to sleep feeling as if everything was going to be okay.

The next morning, I was up early and went out to the garden. The sky and the water were wonderfully blue, with only a slight breeze to push the puffy white clouds around.

I met Loren at the dock. I saw her standing up front, looking anxious. She was the first one off, loaded down with a long clothing bag and a large purse. I took the bag from her as we hurried to the car.

"Did we get the white roses?"

"Of course, Loren. Calm down. Everything is taken care of."

"They're always loose ends. Too many," she said and blew wisps of hair off her face. She looked frazzled, even feverish.

"Are you feeling alright?" I'd never seen her so agitated.

"Fine, fine. I only want to make sure this goes off. I mean not one misstep."

"It will." Then, "You sure you're okay?"

"I'm fine," she barked, annoyed. "Stop asking me every five minutes."

"I'm concerned that's all; don't bite my head off."

"I'm sorry, I have a lot on my plate right now," she turned to me. "It's important to me that everything goes right."

"It's important to me too," it snapped out of me; I couldn't help it. She wasn't the only one feeling the pressure of this night. "We're set," I said for what felt like the hundredth time. "Mom will be making breakfast, and while we're eating, we can surprise them with the tickets."

"Right. Let's go."

Starting the car, before pulling off, I turned to her with one last thing – an important thing at least for me - for her plate, "Did you make sure there's no water on the table to be wasted? They can get it from the bar if they want it."

Loren sighed heavily as she stared fixedly out her window. "Of course, I did. You'd never get over it if I hadn't."

I drove us home without another word.

The parents were, of course, glad to see her. Our mother had made Loren's favorite things for breakfast: apple muffins with real pieces of apple, eggs Florentine, and fresh fruit.

We kept the two company except for the occasional short outings on our own, me riding my bike around the island and sitting on our dock watching the boaters, jet skiers, and paddle boarders enjoying the smooth, calm seas. I wasn't sure what Loren spent her time doing. In the afternoon, we cleaned the house.

Over a late lunch of salad and shrimp, my mother tried to pour me another cup of coffee, and I stopped her, "No thanks. There's no time." I stood up, "Mom and Dad, I have a surprise for you. Remember when you told us how much you wanted to go to the Randolph show?"

I held up three golden tickets with their black, elegant lettering and announced, "We're going."

"What?" my mother's hands flew to her mouth in shock. She stared at my father, who looked just as taken aback before, she turned her shocked gaze on us.

"How in the world? The show's been sold out for months - was sold out within hours of being announced. Carol McAvoy has had her tickets for six months."

"Loren's connections, of course," I gestured toward my sister, who sat unusually quiet, a meek look on her face.

"I knew how much you wanted to go. I called everybody until I got you those tickets. Why shouldn't you go? It's the best show in town, and you have to see it."

"It's terrific," our father said and got to his feet, hugging each of us in turn.

I glanced at the clock over the six-burner range, "The openings in an hour and a half. It gives us just enough time to get ready and get there."

"How am I supposed to get fabulously dressed in thirty minutes?" Our mother turned to Loren and gently pushed a strand of hair behind her daughter's ear. "You're not going?"

This was a gesture I'd seen her do a thousand times since we were kids. It was one of 'their things'. I saw it now, the actual 'thing' was that they were friends and had always been while she and I were not. We didn't have anything unless it was the journaling. Though I didn't think my mother saw it as something just between the two of us.

"No, I could only get the three tickets. And anyway, I'm exhausted," Loren yawned for good measure. "This was a hectic week. You three go and have a good time." She flashed one of her mischievous grins. "On me. I'll take care of the dishes. Go now and get ready."

"Yes, get a move on, you two, get dressed. We don't want to be late. I'm sure your friend Stephanie Carrington will be there on time, Mom."

"She's on the museum board with Theresa Heinz and she'll repeat it every twenty minutes if you let her." She gave my father a gentle push out of the room. "I still can't believe it," she said on the way out. "Stephanie's going to flip her wig when we show up."

Loren retrieved her phone from her bag while I cleared the table.

"We'll be back at four-thirty," I said and glanced at her. She was typing a message, an anxious look on her face. "Loren," I caught her attention. "Anything going on I should know about?"

"Nothing. Everything's on schedule."

She picked up the placemats, and when she had them stacked in her hands, she fumbled them, dropping them to the floor.

"Fuck," she said, staring down at them for a few seconds before stooping and grabbing them up.

I wondered at the cause of my sister's nervous clumsiness.; she usually had the nerves of a tight rope walker. Her acting so strange was beginning to jangle my nerves. Why did she have to start acting weird today of all days, I thought ungenerously, when we had so much going on.

I left her in the kitchen and went to get dressed. Thirty minutes later, we were ready to go. My father appeared first wearing a Tom Ford dark blue leisure suit and a cream-colored shirt that made him look distinguished.

My mother wore one of her favorite outfits; a light blue Bagley Mischa boat-necked dress. And with her white-blond hair and creamy, lightly tanned skin, she reminded me of a younger Helen Mirren. I'd changed into a flower print dress and left my hair down.

"You guys look great," Loren said and opened the front door for us. "You're going to show up everybody there."

"You sure you can't go?" my mother asked while taking her white clutch bag off the hall table.

"Come on," I said impatiently. "The traffic getting up to the center will be heavy. We'll take your car, Dad."

Outside, I was opening the car door for my father, who'd decided to sit in the backseat, when an elderly Volkswagen wagon stopped in our driveway. A young woman got out before retrieving a large, white box. Written on the box in scrolled letters was one word: Ramona.

Walking down the drive, I met her and took the box with a polite, "Thank you."

As she drove off, I went back to the house and deposited the box on the hall table before returning to the car.

"What's that?" my mother asked.

"Nothing much," I answered and backed the car out the driveway and onto the road.

My mother didn't pursue the subject, which was unusual for her; I figured she was too eager to get to the show to worry about a package. I glanced at her as she pulled open the car's vanity mirror and checked her face.

# CHAPTER 39

It took us twenty-four minutes to get to the part of the island where the newly built Jose Simones Ferreira Arts Center sat, a trip that usually took twelve. The traffic up the newly named Ferreira Drive was heavy, with a long line of cars making their way up the road.

The center, which boasted a huge cardinal gallery and three smaller ones, housed a collection of three hundred plus various works from paintings to sculpture, many gifted by the philanthropist David Geffen who had a home on the island. The curator had been snagged from the Museum of Modern Art in Manhattan, and the center featured not only the galleries but also performance spaces and even a small theatre.

The Ferreira was a gift to the island. The Heinz family (yes, the ketchup Heinz) had donated fifty-eight percent of the two-hundred eighty million dollar construction cost and had been rewarded by the institute being named after their patriarch.

I believed the Heinz's got their money's worth. The Ferreira, as it was called, though small in scale compared to other museums, was magnificent. It had been designed by the late Zaha Mohammed Hadid, the Pritzker prize-winning architect whose sensationally imaginative designs were featured in buildings around the world. The Ferreira was a testament to Ms. Hadid's immeasurable talent and the island's stunning natural beauty.

The building seemed to float in the air in a kaleidoscope of colors. It was made of steel and a unique kind of glass from what I'd read. A glass that was as thin and light as paper but had a tensile strength that could fight hurricane winds without shattering.

One of the attributes of the new kind of glass was that it seemed to absorb the elements of wind, rain, and sun to become a natural element itself; as if it had grown up from the soil it stood on, like a grand tree, a part of the natural world, the island's world; this was its jewel.

I pulled behind the row of cars at the front entrance, where a line of valets in black pants and starched red shirts opened car doors, letting out guests. We idled behind a gun-metal gray Range Rover Evoque as one of the valets quickly opened the driver's door, letting out a man around my age.

The man tossed his keys to the valet before striding importantly down the sea-shell crushed path to the fluttering glass doors, which were held wide open for the arrivals.

A smiling young man opened our doors. I handed over the keys, and we moved down the path, stopping briefly at the doors, which were uniquely shaped like sea waves outlined in gold ribbon. As we stepped into the sun-lit atrium of the center's first level, guests milled around in the splendor of one-percenters and moved from gallery to gallery, enjoying the works.

A man in a black tie appeared seemingly out of nowhere. He held out a silver tray, "Your ticket, please," I laid down the tickets. "Thank you," he handed each of us a decorative program. "You'll find the art wondrous and beautiful and there is an exquisite repast available for your pleasure in the Ellis Club Room. Enjoy it all."

With a bow, he was gone.

The main exhibit was being shown in the largest gallery, the work of renowned artist, Michael Liam Randolph. He was a painter and sculptor whose work was featured in the Louvre, the Balboa in Spain, and the MOMA in the city.

I'd seen his work at the MOMA, the abstracts, where the colors were so vibrant that they appeared incandescent and magnificently rare. The fact a person could create such beauty had brought tears to my eyes. His work was reminiscent of Matisse, yet with its own depth and flare. We walked into the main space along with a small crowd and stopped dead in awe. The paintings appeared to be floating.

"It's breathtaking," my mother said in awe.

We wandered around in humble amazement, staring at the works which were hung on glass rods; I suspected it was the same glass used for the building. It gave the paintings the magical appearance of being surrounded by light and air.

"I love this one," my mother stopped in front of a work titled "The Art of Love." It was the picture of a nude woman on her knees, her flesh-shaped Rubenesque as she glanced solemnly over her right shoulder. It was only her, and there were no other objects in the frame. The central focus was her.

The background was a fierce splash of red, burgundy, and blue-black with a depth of color so rich and vibrant it took your breath away. This was the magic of Randolph's work.

"It's magnificent," my father stared at the work for long minutes before turning and kissing my left cheek. "Thank you for bringing us here, my Golden girl. This means a lot to us."

"You're welcome, Dad," I said, thinking how what was to come for them later would top even this.

We moved slowly from one painting to the next. Everyone seemed mesmerized by the work. After a while, I saw people leaving the gallery and heading for the repast. Stepping away from my parents, I took a quick peek at what was on offer. Though I was positive they wouldn't want anything to eat, they might accept a small aperitif; I hoped they would because it would take up more time.

Back with them, "They're serving drinks in the other room."

"Sounds nice," my mother said, smiling as she waved at a couple of familiar faces. "Let's have one."

We left the cardinal gallery and moved into the gallery where the food and drinks were set up. There were tables laden with all kinds of finger foods along with a long portable bar manned by two bartenders. While my parents waited to be served glasses of white wine, I stepped away and called Loren.

She answered immediately, "How's it going?"

"So far, so good," she sounded breathless. "Everyone showed right on time, doing what they're supposed to do."

My arm was grabbed; startled, I turned to my mother.

"Jesse, are you coming?" She gestured toward another gallery. "Mr. Randolph is right in there. He's greeting and talking to the guest." Her face was prettily pink with excitement.

"I'll call you back," I said quickly into the phone.

"Keep them out a little while longer," Loren got in before disconnecting.

"He seems very accessible. I never expected it from such a famous person - you know how Richard sometimes behaves. I heard someone say he'd recently finished a work that's going to the Louvre."

"Let's go meet him then."

**CHAPTER 40**

Taking her arm, I shuttled her out of the room with my father following.

"No," she demurred. "There are so many others waiting."

"We have the time, Mom."

The artist was holding court with a substantial group of people who appeared to be star-struck. He was a tall man with a lean ropiness that nevertheless appeared strong. He was in his early sixties with salt-and-pepper hair, mostly salt, and was dark-eyed with tight, sharp features. I noticed his hands were as thin as those of a pianist.

He stood laughing, talking, and signing the programs offered to him. We stood in line, and when it was finally our turn, I introduced my parents and myself. He was delighted to meet my father.

"My son's in his first year at Harvard and is on the crew team," Randolph said, shaking my father's hand vigorously. "He raves about the scullers you designed,' They float on the water, not through it'. This from my eighteen-year-old kid, his exact words," he laughed.

"My wife and I enjoy your work very much, Mr. Randolph."

"Please call me, Michael."

"Our little town is thrilled to have you here."

"Your show was a present from our daughters," my mother added.

Randolph turned to me, "How lovely you are and good to your folks. Would you honor me by having a drink with me? The center kindly set aside a small area for me to take a break without being interrupted," he grinned conspiratorially. "There's even a guard."

I considered the time, thinking we had just enough before saying," We'd love to but only for a few minutes so as not to monopolize you."

My parents readily agreed.

"Great," Randolph slapped his long-fingered hands together.

He crooked a finger at a woman dressed in all black. She stood quietly in the corner like one of Randolph's statues. "Alana, we're going to sit."

"Of course, sir," Alana said. "Follow me."

"Follow her," Randolph extended an arm.

As we were led off by the black-clad woman, I heard Randolph ask my father. "Do you design on paper first, or get it down in your head and go from there?"

We were taken to a sectioned-off area of four comfortable lounge chairs around a glass coffee table of Scandinavian design. A man, made of all muscles, including those in his face, stood outside the area like a human rock. No one uninvited was getting past this man.

Alana came over and spoke to Mr. Randolph, who turned to us, "What would you like to drink? How about martinis all around?"

"I'd love one, very dry," my mother said.

"Is there any other way?" Randolph smiled at her, and my mother did something she rarely did. She giggled.

Alana went away while the artist talked with my parents as I sat quietly, occasionally commenting, though my mind was on the passing hour, nearing the magic hour. When the cocktails arrived, we toasted Randolph and his show which he graciously accepted.

At one point, when my father was speaking to my mother

about one of Randolph's pieces, the man himself turned and studied me with what I recognized as an artist's eye.

"You look nothing like them though I don't want to assume anything or cross any lines."

"I'm adopted."

"Of course, you are. I have a couple of friends who've adopted daughters as well."

"From China or some other Asian country?"

"Well, yes. And as with you, everything worked out fine. All the children get along a seamless transition with no strife. Big happy families. There's another daughter, is that right?"

My mother caught his last question and turned to us, "Yes, her name is Loren." She took out her phone and held up Loren's picture. "This is her."

Randolph held the phone and gazed at Loren's picture, "Lovely. You're a lucky family."

"We are," my mother got to her feet, and so did the rest of us. "We don't want to keep you any longer." She put out a hand, and Randolph took it in both of his. "We want to be sure to see the rest of your work."

"By all means, take your time. It's been a pleasure meeting all of you." He warmly shook my father's hand, "I'll tell my son that I met you. Won't he be impressed?"

We left him to finish his martini and moved off into a smaller gallery where some of Randolph's sculptures were displayed. There were works of bronze and clay, all credited with a simple beauty: a woman brushing her hair, an old woman walking down the street bent under an umbrella, a man sitting on a park bench looking down at his hands.

In the last gallery was a permanent exhibition of New England seascapes by Winslow Homer.

When next I checked the time, it was four-thirty; time to leave. Having lost sight of my parents, who'd gone back for a second viewing of Randolph's paintings, it took me nearly ten minutes to find them putting me on edge; time that had seemed to stretch earlier was now running out on me.

I found them standing in front of a triptych depicting life on the island before the world discovered it. Yet, it was more than that. As I studied the panels, I realized that it was more of a fantasy of what people believed island life should be. These ideas drew people to Nantucket in the first place: a siren song of endless summer days, gently cresting waves, and untouched natural beauty.

"It's the way we love the island," my father said quietly beside me. "The way our hearts see it."

"Yes," I said, feeling that deep abiding love for my hometown, its uniqueness, its old-world New Englandness surrounded by the sea. "But things are different now," I said, realizing the sad truth of my own words. Then, "Have you both seen enough? Ready to go?"

My mother raised an eyebrow at me, "I just saw Diane Melner; I was going over to chat with her."

"Aren't you going to have lunch with her at the club tomorrow? So, you'll see her then." Diane Melner had been invited to the party and would be on her way there now. "And anyway, my feet hurt, Mom. I'm ready to get out of these shoes."

"It wasn't my fault you chose to wear those sky-high heels."

"They go with the dress."

"But you knew you'd be walking a lot."

"I'm feeling a little tired," my father intervened. "I think we've seen everything anyway, and when the center officially opens, we'll come back, Lil."

"Alright," my mother accepted with some ill grace. "Let's go then."

# CHAPTER 41

As we headed toward the exit, I put a hand on my father's arm, "I left my program in the last gallery and wanted it as a souvenir, "Get the car, Dad; I'll be back in a second."

I watched them walk out before heading for Randolph's lounging area; he was once again holding court with another group of his admirers. I stepped forward, and the massive granite guard stepped in front of me. Waving around him, I caught Randolph's attention, and he broke off talking to a woman who looked to be wearing the right side of a Tiffany cabinet.

"Step aside, please," he said to the wall-of-a-man who did so without hesitation.

"The lovely Jess or Jesse, isn't it?" Randolph asked.

"Jesse."

I realized then that though he wasn't s overly handsome man, he had a presence about him, an aura of being, a special something that surrounded him and drew you to him. Abrams had that same something.

"I know this is last minute Mr. Randolph, but I wanted to invite you, if you don't have any other plans, of course, to my parent's anniversary party; it's a surprise. I'm sure they'd love to have you there."

"How wonderful. You are a good daughter." He called over his shoulder, "Alana," the woman stepped forward.

"I'll try my best to make it. Please leave your address with Alana. Do you mind if she and a few others from my group come along? They help me get through these events without embarrassing myself too much."

"We'd love to have all of you come. It starts at five. We're only twelve minutes from here, at least when there isn't much traffic. I'd better go before they come looking for me."

After giving Alana the information, I checked my phone on the way out. Nothing from Abrams today. Had something happened, I wondered, then told myself to stop it; I had to get my parent's home. I'd get in touch with him later party when the fanfare had died down.

The ride back took twelve minutes as I'd told Mr. Randolph it would, and when we pulled into the driveway, I stopped the car and took a deep breath. There were no signs that more than eighty people were steps away, ready to celebrate a long and happy marriage.

I got out of the car, my father followed opening my mother's door and helping her out. Before they could head toward the front entrance as they usually did, I stopped them.

"I have something to show you round back."

Not waiting for an answer, I started that way. "It just came today, and I'm sure you'll love it."

"What is it, Jesse?" from my mother. "The thing in the box that came earlier? Not another present, I hope. And I thought your feet hurt."

"It's okay, Lil, it'll only take a moment," my father put a hand at my mother's waist, gently propelling her forward before asking. "Do you hear Dean Martin?"

We rounded the corner of the house, and I halted at the sight before me, causing them to bump into me.

Backdropped by the sloping grass down to the water and bordered by my mother's lovely profusion of flowers sat a giant pavilion with glowing lights. From cleverly concealed speakers, Dean Martin crooned, 'I Have But One Heart'; while in front of us stood a crowd of people smiling, clapping, and hooting at the struck-dumb look of shock on my parent's faces.

Loren appeared beside us and threw her arms around them as she looked at me, "One, two…'" we counted in unison, then sang out. "Surprise, Happy Anniversary, Mom and Dad!"

We stepped back as family and friends crowded around them. My mother's hand had gone to the top of her head as if her disbelief would send it popping off. Her mouth moved in garbled, stuttering speech as she tried to get words out to all the friends and family around her, congratulating her on being married for thirty-five years. My father had at first paled, then turned beet red at the overwhelming press of attention from the many people in his life.

"We pulled it off, Loren," I said and took her in.

I'd never seen my sister looking more beautiful. Her eyes sparkled with a bright light of intense expectation. She radiated an exquisite loveliness from the top of her shiny blond chignon entwined with small golden, white flowers sprinkled with tiny diamonds to her white Jason Wu dress that was almost a gown. Loren was luminous as a fairy tale princess in a storybook. As if the world was hers. But then, wasn't it?

A series of chimes were heard from the pavilion, and as everyone turned to look, a line of waiters filed out carrying silver trays topped with filled champagne flutes they eagerly handed out.

Loren held up her glass as all eyes turned on her admiringly. Her boss RJC appeared and began taking pictures.

"To you, Mom and Dad, for the love you've always shown us and for the love you have for each other. We want you to know how proud we are to be your daughters."

"Happy thirty-fifth Anniversary," I chimed in.

We all took a sip as our parents went into each other's arms for a chaste kiss that caused thunderous applause to erupt from the guests.

Looking at them, at their sweet kiss, I thought of Abrams; I couldn't help it. I'd felt love in his kisses; I'd tried to convey my love for him in mine. At this moment, watching my folks, I knew I wanted the same thing with Abrams someday. I closed my eyes and wished for it like I had when I was young and wished with all my heart to be accepted and loved like Loren was.

Someone touched the center of my back, and I jumped in what felt like fright and turned; Loosha was there.

"I give it to your sister," she whispered. "She's no wallflower."

"Hey, I'm glad you made it," I said. She was dressed as lovely as I'd ever seen her; in a scooped neck blush pink dress, so light it was almost white, a thin white belt that emphasized her curves as the dress descended past her knees to a swishy hem that moved when she did. "You look beautiful, girlfriend. Come with me; I need to change."

Putting my arm through hers, we walked toward the house greeting family, friends, and acquaintances. We were met by Ami, Jack, and his pretty wife, Elissa.

"It turned out better than I thought," Ami said, looking around, "wonderful as a matter of fact."

"We make a good team," Jack said. "Maybe we should think of expanding our services?"

"No way, Jacky-boy, this was a one-off to help our Jesse."

"This wouldn't have been possible without your guy's help," I said "thanks, you two."

"We'll toast each other when you return from putting on your party dress," Ami twinkled at me.

Inside, I quickly changed before lightly dabbing my new perfume on the insides of my wrists and behind my ears.

At the sight of me, Loosha whistled, "Dude, you look good enough to take to Chinatown. I can say that because I've been there, and I'm Chinese."

As we headed back out, we met Loren coming through the

sliding glass doors with a group of people hanging on her every word.

She studied me for a long minute, "That's a cute dress, sis. By the way, Auntie Erin and Sam are coming. I'd better get out of the way," her lips twisted sardonically, "they might run over me getting to you."

She left with the group trailing after her.

"She's such a bitch," Loosha said as we exited the house. "She's jealous because she's not their favorite."

"Loosha," I warned and smiled at my favorite relatives who were moving toward us.

"Hi, Uncle Sam," I hugged him before stepping back to admire his handsomeness in the summer yellow vest he wore with no shirt over dark pants.

"You smell great," he said.

"Jesse, my love," my Aunt Erin planted tiny kisses all over my face as she used to when I was little, making me laugh. She'd always made me laugh, which was only one reason we were close.

Before me, she'd been the 'different one' in the family, who went her own way, who lived her life unapologetically, with who she loved. Then when I'd come along, we'd become the 'different ones', and that had connected us because we understood what the other had to go through, deal with, turn the other cheek to and it had made us forever close.

"Hello, Loosha," they said in unison.

"I love your dress, honey, " Erin said. "You look gorgeous," she gazed at me narrowly, "and with an added glow from something…"

"I'm glad to see you both, that's all. You look great, Auntie." She did in a yellow pants suit with a lime green shirt. She had a runner's physique, making her a taller, narrower version of my mother.

"How about coming to us in a couple of weeks? It's been too long. We'll have a barbecue in your honor- fish and vegetables, of course."

"I'd love to; I meant to visit. I miss you guys."

"We love and miss you too, Jesse baby," she patted my cheek affectionately. "You and your sister did an amazing job with this party."

"It was mostly Loren."

"Stop the modesty."

Loosha rolled her eyes, "Please stop."

"It's settled then; you'll come and hang with us for a while and -- "Sam began when there was a sudden commotion, a flurry of activity coming around the side of the house. "What's going on? Something happening."

# CHAPTER 42

As the sound of applause and excited voices reached us, I understood it then. "Randolph must be here, he came after all."

At that instant, a crowd of party-goers and hangers-on rounded the corner and at its center was the great artist along with his numerous entourage. He was grinning and shaking eagerly outstretched hands while stopping here and there to have his picture taken with some of the guests.

He wore a white suit with a white shirt and white shoes. I decided it took a brave man to wear all white, one who enjoyed being the center of attention, and Mr. Randolph seemed to already be enjoying himself immensely. He beamed at my parents, who'd broken away from their guests and come forward to greet him.

Loren appeared, and I watched her introduce herself. Our mother, her face awash in pride, wrapped an arm around Loren's waist as Randolph took Loren in with interested eyes.

"There she goes, charming the world," Loosha said beside me.

"Well, she's good at it."

Loosha sniffed loudly, her only response.

"I'd better go and re-check the dining situation."

We entered the pavilion and saw Loren hadn't missed a trick. The inside was extraordinarily decorated, from the gleaming dark wooden floor laid underfoot to the huge chandelier overhead. Round, damasked covered tables sat on the floor. Their gleaming silverware and shiny glassware sparkled around the room while the elaborate flower centerpieces of roses - primarily white - mixed in with yellow, red, and lilac threw color around the room. 'Us By The Sea' stood on its easel in a far corner covered by white sheeting.

An over-the-top stocked bar was set up on one side. One long side of the wall was open so people could catch a gentle breeze and look out at the ocean as they waited for their drinks. Music floated from hidden surround sound speakers, the dreamy tones of Duke Ellington, one of my parent's favorite musicians.

As the guests partook of the plentiful hors d'oeuvres, waiters in white dinner jackets served cocktails while others helped ready the dinner service.

"You two did good," Loosha said.

"Are your parents coming?" I asked after I'd stopped to chat with one of my father's former protégées.

She shook her head, "They usually take a trip back to Iceland when I return home."

"China's not your home."

"It's where I was born. Where I came from. And so did you."

"When was the last time you talked to them?"

"A few days ago or was it a couple of weeks?" she shrugged, unconcerned. "I forget."

She hadn't forgotten; I could see it in her face. She hadn't spoken to them or anyone else in her extended family, or mixed-race family as she called them, for a couple of months, if not longer. Loosha did this every time she went in search of her birth family. She'd once told me it was her way of mentally separating herself from her adopted one and preparing herself in case - by some miracle - she found her real one. As she once said to me, '...found those who lost me.'

"You could at least call," I said, and she didn't answer. "I have to start circulating and thanking people for coming. We'll have a drink together before the night is over."

"How about two," Loosha said. "I'll go chat with your Mom and Dad."

Circulating among the guests, speaking with friends and family, I chatted with RJC and then with Mr. Randolph, who held both my hands as we did so. I basked in my parent's happiness as the day started to drop to a starry night, and even though I hadn't heard from Abrams, I didn't dwell on it because everything else was perfect.

A woman with a stylish Afro and a cell phone in each hand came up to me.

"I'm Trina, the event coordinator. We can start serving dinner soon if you like. We must have the toasts and speeches first."

The speech, hell, I hadn't prepared one word. I'd determinedly put it out of my mind and had successfully done so up until now, and now it was here. My stomach flipped sickly at having to speak in front of these people while they stared at me.

Trina spoke into one of her phones, "Loren, everything's ready." She listened, then looked at me, "She said to wait fifteen minutes."

"Why?" I turned away from her without waiting for an answer. "I'll get her so we can get this over with."

At the house, I found Loren in the kitchen, texting and pacing the floor. Her face was mobile as fascination and frustration warred across it.

When she saw me, "Oh my God, it's time Jesse, I have a surprise."

"What next? Wasn't the painting enough?" I asked.

"You'll see. Everyone will see. Let's go; we can start seating everyone for dinner."

We went back outside through the garden, where a few people still lingered, and into the pavilion filling up guests. The smell of great food permeated the air. Our parents sat at the head table that featured a sign etched in hearts and flowers that read simply: LOVE. The guests were settling down at their assigned tables in anticipation of the meal and dedications to come.

Loren moved to the center of the floor as the music stopped and the chiming of bells rang out. It immediately quieted as Trina handed her a small microphone and a tall glass of champagne as I stood nervously on the side, dreading my turn.

"There could be no me without you," Loren began causing laughter from the crowd, "everything that's good in me, I owe to you." She turned toward our parents as some of the guests nodded in agreement. "You've always been there for me. Not only do I love you; I admire you both and feel blessed to be your daughter." She raised her glass, "To you and your forever happiness."

She ended with a sip of champagne and a loud round of applause from everyone in the room, or so it seemed to me.

Loosha, who'd come up behind me without my realizing it, whispered in my ear, "Your turn."

Trina was there a glass of champagne, and the mike held out to me. Loren had gone over to my parent's table, where she stood between them, her arms around their shoulders as they all stared at me.

I swallowed the tightness in my throat as I raised the glass to my parents, "They say -" I began nervously.

"Louder," someone on the other side of the room called.

"They say," I began again, only a bit louder. "Blood is thicker than water. Mom, Dad, though your blood doesn't flow through my veins, my love for you both runs through my heart." I broke off as tears clogged my throat and slid down my face.

"I've loved you from the first time I felt your arms around me. I could never have asked for a more loving, more glorious people to be my parents, my family with Loren as my sister. I love you and always will. Thank you for choosing me."

I drank to them, and so again did everyone else. I finished off my champagne before joining my family.

She said to the room, "More speeches later, everyone, enjoy your meal."

The voice of Carly Simon, another one of my parent's favorite musicians, filled the air. Colored lamps, strung throughout the pavilion, came to life as some of the guests got up to dance while waiters served the feast. I saw Loren suddenly exit the pavilion with Trina on her heels as I went to sit beside my favorite relatives.

Erin, who was eating from a plate of sliced fruit, asked, "When are they going to give a speech? Your mother is bursting at the seams to give a shout-out," she said making us laugh.

"After dinner," I said when we heard again a flurry of activity coming from outside.

"Another celebrity?" Sam asked.

Flashes of light and loud voices reached us. My parents left their table with Loosha following along.

"Another surprise?" I heard my mother ask. "I don't think my heart can take anymore," she sounded half-joking and half-serious. More guests followed them out, eager to know what was going on.

Sam, with a look of concern on his face, asked, "Someone have an accident?"

A sting of panic hit me. I looked around for Loren and realized she hadn't come back inside. I headed out to find her and ran into another crowd coming toward me, this one was larger than the one that had surrounded Randolph. Camera phones were snapping pictures as excited voices and shouts of surprise filled the air.

"Jesus," Loosha was there and gripped my arm tightly. "What the fuck?"

At the tail end of her words, the crowd parted, and there was Loren, hand-in-hand with a man I instantly recognized. I knew.

"It's him," I said, feeling as if I'd turned to stone.

Loosha heard the disbelief in my voice, "Him, who?"

"Abrams Harrington – Allen...

"What?"

"...with Loren."

# CHAPTER 43

The words fell out of me like ice-covered stones even as I felt heat engulf me in a tsunami of disbelief. Sweat poured down my face, my head swam in total confusion and terror, and I began to fall; Loosha caught me before I hit the ground. I saw them clearly and realized what I was seeing was not a hallucination. It was truly Abrams and Loren. Together. Hand-in-hand. Abrams was dressed in a spectacular black tuxedo, white shirt, and black bow tie. He was unsmiling as they headed into the pavilion.

"It can't be; I'm not seeing this."

But, of course, I was seeing it all. Loren with Abrams. My Abrams. My parents followed them amid the camera flashes, animated voices and shouts of: Abrams! Loren! They looked just like Prince and Princess Charming, I realized. While I stood looking on, shattered.

"Holy shit, " Loosha gasped belatedly. "They're together."

I stormed past Loosha, almost knocking her down, and into the pavilion straight for them. I wanted answers though I couldn't imagine what they could say that would make any sense because nothing made sense, especially the fact that Abrams was here, not with me but with Loren, my sister. Our parents stood beside them as folks moved up to shake Abrams's hand and talk to him, undoubtedly about his mother and her presidential candidacy.

Loren stood close, basking in it all. How could she do this to me?

I thought furiously as I cut through the guests, ignoring people who tried to stop me for a chat or congratulate me on the party's success.

"Abrams," I stopped a few steps away.

They turned and looked at me, and as I watched, the color dropped from Abram's face until he looked lifeless.

"Jess -," he began, then tried again. "Jesse?" His words came out in a croak, "What are you doing here?"

"What's going on?" Loren stepped between us. "You two know each other? Jess?" she stared at us. We all stared at each other, a stunning tableau in a crazed world of our own. My thoughts whirled, then skidded to a halt as my fingers went involuntarily to my mouth in realization.

"You're here because of her invitation. You're the special person she -"

"How'd you know Jesse?" Loren asked again. Her face had hardened, and her gray eyes were ice-cold.

"Abrams, you didn't tell me you'd be here," I said.

"You never mentioned an anniversary party to me."

"I must have, Abrams."

"No or I didn't put it all together."

"What the fuck is going on here?" Loren raised her voice, angry that she was being ignored. "I didn't know you knew my sister."

""I didn't know you two were sisters," Abrams said, still speaking to me. "You never mentioned a sister."

Loren faced me, "What's going on here, Jesse?"

Our parents looked from one to the other, twin looks of deep concern and bewilderment on their faces.

My mother spoke to me first, "What's going on between you two?"

"Jesse knows Abrams," Loren said indignantly.

"It's more than just knowing him," I shot back.

"I need to talk to you alone," Abrams said.

"Yes," Loren and I said simultaneously.

"He meant me, Loren, not you."

"Why would he want to talk to you?" she said stridently.

"Stop it, you two," our mother snapped sharply as her gaze flicked unhappily toward the guests who were hanging on our every word. "This is unseemly. Undignified. Everyone is looking at you. Let's go into the house."

"I'm not going anywhere," Loren's entire body had stiffened as one hand balled itself into a fist while she raised the other and pointed an accusing finger at me. "Jesse is acting crazy, which is no surprise at all. This is crazy."

"I'm not going to listen to this," I turned away.

Abrams grabbed hold my arm, halting me. Loren then grabbed Abrams's jacket, stopping him; we were frozen statues on display as if honed by Randolph's clever hands.

I un-thawed first, and abruptly, without hesitation or thought, I pushed Loren. My right hand went to the softness of her belly, and even though it wasn't a hard push, she went stumbling back away from us - him - as some of those around us gasped in surprised dismay.

I'd never done anything like it in my life, never touched her in anger and the enormous shock of it ran through me even as Loren tripped over the hem of her dress and would've fallen if Abrams hadn't caught her. She threw her arms around his neck and clutched him as if she were drowning as she smiled at me.

I ran then, pushing past guests who tried to speak with me or were taking my picture with their phones. I headed down the beach, where I dropped to the sand and sobbed hard, wild with grief, so much so that I pulled at the long length of my hair in distress. The actual physical pain of their betrayal – his betrayal - caused me to shriek in turmoil.

I burrowed into the sand like some wounded thing and lay there for a long time. When I finally opened my eyes, I tried to see the darkening ocean through the darkening world but was blinded by a cascade of tears and an overwhelming sense of loss. I should have known I was going to lose out. After all, I was the darker sister while Loren was the light. All she had to do was want, and it was given to her even if it belonged to someone else - to me.

I painfully pictured them together on magazine covers, trending online, at film openings, and their picture in the society section of the Times. Everywhere. Abrams was wearing a beautiful suit; Loren in a stunning white gown, holding each other, grinning into each other's up turned face. Married. Happy. The prince and princess. The perfects. I could see them so clearly in front of me, so real, so sure. So inevitable. Had they slept together? As this hurtful thought hit me, the pain inside broke through to a moan.

It had been too good to be true - he was too good to be true. My sister with him, the love of my life. But was she my sister? There was no blood between us and nothing between us now. What had once been there? What had we truly meant to each other? I'd been the one who'd worshipped her from the beginning because she was born into them; she had always belonged to them. I'd had to earn their love by blood, sweat, and tears. And not only my place in their family but in the world as their adopted daughter, the other sister, the Chinese one. I'd always been second class and hadn't fully realized it until this traumatic moment.

Should I give in and concede to Loren? The better sister, daughter, woman? She had it all while I had no one. It was as if I didn't exist anymore, which made sense; I'd disappeared the moment I saw them together.

"Jesse?"

Startled, I sat up and, through my tears, saw Abrams there. He stood a few feet away. He'd come after me.

"I swear to you," his voice was ragged as he moved carefully toward me. "I had no idea about any of this; let alone the fact you two were related."

I stepped toward him, "It's on me too, I never said I had a sister.

But it's beside the point isn't it, Abrams. You're here with another woman when I thought we were together. My own sister to top this madness off. I was warned but I didn't listen and it's what I deserve for trusting someone like you, a bastard and a liar."

"Goddammit, Jesse, I didn't know for chrissakes because Loren told me her sister was dead."

"Shut up," I put both hands to my ears. "I don't want to hear anymore. Go away. Go."

He pulled my hands down from my ears and held them tightly. "You have it all wrong. There's nothing between us on my part."

"Jesse," we both looked around, and there was Loosha running down toward us and yelling at us in Mandarin.

I shook off Abrams as she reached us.

"Get away from her, you asshole," she said in English and pushed Abrams away from me before screaming at him, "Ni hun dan," 'you asshole' in Mandarin.

She stepped in front of me as Abrams came toward me while Loren and our parents appeared and stared down at us.

I turned away from my friend and family and ran toward the ocean, away from all of them.

Of course, it was Loosha who found me later, sitting on a rock out in the dark water, and somehow got me home to Staten Island, where I shut myself away for five days. I refused to take calls from anyone, including Aunt Erin and especially Abrams. I spoke once to Clarence at the office and told him I was so ill I might have to be hospitalized, which felt very true to me. In my mind, I was more than sick; I felt gutted as if I were dying as I did when Yolanda was murdered.

At one point, I remember asking Loosha as we drove away, "Do you have anything?"

"Like what?" She'd asked while glancing at me in alarm.

"I don't care. Pills, coke, ecstasy. Anything, just something strong. I used up the last of my Percocet a year ago."

She hadn't given me anything. Instead, she'd tried her best to stop my downward spiral, which took me from couch to bed in fits of pain and sorrow. The only thing I managed to do physically was write in my journal. Pages and pages of scribbled angry, tearful, revengeful, pitiful thoughts that were half coherent and half-crazed rantings.

# CHAPTER 44

On the fifth day, Loosha let herself in with the extra key I'd given her making me wish I hadn't done that.

"You have to stop this crying, Jesse; this lone pity party," she said as she stomped around the living room, pushing aside half-empty cups of wine, an uneaten plate of toast, and the party dress now torn and stained and rolled into a ball. "And accept the fact they're together."

"I can't. I won't. I met him first," I said, exhausted from the tears and my 'lone pity party,' as she called it.

"Loren met him long before you did."

"I loved him first."

"Maybe. But it doesn't matter; she has him now. You've got to get over Abrams; I mean totally over him."

Grabbing up the ripped-apart dress, I used it to wipe at my tear-streaked face. "I'm sick." Meaning heartbroken, though, I knew my friend wouldn't appreciate that differential, "Go away."

"You shouldn't have given me a key if you didn't want me to use it."

"Another stupid move on my part. It's all I seem to do lately. So, where does all this leave me? By myself. Forever alone." I blubbered snot.

"You stop this right now, Jesse; I'll show you why -" Loosha pulled a magazine from her bag and held it up, the cover facing me, "This is why."

It was the latest copy of US Magazine, and on the cover was a picture of Loren and Abrams; it looked to have been taken as they walked down the street; he with his head slightly down while Loren was looking directly into the camera. The headline read: The New Camelot Couple

"Oh, no," I moaned. "It's real."

"I'll tell you what," she tossed the magazine to the floor. "Put them both out your mind, get off this couch, pack up and come to China with me. Get away from all this mess."

I shook my head on the stale pillow, damp and cool from my tears. "I have to think."

"It's all you've been doing for days, thinking about them, and it's causing you nothing but heartache."

"I could just –" I took the pillow in both hands and flung it across the couch, "both of them."

"See," she said, pointing a finger at me before slumping into a chair. "For the last time: get over it, Jesse; you and him were impossible from the get-go. You should have realized that when you found out who he was."

"Go away, Loosha," I rolled over on the couch with my back to her. "Take your trip."

"Come with me," she said and when I didn't answer, she left me alone.

The next thing I knew, there was a pounding at my door, then my doorbell was ringing nonstop while my phone - set on vibrate - buzzed incessantly. I tried ignoring all of it until I realized that whoever was at the door was not going away.

I hefted myself up and stumbled to the front door.

"Go away," I yelled at whoever was on the other side.

"This is your mother, and I will not. Open this door right this second, Jesse."

Unable to help myself, I did as I was told. My mother swept in and looked me over, "Oh, Jesse honey; what have you done to yourself? You look terrible."

"Where's Dad?" I asked, closing the door after her." I felt a stab of disappointment that she was here instead of him. Fear was there, too, which was always underneath, the kind I never explained to myself because I couldn't.

"He's waiting in the taxi."

I was stunned by this. A taxi? They had come all the way from Nantucket and then had to get a taxi to my house.

"Why didn't you call?"

She gave me a half-angry, half-exasperated look, "We did. You aren't answering your phone."

"What do you want?" I asked baldly.

"Your father and I have been very worried about you."

I caught the fact she didn't mention that Loren had been worried too.

"You're taking this thing way too hard, Jesse." She suddenly softened, "Come sit down, and I'll make you some tea."

She led me back to the couch. On her way to the kitchen, she straightened up the living room. I sat quietly until she returned with a cup of tea, half a turkey sandwich, and a small salad on a tray, she placed on the coffee table.

She looked good in her light make-up and what she called one of her 'traveling suits;' this one was robin egg blue. She sat down next to me and to my surprise, pushed a strand of my hair behind my ear just like she did for Loren.

"When did you last wash your hair? You need to go back to work," she said. "You have responsibilities. Forget about Abrams. Let your sister have this one, honey. She deserves him. Listen," she said with an enthusiastic note in her voice as she took my hand.

"Loosha told me she was going to China on one of her missions to find her birth parents. I was thinking how great it would be if you went along with her this time. Your Dad and I would be glad to pay all costs. You'd get away from here, and that'll do you a world of good, and you've always wanted to see where you were born. I'm right about that aren't I?"

I took a deep breath and let it out along with words I never imagined I'd say to her. "Now, you want to send me back like some parcel you don't want anymore after all these years. It's too late, Mom. I'm not some flawed thing that's unwanted, unlovable.

"Jesse, none of that's true," her tone was hurt, the look on her face tragic. "Why are you treating me like this after I came all this way to try and make you feel better, to get you to pick yourself up just as I did when your friend died. But you make it sound as if I have some rancid motive and not your best interest at heart."

"Mom, just forget it," I swiped at the silent tears sliding down my face and straightened myself up. "I'll think about it; but won't promise anything."

"Good,' she stood satisfied and gathered her purse before saying, "While you're at it, promise to break off any contact with this Abrams. Even pretend, honey, if you have to

I felt the tears again, but this time, they were tears of anger. How dare she try to get rid of me now, send me back like some parcel she didn't want after thirty years. It's too late for that, Mom, I thought; I'm not some flawed thing that needs to be sent back as unusable, unlovable.

Swiping at my face, I drew myself up but only said, "I'll think about it. But won't promise anything."

"While you're at it, promise to break off any contact with this Abrams. "Even pretend, if you have to that it's all been a big misunderstanding, that whatever took place between you two was taken out of context, spoken during the heat of the moment and meant nothing at all." She stared at me solemnly, "So when you see him and your sister together, it won't hurt you too much."

I wanted to do the opposite of crying this time and laugh hysterically as if she'd told me the world's funniest joke. "You'll have to go, Mom," I got to my feet. I'd had more than enough of her and couldn't take a second more. "I'm going to do what you said right now and go to work; I've been away too long."

I took her arm and lead her to the front door, where I pulled it open and walked her quickly outside, where my father waited beside the cab.

"How's my Golden Girl?" he whispered at the top of my head as he took me in his arms.

"Not so golden," I said dry-eyed. "I'm going into the office today."

He nodded, his gaze penetrating and deeply burdened with a dark concern.

"Don't worry, Dad. I'm alright."

"You sure?" The dark concern was still in his eyes, it softened me for a moment.

"Yes, I'll handle it. Take Mom home, and I'll call you later."

He opened the cab door for my mother, who halted in front of me before getting in, "We love you and only want what's best for you. We always have."

I didn't say anything else, only watched them drive away. I thought, what's best for me; Abrams is best for me, but they don't want me to have him. I was tempted to go back to bed; I physically hurt, and not just in the heart; I knew it was grief, but if I continuing to wallow in it, what would that solve? Not a thing; it wouldn't change anything. Abrams had been cut out of my life with a machete, and I appeared to be the only one bleeding from it.

I took a shower, dressed, and went to catch the next ferry into Manhattan.

In the terminal, I walked past a newspaper and magazine stand and stopped to stare at the cover of the Daily Mail, which featured Abrams and Loren together.

Seated alone in the almost empty lower deck, I checked my phone. There were calls and messages from work, not too urgent though I wouldn't have cared less if they were. There were eight texts from Loosha, ranging from: 'He's a jerk, kick him to the curb' to 'Get the fuck over him; he's not worth two dead flies.' There were twenty-two calls and messages from Abrams; I deleted everything.

Staring out the window at the gentle wavelets that heralded us along, I wondered how only a few days ago, I'd been thrilled to be alive. Today, I felt the end of everything.

# CHAPTER 45

When the ferry pulled into Whitehall, I sat and waited for the other passengers to disembark. I finally walked slowly up the stairs to the main deck feeling a hundred years old. People milled around waiting to get on while stragglers were trying to get off; I paid no attention to any of it; I only waited my turn; closeted within myself.

A small commotion erupted; I heard it but didn't look around until I heard my name called not once but twice from somewhere in the crowd.

"Jesse," startled, I looked up then, "Jesse."

Abrams was pushing toward me, his handsome face haggard and disturbed.

A woman bumped into me.

"On or off," she said gruffly.

Before I could do anything, Abrams reached me and pulled me into his arms. I resisted, not knowing what to do, how to feel, what to say. We were the only two left on the platform, the ferry having carefully pulled away from the dock with the people on the outer deck staring at us.

"Maybe we should run away together. Leave. Disappear into our own world," he said desperately into my hair.

He pulled back and stared at me when I still hadn't responded.

"I've been calling you night and day. I got rid of those guards to be on my own. I've staked out this terminal for the last few days hoping you'd show. I showed up at your house, and your friend told me I'd better leave or she'd call the police. Why won't you say something, Jesse? Yell, scream, hit me; God knows I deserve it."

"Say it," I finally said with no elaboration. "Say it."

"She never had me. It was always you, Jesse," he said with so much heartfelt emotion that I instantly believed him, "From that time in Mr. Kirby's', it was always you. And I didn't realize it until I thought I'd lost you. I love you. Until the day I die."

I closed my eyes as my body sagged against him in relief, feeling whole and sure of itself again as I put my arms around him, and we held together.

"God help me, I still love you too, so much. It wouldn't work; we can't run away. If you were someone else, maybe, but you're not. You're Abrams Allen Harrington, your mother will be the next president, and you'll be by her side."

"I didn't know -"

"Please, don't say it again."

"- she was your sister. We were briefly introduced, and she never talked about you. Like I told you, she said her sister had died.

"You two were together."

He shook his head, "No. We met, went out, and had our pictures taken. If we were even in the same room, people began putting two-and-two together when it wasn't that way at all but denying it only made it worse. I didn't want it to go any further, but I didn't' want to hurt her either and wrongly went along; that's why I ended up at your parent's anniversary party; I'd promised and saw nothing in it, but that was before I met you and fell hard."

"She's in love with you too."

"I can't help that; it's not what I want."

What're we going to do about it? I don't want to hurt her either."

"I want to be with you, no matter what comes. We have to tell her."

"Yes, now."

"Let's do it and not waste any more time."

"She's not at home but working. One of Richard's most important shots of the year is going on."

"Let's go," he smiled at me for the first time since he'd caught sight of me. That wonderful smile of his. It bucked me up even more. I was more than ready to confront Loren; I was dying to do it.

"What're we waiting for?" I said, and we practically ran out of the terminal.

One of RJC's three Manhattan studios was located on Central Park South, where some of the most expensive real estates in the world resided. RJC's studio made up the entire top floor of the Etienne Building, of which he was part owner. The rest were condo units that went for eight million dollars and up with amenities that included roof-top infinity pools, two private chefs on call, twenty-four-hour armed security, and a full-time nanny service.

We stepped out of the cab in front of the building which was stained glass-fronted so that it sparkled with color. Four dark-suited men stood at their post in front of the building's entrance; confirming that Richard was photographing one of the most famous people in the world today.

One of the men escorted us inside through the lobby of polished tile and dripping chandeliers. We stopped at the lobby desk where another security guard typed my name into a keyboard, and I knew he was messaging Loren. I'd been to the top floor a couple of times, so my name and identification information were already listed in their security files.

"Tell her Abrams is with me."

He didn't look up; he just kept typing and then stopped. We

stood there silently waiting for a response that was a few minutes in coming.

The man finally said, again without looking up, "Please take elevator seven."

There were eight elevators for the building, four on the right side for the residents, and the other four on the left were Richard's private elevators, which didn't work unless security allowed you inside. Each set of doors was a different, golden art deco design; number seven stood open, waiting for us. Abrams and I stepped inside.

# CHAPTER 46

We didn't speak as we rode up to the top floor. Could I do it, I wondered? Could I confront her, not my blood sister, yet still my sister, whom I've loved from the very beginning and over a man? But not just some man; I glanced at Abrams, who gave me a brief smile, but Abrams Allen. Would I fight for him? Fight her for him? I closed my eyes for a few seconds as if in prayer because the answer was: Yes. Sister Light versus Sister Dark, the irony of it was frightening.

Richard's floor was divided into four sections. His apartment stretched across the entire building and consisted of two bedrooms, a large kitchen, dining and living spaces, a huge studio, and a three-room office; it was a complex unto itself.

The elevator doors opened onto a crowd; a coordinated circus is what we stepped into: a show with its cast of characters all there to perform for the guest of honor, the person readying to have their picture taken.

Kendrick Lamar's music played from hidden speakers as racks of designer clothes and cases of accessories were being wheeled through the rooms. Tables groaned with food and drinks, and bunches of flowers were placed here and there with emphasis on their abundance. Make-up artists and hair stylists floated around the room waiting to be used, and they were all there for one purpose only, to make sure Richard's latest project was an overwhelming success. They glanced at us, then back to the person at center stage.

This person stood talking animatedly with RJC while every-one else circled them like planets circling the sun. His subject was the famous-of-the-famous and recognized immediately by almost everyone on the planet; she was Oprah Winfrey, who laughed warmly at Richard's chatter. She would feature in his next highly anticipated show and next book, and these facts alone had already significantly raised his status to newer heights.

A man, his head shaved clean except for a top-knot of short dreadlocks, greeted us. Holding a tablet, he addressed Abrams, "We knew you were on your way up, sir. Ms. Winfrey would like to say hello."

Frowning, Abrams said, "Is Loren here?"

"Yes, sir, she's seeing to a few calls and will be with you in a moment."

"Abrams," I touched his arm. "I'll get Loren, and we'll try and find a quiet place to talk."

"You sure?"

I nodded, and the man led him over to Ms. Winfrey, who hugged Abrams before dropping into conversation with him. Richard took pictures of them, and with their phones, so did a few other people.

I looked around for Loren and saw her walking up to Abrams, she kissed him on the mouth before slipping an arm around his waist and putting her other hand on his chest. She, of course, looked beautiful in a bubble pink jumpsuit, her blond hair cas-cading down her back, having dressed in honor of their important guest.

Oprah beamed at them, "You two are delicious together. You're a story for 'O' - Sweet Love or something like that; I'll call your office, Abrams."

More pictures were taken of the three. I hated it and started toward them, toward Loren.

My heartbeat tripled at the coming confrontation, yet determination kept me going; we had to have this out. I needed this settled so that I, we, could get past this and get on with our new normal as sisters, whatever that new normal was going to be.

Loren saw me coming, disentangled herself from them, and met me halfway.

"We have to talk."

She looked me up and down; her smile for Abrams and Oprah was gone as if it had never been.

"About what? The fact you're suicidal?"

My mouth dropped open in shocked surprise before I fumbled helplessly over my words.

"I was never out of my head," my voice rose; a couple of people glanced at us. "I was grieving."

"Keep your voice down," she glanced around. "What's the matter with you?" She studied me as if she'd never seen me before." You're not as passive as I thought, are you, little sister?"

"I can stand up for myself and for what I want."

"Can you really?" she asked as people passing through to other parts of the apartment stared at us as they went by. "If we have to do this, let's go somewhere more private."

I followed her into Richard's living room where Loren wasted no time.

"Is Abrams aware you once had a nervous breakdown and was in Bellevue Psychiatric?" she asked silkily. "Does his mother and her campaign people know?"

"Why would it matter to them?"

"It would be pretty shitty if her campaign for president were rocked by some crazy woman who knew her son."

"None of that's true," I controlled myself with effort. "Loren, I understand your anger…"

"Don't you patronize me," she stepped toward me as the door opened and a line of people entered, laughing with drinks in their hands. Abrams was a few steps behind them.

"I've been looking everywhere for you," he said, his gaze zeroed in on my face and demeanor.

"I texted you, Abrams, and you didn't get back to me," Loren said as he turned to face her.

"I told you to stop, Loren. There's nothing between us," he said softly, in an effort not to hurt her. "There never was, not the way you wanted it."

Loren went pale as her grey eyes shimmered with abrupt and unshed tears.

"You don't know what you're saying, Abrams."

"Yes, he does," I cut in.

"We can't talk here," Loren interrupted as her phone buzzed. "I'm needed out in the studio; you see how busy we are? I can't handle any of this right now."

"We have to settle this," I insisted, "Today, if we're to get on with our lives."

Color suddenly suffused Loren's face until she was the color of her suit, and I recognized anger sweeping through her, "This is an important day for Richard, and I'm not going to ruin it fighting with you. I'm on my way home to rest before the full shoot. I'll meet you there to finally get this all out."

Her eyes swept over us both with a kind of contempt I hadn't a clue my sister was capable of, "I'll show you how wrong you two are for each other. Now, get the hell out, and don't let any of the media people see you leave."

# CHAPTER 47

We left without speaking to anyone else and took a cab to Loren's apartment. We didn't speak until we got halfway there.

Abrams turned to me, "Here's the plan: we talk -"

I shook my head, "I have to talk to her first because I hope some of the closeness we shared is still there. We're family despite everything. I can get her to understand how much we love each other and want to be together."

He hesitated, "She doesn't want to listen, Jesse. Loren's made up her mind that we're making a mistake and will do whatever she can to stop us."

"She'll listen to reason, trust me."

"Alright," he said reluctantly as the cab pulled up in front of Loren's townhouse. "I don't believe you know her as well as you think you do, but we'll do it your way first."

We walked up to her door hand-in-hand, "Here goes," my voice was shaky with anxiety.

"You said yourself: it's going to be alright."

I didn't say anything else; I looked toward the apartment and saw Loren watching us from the window. I tried the door, but it was locked. I knocked even though she knew we were outside. A few seconds later, she opened up without a word, and we stepped into the foyer.

We stood there until I said baldly, "I'm not going to fight with you over Abrams."

"I met him first."

"I loved him first," I countered.

"Stop it," Abrams intervened sharply. "There's not going to be any fight."

"Can the two of us talk first, Loren? Just between you and me, us sisters."

"Me and the crazy sister," Loren said.

"What?" Abrams asked.

"There's even a video of her being crazy," Loren looked at him calmly. "Not just crazy -" she made a striking motion across her throat. "- suicidal. She tried to kill herself. She never told you that did she?" Loren asked matter-of-factly.

"How's that going to look, Abrams? You involved with someone who'd once been suicidal? Maybe still is. How's it going to play in Middle America? You want to be president someday, don't you? How will it happen when you're involved with someone like her? I don't understand wanting her when you could have me."

"Stop it, Loren," I screamed at her.

Abrams put an arm around me, "Nothing you can say will change the fact: it's Jesse, not you."

She turned abruptly on her heel and walked away as if I were recalcitrant children she was tired of dealing with. I put a staying hand on Abrams's chest and followed her into the kitchen, where she went to the wine rack and took out a bottle. She opened her knick-knack drawer, found a bottle opener, opened the wine, got down a glass, and filled it without asking me if I wanted any.

"I can't fucking believe he'd want you over me," she said after taking a long swallow of the liquid.

"All I want from Abrams is his love."

A pitying look settled onto her face, "Jesse, all you can do for him is cause him a lot of embarrassment and pain. Come on, sis, be reasonable. You've always been realistic. Why are you giving that up now? No one should know better than you not to get in my way when I want something."

She gestured at me with the wineglass stem, "He knows you're adopted, of course. Do you know how Mrs. Harrington's enemies can use that against her and Abrams? They did it to Senator McCain, and did he become president?"

"You have to think of somebody else instead of yourself. You're just plain selfish trying to keep him from the world when he'd have it all with me."

"You're delusional, Loren," I said, barely holding back my anger. "You don't love him; all you want is a reflection of yourself."

"Stop that love business; it sounds stupid coming from you," Loren said with a derisive twist of her lips. "You were always so simple."

She put the glass down hard enough to break it, her features I'd always thought the essence of beauty, were just stubborn, aggrieved, and twisted; a reflection of what truly went on inside her. She reminded me of a gorgon out to turn anyone to stone, strike them down, if they didn't bow down to her.

"I believe that when Abrams figures it out, adds it all up: what he can lose with you versus what he can gain with me, he'll come to his senses. What does he know about you anyway? While I know everything."

"Everything, Loren."

She suddenly smiled brilliantly at me and smoothed back her already smooth white-blond hair as if it had been moved by an ill wind. She put both hands on the table and leaned over it toward me as if she was ready to divulge the juiciest secret of a lifetime. And I guess she was.

"Not when he finds out you were the product of a rape."

Her words staggered me back as if they had literal weight as she tossed them at me like hand grenades. She laughed merrily at the look on my face.

"Your birth mother was young, couldn't take the humiliation of keeping her rapist's child, so she left you on the orphanage steps and disappeared forever."

"You're lying."

"All those journals my mother keeps," she said off-handedly as if it wasn't important. As if what she had said hadn't tilted my world off its axis. "Well, in one of her books, she wrote the entire story of your being - a sad tale believe me. How the woman left the note telling of the rape and how she couldn't bear to look at you. Ask my mother about it; it's time you finally knew the truth. All of it. "

"Another thing:" she said, a repugnance that etched every word, "you are not my sister."

"Loren, what --" I couldn't get the words out; her tsunami of a revelation had jolted me to my core so that the room, the world, tilted on its axes; I swayed at my sudden dislocation.

"My real sister is dead. You should read some of Mom's journals, Jesse, such a treasure trove of juicy information. Of course, you'd be surprised at what they've kept from you, always for your own good. So, I'll fill in all the blanks for you. Her name was Lucy. She died when she was two of SIDS. It's why Mom loves that picture, "Us By The Sea." It reminds her of Lucy and me while you're nowhere to be found."

I didn't say anything. I couldn't; even breathing was a heartbreak.

"Lucy was gone, and they brought you home to take her place," she gave a short, derisive laugh. "My God, as if that could ever happen."

"You're lying," I whispered, barely able to speak.

"From what she wrote, they couldn't have any more children because 'my mother, not ours' had developed large fibroids after Lucy and had to have a hysterectomy. No more babies. So, they bought you instead."

The tears I'd been holding back forced themselves out and down my face. I still couldn't speak though I felt the absurd need to apologize to her, tell her how sorry I was that I wasn't the sister she'd always wanted.

"I loved Lucy so much, you see; I never forgot her."

"They never told me."

"She lived, then she died."

"Why wouldn't they tell me?"

"Because you'd think you were a replacement for their dead daughter when you weren't a gift to our family but the exact opposite."

"They could have said something."

"But they damn well didn't."

Streaks of angry red, stained Loren's cheekbones, and her eyes blazed with hate for me I'd never imagined, let alone seen. She looked like an avenging angel; if she'd had a sword of fire, I was sure she'd use it right then and there to strike me down.

"Lucy walked at fifteen months, had hair the color of summer wheat. She laughed all the time and was just wonderful. She was my very own baby doll. Then came you, always crying, afraid, couldn't understand a word spoken to you."

She suddenly came hurdling around the island counter at me, " Zian is who you were, are: looking different, sounding different, even smelling different. A total disappointment I had to put up with day-after-day," she spat. "You were always being laughed at, bullied, and I had to come to your rescue, protect you because you were so-called family."

The words were hurled at me with such rancid vindictiveness that it jolted the steel in me to fight back, not take this lying down but give it back to her.

"Had to, Loren? Only when you wanted to - when some guy you thought I wasn't good enough for - paid any attention to me," I didn't hold anything back. "Including our father."

She sucked in a breath as we stared at each other, as it all clicked into place; drew together like perfect puzzle pieces, what Loosha had always said about Loren, what Ari and Jack believed: that she had never cared for me at all. Never. "You've hated me all this time while I – "

"You -," she snarled, the word fueled with a rage that had built up over time, over the years, and was finally free and spewing forth. I was finally learning how she had always felt about me, a deep loathing she'd hidden so perfectly until now. The thing with Abrams had released her.

"A stranger who invaded my home, my family. And now you want to take Abrams away from me!" she ranted as she hurled herself at me, going for my face.

I staggered back, slipped on her polished floor, and caught myself on the island as a lifetime of prejudice, snide comments, turning-the-other-cheek, being different, unacceptable flashed through me until I blazed like a phoenix rising with a kind of fury I'd never felt in my life, and met her halfway.

Our hands were at each other when the kitchen door flew open, and Abrams was there forcibly pushing us apart. Loren landed against the counter, smashing her hip and almost falling while I hit a counter stool, causing it to topple over.

"That's enough," Abrams roared.

Turning toward me, he wrapped his arms around me and forced me back away from Loren. She took a step toward us and spat before she turned and ran out the room.

We went after her, but she'd already reached the top of the staircase and disappeared into her bedroom. As we reached the landing, she barreled out with the gun in her hand and pointed it at Abrams. Without thinking, I jumped between them and grabbed the barrel.

"No," he screamed as his hand whipped around me and grabbed Loren's wrist.

She pulled the trigger.

The bullet flashed across my cheek, a heated razor blade as blood, hot and wet, hit the back of my neck and head; Abrams's blood. He dropped straight to the floor, clutching the side of his neck as blood pumped from his torn-out carotid artery in a freshet of red. Dropping to my knees beside him, I watched him die.

Loren stood there holding the gun, looking dazed. I wasn't dazed. I reared up and took hold of the gun, trying to wrestle it from between us when it fired again. I still didn't let go; instead, I rammed it and her backward, back against the railing.

We slipped in the blood, the gun dropped, and somehow, Loren, whose door I would sleep up against just to be near her, whom I once loved more than I loved myself, my sister: fell over the banister.

I reached for her flailing hand and tried to pull her up, but the pain in my side was too much; I hadn't the strength. I tried harder as something let go of me and gave out with blood. I let her go with a wail of pain and hopelessness and heard her scream, then the thud below. I heard it a long way off, for a long time, so that in the end, neither of us got Abrams. We are all lost in love, in life. We all lost.

**CHAPTER 48**

"Hey," Sam shook Erin out of her fretful doze. "How could Jesse have written the last few pages?"

"She didn't," Erin said, slightly confused but coming out of it, she quickly sat up. She looked at the last written pages. "It's Lillian's writing. Lillian's version. She must have read statements and reports talking to people who would talk and put together what she believed happened, re-imagined it, and written these final words. Jesse's words. "My poor sister and Martin too, he'll never be the same. None of us will be."

Sam smoothed the last blank pages. Forever to be blank, he thought. The end. Or was it?

"You think we'll ever know what really happened? Happened to Jesse?"

Erin didn't answer, deep in her thoughts, of the lovely girl who'd only wanted to be loved for herself and who'd crossed oceans to be part of their lives.

She stood and moved to the window, "The storm is over."

# EPILOGUE

The sky was blue; it was warm though the signs of fall were everywhere across the island, in the red huckleberry leaves and the golden leaves of the - tree. Lillian sat alone on the bench, watching the sunset over the ocean. Jesse stood, not seeing the brilliant splashes of color; her eyes were on her mother. It had been a long time since she'd seen her.

Maybe it was her daughter's still presence or a mother's intuition that made Lillian turn and stare at her.

Jesse took a step forward, "Mom?"

## THE END

# ABOUT THE AUTHOR

Lori Ann Mathews is the author of *You Don't Know Me* and *Begin At The End*, Detective Owen Story novels. She is the founder and CEO of LAM Productions and she lives in the Midwest.

www.ingramcontent.com/pod-product-compliance
Lightning Source LLC
Chambersburg PA
CBHW061335160726
47995CB00001B/34